The Nashville Bet

SHANA GRAY

HEADLINE
ETERNAL

First published in Great Britain in 2018
by HEADLINE ETERNAL
An imprint of HEADLINE PUBLISHING GROUP

1

Cataloguing in Publication Data is available from the British Library

ISBN 978 1 4722 6005 5

Typeset in 11/14 pt Minion Pro by Jouve (UK), Milton Keynes

Printed and bound in Great Britain by CPI Group (UK) Ltd, Croydon, CR0 4YY

HEADLINE PUBLISHING GROUP
An Hachette UK Company
Carmelite House
50 Victoria Embankment
London EC4Y 0DZ

www.headlineeternal.com
www.headline.co.uk
www.hachette.co.uk

Shana Gray is a hybrid author who was first published in 2010. She has written contemporary erotic romances for multiple publishers, including Harlequin Blaze, Random House, and Headline, and is also an indie author. Her stories range from scorching quickie-length to longer full-length novels. Shana's passion is to enjoy life! She lives in Ontario, but loves to travel and see the world, be with family and friends, and experience the beauty that surrounds us. Many of her experiences find their way into her books.

Visit Shana online at www.shanagray.com and connect with her on Twitter @ShanaGray_ or via Facebook www.facebook.com/authorshanagray.

By Shana Gray

Working Girl

Girls' Weekend Away
What Happens in Vegas
Meet Me in San Francisco
The Nashville Bet

I decided to set this book in Nashville after having a wonderful lunch with my editor Kate Byrne, in London, England, this past February. It was so amazing to meet and spend time with you. The look of delight in your eyes when I told you I was considering Nashville made it impossible for me not to dive into the country music scene. This book is for you. xo

Acknowledgments

There are always so many people to acknowledge when writing a book. The usual suspects, Louise, Kate and Kristin (blows kisses) please know that without you guys . . . well . . . the book(s) wouldn't have been brought to life. Behind the scenes are so many others that touch the pages, and each have an important role as well. I thank you.

I did a whole lot of marathoning *Nashville,* so I could capture the feel of the town. In the process, I fell in love with the show, and while Deacon is awesome . . . I was team Luke LOL.

For the musical bits, I was able to count on some friends from long ago that still rock the tunes after all these years.

I hope you love Ava and Chase's story as much as I do.

See you in Monaco!

Shana xo

The Nashville Bet

Chapter 1

The plane began descending and Ava wriggled a little with excitement in her seat, earning a strange look from the college kid next to her. Most travelers preferred the aisle seat so that they could get out easily, but not Ava. She loved to see where she was going, all the new possibilities and adventures that were awaiting her. This particular trip was going to be off-the-charts fun! Nashville and CMA Fest had been on her bucket list for a while. There would be multiple stages, many different performers and all the country music she could ever want!

Flight attendants did another pass of the aisles and she handed over her soda can to be recycled. Had to do her bit to save planet Earth! The plane twitched in the sky with a bit of turbulence and Ava gripped her knees. She loved to fly because it took her places, but she preferred the skies to be calm. Otherwise, she got a little nervous and every noise the plane made was the sound of impending doom. She gazed out the window, taking deep breaths to calm herself, and thought of her friends, the sisters of her heart, her college buddies.

Everything had been rather last minute. Her boss, David, had booked a kick-ass suite for CMA Fest at Nissan Stadium, but a sudden family emergency meant he couldn't go. He offered the suite to Ava and told her that he'd finagle extra tickets for her friends as a thank-you for her work on their latest project. Ava had been all over that and her friends had jumped at the chance to watch amazing country acts in luxurious – and air-conditioned – comfort. Ava loved all music, and Celia, Bonni and Fredi also loved country music so Ava had no doubt this trip was going to be a blast.

Celia and Bonni had taken over planning the itinerary. It made her friends happy to be in control of things so, since it didn't matter as much to her, Ava was fine going along with the flow. Tonight they were killing two birds with one stone by going line dancing and meeting up with the guy with the extra tickets. He was a friend of a friend of David's who apparently lived in the area. It was going to be a whirlwind trip, really. The CMA Fest ran until Saturday with three days of concerts in many different locations. Ava knew they wouldn't be able to see all of them, but it sure was going to be fun!

Bonni had made noises about 'Why can't this guy just leave us the tickets at the hotel?' but Ava didn't mind. She knew everything would work itself out. Besides, she had his contact info just in case something went awry.

The plane leveled out as it continued its descent. The sun was low in the sky and Ava saw shards of its golden light glinting off miniature-looking buildings through the window. Seeing Nashville on the horizon filled her with a powerful sense of 'coming home.' Ava had happily grown up country in a small farming town out in the Midwest, but college, and her friends, had shown her a bigger world. There was so much to see, to explore. She still went home for holidays, though, but that time was spent catching up with her family and finding out the latest news, not going to the nearest honky-tonk and cutting loose. She was looking forward to reconnecting with her roots.

As a child, Ava had sat in her grandfather's workshop while he puttered about doing some woodwork and old-school country music played through tinny speakers, accompanied by the sound of sandpaper against wood. She couldn't hear Patsy Cline without thinking of him. Ava still preferred the big female country artists like Carrie Underwood, Shania Twain, Miranda Lambert and Faith Hill. There was no denying, though, that country music was still dominated by the boys. Many of the so-called 'bro-country' songs didn't appeal to her at all.

The college kid leaned forward to push his backpack more securely underneath the seat in front of him. When he sat back, his legs spread wide, and Ava moved closer to the plane's wall to avoid touching him. She was sure he didn't mean to manspread, and they were almost on the ground so it wasn't worth the awkward conversation to ask him to move back into his space. Still, this was just another sign that there were no more considerate gentlemen left.

Bonni and Celia had found their happily ever after on previous trips. That left just her and Fredi to find theirs. Ava had gradually become so disappointed in the male species over the years it had been hard not to just give up on finding her true love. But no. Those were quitter thoughts and she refused to let go of her dreams. Ava would never, ever let herself think otherwise. She *knew* the man of her dreams was out there. One day, somewhere, somehow, she would find him. Now, if that wasn't a country song in the making, she didn't know what was.

Country music was all about storytelling, and telling love

stories was one of its favorite things to do. Whether it was swearing to always love someone, feeling a slow and steady rush or celebrating still going strong, there was a song for every feeling, every situation. Country music had such a strong romantic flare and Ava loved the heartbreaking tales. She was a sucker for them, even though she invariably cried. And Nashville! It was the heart and soul of country music.

Ava squinted and looked at the city below. Not long now until touchdown. She was meeting Fredi on the curb outside Baggage Claim, since it was the easiest point of connection without Fredi having to park. Her friend was driving up from Florida, saying she needed the time away from her job as a wedding-dress designer.

'Endless hours in the car is my peace,' she'd insisted.

Out of the four of them, she and Fredi were the most opposite. Ava chose to give people the benefit of the doubt and to see the good in them, while Fredi took a more cynical view of life. Ava sighed and sat back in the seat, letting the sun bathe across her face. The plane banked sharply, the light turning to shade, and she heard the wheels come down. Touchdown was easy, the taxi to the gate uneventful, and disembarking the plane was the typical shuffle down the aisle.

She pulled her phone out of her purse, went to the group chat with her friends and typed, *Nashville, I am in you.* Then she skirted a family who had stopped at the end of the jetway, trying to organize their screaming kids.

Ava's long legs took her swiftly through the crowd that was dawdling along. She had on runners instead of her preferred heels so she could fly through the crowd easily, teamed with flattering skinny jeans and a butter-cream-yellow blouse. She flipped her hair over her shoulder, wishing she'd tied its thick auburn mass up into a bun. Her skin felt coated with sweat and grime and she was eager to shower to get the airplane cooties off her once they arrived at the hotel.

Ava was a bit of a clean freak. No, she wasn't a germaphobe, but she did her best to avoid any while using public transportation. A flight attendant had told her once to always wipe down her seat and tray-table before departure and she had taken the advice to heart ever since. More than once she'd gotten sick after flying, and the last thing she wanted was to come down with airplane crud while on this trip.

In addition to her purse, all she had packed was a carry-on so, after weaving through the crowd, she waited patiently by a pillar near the doors to the kiss-and-fly pick-up. Her phone buzzed and she read the message. Fredi was just driving into Arrivals.

Ava rushed outside and watched for her. She looked over the heads of the people standing around her and smiled when a candy-apple-red Volkswagen Beetle zipped around the other cars and into the Arrivals area.

Ava raised her hand and stepped off the curb. Fredi screeched to a halt, the sound echoing off the walls. The back hatch popped up and Ava fired in her carry-on, slammed the hatch shut and climbed into the front seat.

'Ava! It's so good to see you, girl,' Fredi greeted her while looking in the rear-view and side mirrors, waiting for a break before bursting back into the traffic, blaring the horn.

'Thanks so much for picking me up. It sure beats taking a taxi to the hotel.' Ava settled in the seat and put her huge satchel, which carried everything she could possibly need, between her knees on the floor.

'You know it's no problem.' She put on the indicator and instructed Ava, 'Hang on to your hat! This place is a zoo, and I want to get out of here.'

Fredi pulled a Mario Andretti, quickly cutting out from

between a couple of cars, around a pole that reminded you to watch for pedestrian traffic, and then they were shooting out the other end and away from the airport.

'One day, Fredi – one day – you're going to get in a crash,' Ava told her as she pushed herself harder into the passenger seat, her feet braced on the floor. This reminded her exactly why she wasn't a fan of driving with Fredi.

Fredi huffed. 'I can't stand traffic. People are stupid and don't know how to drive.'

'But you should drive defensively, not aggressively.' Ava hung on to the door handle and gritted her teeth.

'I *am* driving defensively, and look, it worked! We're free of airport hell.' Fredi leaned into the steering wheel, gripping with both hands. Her gaze was flashing between the mirrors and the road ahead. Ava wondered why she still held so tightly to the wheel, since they were through the traffic. Then again, Fredi had been just as intense a driver back in college as she appeared to be now, whether stuck bumper to bumper or racing down an interstate.

'No, you weren't, you were being aggressive. Other people have places to be, too, you know. Like picking up dinner for their family or maybe taking a kid to ballet. We're not in any hurry, so what does it hurt to be courteous to other drivers?' Ava said earnestly.

'Spare me the sunshiney BS, Ava. I'm the one bringing you to the hotel. Otherwise, you'd been stuck in a germ-filled Uber or a cab.' Fredi cast her a smug glance.

Ava said, 'You're right. Even your crazy driving is better than a taxi. Do you know what time Bonni and Celia are getting in?' Ava closed her eyes when Fredi whooshed around a slow driver. 'Careful! You're going to get a ticket.'

'Won't! And they could be at the hotel by now, but I've got a feeling they'll be a little bit later. Landon was in Europe some-where in a meeting that ran late. He went back to Cali so he could watch Celia's kids, much to her ex's displeasure, and, can you believe that man? Still causing all that drama about cus-tody and delaying the court case when, clearly, the kids are better off with Celia and Landon. Anyway, then Celia took the jet to get Bonni from Virginia before they flew here. Tough life, huh?' Fredi said, keeping her gaze fixed on the road ahead. 'Flying around in the Bryant corporate jet.'

'Well, I don't think they do it often.' Ava ran her finger along the crease of her jeans, wishing Fredi would be less critical. 'But I bet it's handy being in love with uber-wealthy guys.'

However, personally, Ava didn't care if her future Mr Right was a billionaire or a handyman. All she wanted was love, devotion and a future with a man who would treasure her and treat her like a princess. Someone she could pour all her love into. He had to be out there, somewhere, didn't he?

'Ha, I bet so, too! But not even the luxury of a private jet would entice me to hitch my wagon to a man's mule. What's the point in love and marriage? Just a road to disaster,' Fredi replied cynically.

Ava drew in a soft breath and held it; she didn't believe Fredi's take on love for a minute. Ava was all about passion, togetherness, love at first sight, being swept off your feet. Fredi designed wedding dresses for a living but was the Romance Scrooge. It was irony in its purest form. Maybe one day Fredi would see the light and open herself up to the universe. Ava let the breath she was holding puff out between her lips and turned to Fredi. 'He – the one – has to be out there somewhere, doesn't he, Fredi? I mean, you see it every day.'

Fredi lifted a finger off the steering wheel, somehow making the small gesture imperious, and Ava paused.

'I have told you guys many times, I don't believe in happily ever after. Love is just a word—'

'Until two people make it something special!' Ava interrupted her.

'No, I don't believe that. I see these brides happy and miserable and stressed and everything under the sun. They're all a hot mess from planning a wedding, and how many of their marriages stick?' Fredi shook her head, making her long curls bounce around her shoulders and down her back. 'Not many, I'm afraid. So, nope, it ain't for this chick.'

Ava fell silent. She thought so differently than Fredi. Love was everything. How could anyone go through life without love?

'Fredi, I want someone to take my wagon. I want a big love. I want to find the man of my dreams.' Ava stared out the window, feeling a surge of sentimentality, and thought about how wonderful it would be to find her soulmate.

'Do you think I don't know that, hun? If I could make it happen for you, I would, but c'mon, there's a billion people in the world. Even if soulmates were a real thing, the odds of you finding yours among that many people is completely unrealistic. But maybe it's like when you purposely go shopping because you *need* that particular dress. You'll never find it. But when you're not looking, *boom,* there it is.' Ava turned to watch Fredi, thinking about her words.

'You don't sound overly optimistic.' Ava couldn't let herself feel low; it would ruin their weekend. 'Listen, if – no, *when* – I find my tall, dark and handsome, I'll be shouting it from the rooftops.'

'Oh, I know you will. So long as he makes you happy, I'll be his biggest fan in the world,' Fredi said. Ava felt an inner warmth chasing away her blueness. This is why they had been friends for so long: Fredi's unshakeable loyalty.

'I know it,' Ava replied. 'And I also know that you'll find your other half one day, too.'

Fredi rolled her eyes, but said congenially, 'So what kind of guy are you looking for these days? The kind who looks mighty fine in a three-piece suit?'

Ava closed her eyes and let her dream love conjure up behind her eyelids 'He has dark hair, neatly trimmed, and he's clean-shaven with bright blue eyes to contrast with his dark hair and eyebrows. He's well dressed . . .' Ava hesitated, a bit surprised that the image had begun to fail her.

'Blue or white collar?' Fredi asked her.

'Oh, in the long run, it really doesn't matter, but I think there's nothing sexier than a man in a tux or a well-cut business suit.'

'Then why haven't you found him yet? You work around those tight-ass types all day. You'd think one would catch your attention.'

Ava shook her head. 'Nope. They're all either married, players or gay.'

'Then where do you think you're going to find your magical man? Maybe you oughta get out of Nowheresville, Iowa, and move to a bigger city to find him.'

'I've thought about that. Trust me. But my contract with Edbridge is for another year, minimum. If I leave before then, I owe back the signing bonus, their three per cent matching for the pension and the year-end bonus I'm entitled to. The financials just don't add up. So I'm staying there for at least another year. Plus, I really like David, he's a great boss, and if I stay longer, the bonus dollars will go up until—'

'Whoa, okay, I get it, calculator brain. You make my head swim, spouting off numbers like that. You got it all, you know? Beauty and brains. It'll take a damn unicorn of a man to be worthy of you.'

Ava was stunned. After all these years, since their first meeting in a college class, it was the first time Fredi had ever expressed a sentiment like that. She was touched beyond words. 'If you weren't driving the car, I'd tackle hug you.'

Instead, she reached out and squeezed Fredi's shoulder. Fredi wasn't one for showing affection, but she turned and gave Ava a smile. 'It's true. Anyway, there's probably a load of Nashville suits around, label guys, A&Rs . . . maybe you'll find him this weekend.'

'Ha! Wouldn't that be something? Our previous girls' weekends were certainly lucky for our friends. But you know what? I think you're right. As long as I'm looking, I'll never find it so, as of now, I'm no longer looking!' Ava declared triumphantly. She had tried online dating, going to bars, blind dates – practically everything. Maybe it was time to try not trying. Or something like that.

'Oh my God! I don't believe that for a second. You not looking for your dream man is like you trying not to breathe. Fat chance.' Fredi flicked on the turn signal and roared down the highway off ramp.

As Ava clutched the door handle again and tried to remember the prayers she had learned long, long ago in Sunday School, she acknowledged that Fredi had a point. When was she ever *not* looking for love? Her luck in the love department was so, so bad. But this trip would be just the thing to turn her luck around. She just knew it!

Chapter 2

'Wow, what a place!' Ava stood in the center of the Opryland Hotel. She gazed up at the high glass ceiling and turned to take it all in. The ceiling was magnificent. 'Wasn't this hotel flooded a few years ago?'

'Yeah, I think so. But you certainly wouldn't know it now.' Fredi stood beside her and looked just as impressed.

There was a buzz and energy in the lobby of the hotel that infected Ava. This was going to be such a fun trip! Maybe they'd even see a celebrity, like Keith Urban! Nicole Kidman might be with him, too. Or Faith Hill and Tim McGraw. Now *they* were a couple in love.

Once they picked up the extra tickets from David's friend-of-a-friend, the weekend could really kick into gear! It was going to be amazingly fun. They would have a great time being back together and going out on the town, seeing all the different concerts.

'Are we doing that bar thing tonight? I think there's line dancing. And we're in Jack country – we really need to do a distillery tour.' Fredi nodded, quite serious in this announcement. Then she pulled Ava over to the left. 'Let's check in. We should get things sorted before Celia and Bonni get here.'

Ava let Fredi tug her along, as she was agog at their surroundings. 'This atrium is fantastic! Don't you think? I can't wait to explore it more. Look at those fountains – the water is hopping between them.'

'Focus, Ava.' Fredi nudged her closer to the registration desk.

'What? Yes. Let's see what Celia has planned for us.' Ava opened her satchel and ran her fingers down the spines of the leather planners neatly organized inside. She selected a lovely, worn, deep burgundy one and pulled it out. She flipped it open to the page with a fun butterfly page-marker and today's date on it.

'Oh my God, how many planners do you have in there?' Fredi craned her head to look inside the bag. 'And I though Celia was the organizer.'

Ava answered absently as she read the notes she'd made. 'I brought four with me.'

'Four! How the hell can you have four planners?' Fredi squeaked the words out.

Ava glanced up and was surprised to see the shocked look on Fredi's face. But then, not everybody had planner passion.

'What are you talking about? You should know me by now, I'm a planner girl. What's the big deal?' She opened her leather satchel wider. 'One is for personal, one for work, one for journaling and notes, and one for us girls.' She held up the one she had just looked at and waved it.

Fredi shook her head in wonderment. 'I can't understand the draw. I'm organized, but I don't have planners for every little thing. How can you have so many and keep it all straight about what's in which book?' Fredi took the handle of her suitcase and pulled it over to the registration desk. 'Y'know what? It's okay, I don't wanna know. My brain will likely 'splode. Come on, let's get checked in, upstairs and changed. We have a night ahead of us – no, wait, make that a *weekend* ahead of us.' Fredi did a little whoop that made Ava laugh.

Ava went through the check-in process and told the clerk that that Celia and Bonni would pick up their room keys when they arrived. All was in order quickly and Ava handed Fredi her room keycard. She had expected the room to be pre-paid and was relieved that nothing had gone awry. David had told her it was a freebie for her, a bonus for the complicated financial presentation she'd put together for a client he'd been trying to sign for a year. It made her happy that she could surprise her girls with a free weekend away and first-class seats at CMA Fest.

'So, Miss Organized, does your planner tell you what we're doing tonight? Is it the line dancing?' Fredi asked, slipping the keycard into her jeans pocket.

'Let me look. But you have to lead me again. I can't look and walk *and* drag my suitcase,' Ava told her as she flipped her planner open again.

Fredi groaned and grabbed her elbow as they walked through the lobby. 'The things I do.' She led Ava while she scanned the schedule.

'Watch out for the plant.' Fredi steered her around the tree.

'Yes, we're going to a place called the Wildhorse Corral. It's like some kind of double-level building with numerous bars on each floor, line dancing, live music, food. I'm supposed to meet a guy—'

'What, you know a guy who knows a guy who knows a guy? Maybe this is a set-up. Maybe you'll meet a sexy country singer and go have some heartbreakin' sex all night long.' Fredi cackled.

'Wow, you're in fine form today. But ' – Ava nodded – 'wishful thinking, right? Anyway, yes, I'll meet the guy with the extra tickets tonight, since David's friend organized it all. Oh!' A storefront caught Ava's attention. 'Did you bring cowboy boots?'

Ava hadn't owned cowboy boots since she was a kid. They'd been hand-me-downs, scuffed with scars in the leather, as they had been for work, not fashion. She'd hit a growth spurt when she was fourteen and her feet had outgrown the boots. Since she had transitioned to helping her mom with the house and gardens, they had never bought her another pair.

'Of course I brought cowboy boots.' Fredi looked totally affronted at the implication that she might not have a pair. 'I take it you didn't?'

Ava shook her head and stopped in front of the store window, looking at the display of boots. 'I'm a displaced country girl who's now a big-city girl. When would I ever have a use for cowboy boots? But, I should probably get some, don't you think? Wow, look at the incredible selection. Maybe we should stop in there now, on our way up to the room?'

Fredi leaned her head against Ava's shoulder and sighed. 'I feel sorry for you, my friend. You've led such a sheltered life.' Fredi pointed inside the store. 'Of course you should buy a pair, but you'll pay through the nose for them in there. I'm sure we can take you to some cowboy-boot outlet.'

'We might not have time for that. There's a lot to do this weekend.' The fiscally responsible side of Ava knew that Fredi was absolutely correct about the pricing and cringed back, but the boots were pretty and they were here now! Batting her eyelashes at her friend, Ava knew Fredi had given in when she raised her eyes to the sky as if to ask God for patience.

They were entering the store when Fredi replied, 'I know.

It'll be great. But, to be honest, I've been so busy the last week or two with my recent flurry of Bridezillas that all I've focused on was getting here in time to pick you up. I paid little attention to any emails.'

'Don't you worry, it's all good. I know there are a few must-sees, but we do have a lot to take in. I'm excited about the Nissan Center suite we have.' Ava scanned the rows and rows of boots that were so eye-catching and in a rainbow of colors. It was stunning! She had no idea where to start.

'I am so looking forward to that! Most concerts, you're surrounded by a sea of drunk people, so it'll be really nice to drink in peace!' Fredi said, and Ava heard the excitement bubbling in her voice. Fredi was normally chill about things and rarely let herself get enthusiastic, so it was good to see her like this.

Once inside the store, the thrill of buying a new pair of cowboy boots surprised Ava. She put her suitcase where Fredi directed and wandered over to the display against the wall. There were even more boots inside and she looked at them all, thoroughly overwhelmed.

'How will I ever choose?' She reached out and touched the toe of a burgundy-and-yellow set. 'Look at that color combination . . .'

'Every color imaginable can be put together. From plain leather to psychedelic. You're a size ten, right? We'll have you all dolled up like a country girl again, don't you worry,' Fredi said as she surveyed the displays, hands on her hips. She looked ready to embark on a life-saving mission through enemy fire when her cell phone rang. Fredi cursed when she saw the number on the display and snapped a quick, 'I have to take this,' before striding out of the store, irritation written all over her body.

Ava knew it was probably Fredi's boss. The girls had been

trying to get her to go out on her own for practically years now, but Fredi kept holding back. It was a shame that her friend was hiding her light under an unappreciative bushel. Wandering over to the size-ten boots, she ran her fingers along the toes, waiting for a pair to speak to her, trying not to be dazed by the styles, the colors, the carvings and etchings.

Growing up, she had been the very definition of a tomboy but, thinking about how her style had evolved since college, Ava knew that she wanted something girlie. These would not be boots she used to muck out stables or to ride out to look for calves. Her fingers stuttered on a pair and Ava removed one from the display to look at it more closely. It was perfect.

She grabbed the other one and took both to a nearby bench to try them on. They fit perfectly and she felt like Cinderella with glass slippers. Of course, her boots were ruby red with silver rhinestones outlining the etchings, so it was more like Dorothy in *The Wizard of Oz.*

Fredi came back into the shop, shoving her phone into her pocket with so much force, Ava was afraid she'd rip her pants. Wanting to cheer up her friend, she pointed to her boots and said, 'Look, I found my very own ruby slippers.'

Her friend was silent for a moment and Ava could see Fredi trying to realign her mind back to vacation fun. Finally, she said, 'You know in the books, the slippers were silver.'

Ava strutted around the store, saying cheerfully, 'But they probably weren't nearly as cute as my new boots!'

She felt like yelling triumphantly when she saw a reluctant smirk cross Fredi's face. She liked it when her friends were happy. Fredi walked closer to get a better look at the boots.

'Did you bring any dresses? Oh! With your long, killer legs, those boots and a short dress will look amazing. Did you bring one? A fun one?'

'A fun dress? I don't think I packed any dresses. I change out of my dresses and stuffy business casual clothes the minute I'm away from the day job. You know me, a casual girl.' She waved her hand up and down to indicate her current outfit as proof.

'Okay, so you've got jeans, but I really think you should wear a dress with the boots.' Fredi gave her a sideways look.

Fredi was the shortest of the four of them but she was a powerhouse bundled up inside a small package. Ava was just slightly shorter than Bonni who was, like, Amazon height, and next to petite little Fredi, she felt gargantuan.

'Well, we could go shopping for a dress for tonight, but I didn't bring any stockings,' Ava said slyly, knowing the reaction she was about to get.

'Stockings? You don't wear stockings with cowboy boots.'

Ava burst out laughing at the horrified expression on Fredi's face.

'Fredi, of course I know that. I'm teasing. But, you know, I do like to wear stockings and garters, bustiers, all the "girly stuff".' Ava sat back on the bench to pull off her new boots, wishing she could wear them out, but the ruby hotness did not go well with her yellow blouse. She'd look like Ronald McDonald.

'Did you bring any lingerie this weekend? You never know, you might meet a man that makes you feel all smexy and sweeps you off your feet.' Fredi picked up the boots while Ava shoved her feet back into her runners.

'Actually, no, I tried to travel light this weekend.' Ava paused a beat then said, 'Now you have me worried. Maybe I should have packed some sexy stuff.'

'Stop worrying already. What happened to "not looking"?' Fredi held out the boots to her.

Ava carefully took her new boots, admiring the way they sparkled in the overhead lights. 'Hmm, well, it's a busy weekend for us chicks anyway. No time for men.' Ava looked at the price tag and gasped, 'Holy cow.'

'I told you so. Way more expensive in a hotel. You should know that. Do you still want them?' Fredi picked up another pair and looked at the price. 'Jeezus, I should be in the boot biz.' She put them back.

Ava ran her fingers over the finely tooled leather. She loved these boots: they were pretty, the heel wasn't too high and she could tell the leather was of high quality. If vacation wasn't a time to splurge, when was?

'Yes! Glinda the Good Witch may not have given them to me, but they are mine now!'

Fredi rolled her eyes and lifted a shoulder. 'At least you can take them off and you won't be stuck dancing in them for the rest of your life. You won't have time to break them in, though. What else did you bring?'

'Sandals and runners. I'll have to wear them around the room for a while, then. And don't compare an Academy Award-winning movie to an antiquated fairy tale.' Ava petted the boots fondly. They were definitely coming with her now.

'They are called "classics", not "antiquated". I bet if it had been made into a movie, you'd be all over it.'

'Well, the 1948 film *The Red Shoes*, starring Moira Shearer, was inspired by the fairy tale and Roger Ebert gave it four stars. But it has an unhappy ending, so give me the magic of Judy Garland any day.' Ava gave Fredi a bright smile as she walked over to collect her bag, still carrying her precious new boots.

'Well, then. I stand corrected.' Fredi threw her hands up in the air and went to collect her own luggage.

Ava wheeled her bag over to the counter, placing the boots down. She adored them; they were so pretty with the sparkles and nice coloring. Her father definitely would have dismissed them as frivolous uselessness.

'Alrighty then, boots, you're coming home with me.' She dropped her satchel beside the boots and pulled out her wallet.

'That was a fairly painless decision – unlike all your wedding-dress ideas.' Fredi faked a shudder and Ava pouted.

'Get lost, Fredi, you know you love it. And if you want me to get my wedding dress from you, you'd better stop complaining.'

Fredi snorted. 'I could be so lucky.'

They met glances and burst out laughing.

Ava knew full well Fredi would design her wedding gown. It was a given. The only problem was . . . she had no groom.

Chapter 3

Ava was thrilled they were booked into one of the top-end rooms. She was so happy she could show her friends a good time. Bringing them here, for something they loved, gave Ava so much joy. And being in a luxury hotel to boot! Awesome.

Ava stepped aside and let Fredi go in first, wanting to see the expression on her face.

'Wow.' Fredi dragged her suitcase into the living room of the suite and looked around. She nodded her head. 'You did good, girl.'

Ava propped her suitcase up against the sofa, dropped the bag holding her brand-new boots on the couch and walked over to the sliding glass doors.

'Would you look at this view?' She opened them and stepped out on to the balcony. 'We're inside, but it's like we're outside. This hotel is really cool.'

Fredi came out and stood beside her and whistled. 'This sure is the cat's ass.'

Ava heard the door slam and spun around. 'They're here!'

She dashed into the living room to find Bonni and Celia lugging their suitcases and some bags into the suite.

'Hey!' Ava ran over to tackle-hug her friends.

'Your private jet made it, I see,' Fredi said, and joined in the group hug.

This was a norm for them. Group hugs, squeals of delight, jumping up and down, all the general chaos of the first meeting after being apart for a while. There were even a few tears, mainly from Ava. She stood back and happily watched her friends chatter and catch up. This time, she was responsible for bringing everybody together and she couldn't be more excited.

'You guys have to ride that jet sometime,' Celia told them as she put her purse on the coffee table. She made an exaggerated movement with her hand. 'It's not big, but it's posh. It's the first time I've been on it and I think I could live there. Maybe even join the Mile-high Club one day.' She did a little body wiggle and clapped her hands together.

'As if you haven't already,' Fredi replied.

'Wellllll . . .' Celia didn't say any more, just picked up her bag, which had fallen over.

Ava giggled. 'Hey, speaking of which, why didn't you guys pick me up along the way? It would have saved me from flying commercial.'

Bonni and Celia looked at each other then Bonni replied sheepishly, 'Sorry, Aves, didn't think of it. I don't think we're used to being able to use a plane like an Uber yet.'

Fredi gasped in mock-hurt. 'Aw, Ava, if they'd done that, then you wouldn't have zoomed around with me in the fancy-dancy candy-apple bug.'

Ava shuddered for real and regaled Bonni and Celia with how many death-defying collisions had narrowly been avoided while Fredi snooped through their bags. Ava broke off her story when Fredi squealed in delight and hauled out a big bottle of Jack Daniels.

'I love you guys. You never forget. Smart of you to do a booze run. Saves us having to go out right away.' She hugged the Jack with a sublime smile on her face. 'But, you know, we will be going to the distillery sometime over the weekend. I have so decreed.'

Ava watched Fredi take the bottle over to the bar and twist the cap off. 'Shots, everyone.'

'Of Jack Daniels?' Ava asked, surprised. 'I know I can drink most of you under the table, but straight shots of Jack are . . .' Ava shivered. 'It just burns so bad.'

'Don't be such a baby,' Fredi said as she lined up some tumblers she had found behind the bar. 'Don't we always start off our weekends with a bit of booze?' She pursed her lips as she measured out the shots.

'Okay, ladies, get over here. We have to get ready, don't we? Line dancing tonight!' Fredi barked out the orders and everyone was quick to oblige.

'Pre-drinks!' Celia skipped over to the bar and picked up her glass.

Bonni had hers in her hand and Ava took her glass.

The women raised their glasses, clinked them together and, amidst a variety of grimaces, groans and shivers, downed their shots of Jack Daniels.

'Brrr, that's harsh.' Ava said, shaking her head, her tongue hanging out, sucking in some air.

'What's the matter, honey? Is your tongue on fire?' Fredi asked.

'Uh-huh.' But Ava slapped the cup down and indicated with a finger that she wanted some more. May as well start the night out with a bang, she thought. Tonight was the launch of their long weekend together. She was going to have fuuuun.

'Atta girl.' Fredi had a big smile on her face as she gave Ava another generous dollop of Jack. 'Glasses forward, ladies,' she instructed Bonni and Celia.

Ava picked up hers and watched the others push theirs forward for a refill before they clinked their glasses again.

'Now, what is this about cowboy boots?' Celia asked.

'Oh yeah, Ava totally bought some cowboy boots today,' Fredi said, putting the cap back on the Jack and sticking it in the freezer behind the bar. 'Can you believe she didn't bring cowboy boots to Nashville?'

Celia looked at Ava with an expression of wonder. 'How could you not bring any boots to Nashville?'

Ava wasn't going to let her friends' teasing bother her and tossed it right back at them. 'I haven't had any for years and, honestly, it never even crossed my mind. But I definitely needed a pair for this weekend.' She lifted a shoulder and gave them a saucy smile. 'Just be glad I didn't bring my old tap shoes.'

Fredi groaned. 'Now that would be a sight, you tapping away to "Boot Scooting Boogey", or up on your toes doing pirouettes to "Friends in Low Places".'

Ava looked at Fredi and furrowed her brows. 'I would have killed it.'

'I didn't bring any cowboy boots.' All heads pivoted to Bonni.

'What? You did not bring cowboy boots?' Fredi was astonished.

'Nah, these are my favorites and super-comfy. I can cut a rug in them to beat the band or run down a suspect.' She stuck her foot out and Ava glanced down at Bonni's black, low-heeled boots.

'Guys, come look at the ones I just bought.' Ava rushed over to the couch and hoisted the bag. She pulled the boots out and held them up, turning them so the light would catch the sparkles.

The women oohed and aahed.

'They're gorg!' Celia said, taking one and running her fingers over the leather. 'You will be the pride of the line-dancing dance floor tonight. Can you believe we're in Nashville? I'm so glad I learned to line dance years ago, because going to the Wildhorse Saloon is amazing. It's like the Bluebird Café! Famous.'

Ava carefully tucked her boots back into their bag, giving them a final pat. Now she just had to find a dress to go with them. She was excited about going dancing tonight; it had been way too long since she'd danced. And tonight was line dancing! She hadn't line danced since high school, yet she wasn't worried. She may be a city mouse now, but it was time to let her country shine!

Chapter 4

Chase looked at the photo on his phone, which he'd balanced on the steering wheel. Ava Trent. Somehow, he was supposed to find this woman and hand off two of the complimentary tickets he had been given by his label.

He gazed at her image in between checking the laneway ahead of him that would take him from his ranch house out to the highway and into Nashville. All he had to worry about was the deer that might leap from his forest on either side and into his path.

She wasn't his type at all. This Ava wore a business suit that was black and stiff and the hair scraped back from her face seemed to stretch her skin. It was hard to tell the color – auburn? – but he'd never really gone for chicks with that shade. Not that he was going to *go* for her, but still. Yet there was something in her eyes. Even as a two-dimensional image, he could see a mystery in them, and that had him very slightly intrigued. She wasn't plain, but she wasn't gorgeous. Just average.

He pinched the photo wider so he could see better. The

smile was strained on her face, not natural, and for a moment he had the urge to want to see her *real* smile. To hear her laugh. But then, what do you expect for a business-executive profile photo? She was probably some stuck-up, entitled, spoiled city chick who was everything he disliked. She had the look. He'd seen it often and had been around enough high-society debutantes to last him a lifetime. His family reputation had put him in demand as a Marshal – an escort for debutantes. Gone were the days of marrying debs off, but it was still a very serious business and he knew he'd been bait.

His parents hadn't been too happy with him when he pushed back. He'd had enough of the debs, and the last straw was a debutante with drugs stashed in her bouquet at the ball. Now that was a disaster he wasn't willing to repeat. Give him an earthy country girl any day.

Chase realized that, while the woman in the photo caught his interest in a weird way – only slightly, mind you – he was close to deciding he already didn't like her. Talk about jumping to a rash conclusion. He shook his head and tossed his phone into the tray in front of the wide console between the two front seats of his truck.

He'd do the hand-off and then be on his way. But why the hell they were doing it at the Wildhorse Corral was beyond him. His chances of finding her in there were near to impossible since it would be packed tonight. With CMA Fest this weekend, anybody who was anybody, and then some, would likely be there.

He groaned, thinking that he should probably be there, too. Since he was somebody. At least, that's what his agent and producer told him.

'*You need to be seen in these places, Chase.*'
'*Enchant your fans!*'

'Charm the ladies.'

'You're hot right now, but if you want to be Luke Bryan big, you need to make them love you.'

He touched the antique pocket watch he had hanging from his rear-view, the chain carefully wound around the mirror. He smiled, running his thumb over the beautifully carved surface. This watch was over two hundred years old and had been passed down through his family first born to first born, each one taking care of it to ensure its posterity for the next generation. His mother hated that he had it hanging in his truck. 'Anyone could steal it, and your daddy would roll over in his grave,' she harped. But his truck was his escape. Where he could be alone, with his thoughts, his songs, his music.

He reached the end of the long lane and paused, checking both ways before pulling out on to the dirt backroad that hid the entrance to his ranch. He was hugely into privacy. Coming from old wealth, in an even older family that had roots traced back to the *Mayflower* and royal blood from England – which his family chose to ignore, since the American Revolution – he'd learned to keep things off the radar.

He was rather an enigma in the Hudson family, wanting his solitude and his privacy yet singing for the public, the thousands of fans that filled the arenas for his shows. The family wealth had been carefully cultivated through the years, just as this watch had been.

Chase turned on the radio and was greeted by his latest single, 'You Drive Me Crazy'. He laughed; it still felt awkward hearing his voice on the radio. But he had to admit it was a good song. It was one you had to read between the lines of to get the true meaning.

People asked him all the time if he'd written it for a woman and, if so, which woman? The reality was, it was about a dream, a woman he wanted to be with one day. He'd had his fair share of puppy-love broken hearts but it wasn't until he was older that he discovered just how difficult it was to find the *right* woman. One that wasn't all about who he was, his family and wealth or his rising fame. Being famous brought a whole new dynamic, and it was hard to know whom to trust. When he'd been starting out he'd been young and stupid.

Only once had he gotten a little closer to someone; she'd been from the city and, in the beginning, had been fun to be around. But when she tried to move him out of the country and got prickly when he refused to conform to what she wanted him to be, he began to see who she really was. And the demands she'd started to make had been ludicrous. She'd thrown it in his face one too many times that he had more than enough money to give her anything she wanted and leaked some unsavory lies about him on Twitter and Instagram. He'd had enough, so he'd split in the middle of her rampage and headed for the hills. The fallout of her saying he was an alcoholic had been hard to live down and it brewed up other falsities that, thankfully, had all blown over, with help from his publicist and his label. But it had taught him a valuable lesson. Keep life private and be careful who you allow in it.

He had sworn off women until the right one walked into his life. If she ever did. Now, he used alcohol to medicate the void in his heart.

Whiskey was all he let warm him up these days.

Thirty minutes later Chase was leaning against the bar of the Wildhorse Corral. His cowboy hat was pulled low, shadowing his face, and one booted foot was propped on the brass rail. His shot of whiskey sat untouched, the glass between his fingers, and he perused it. Should he, or shouldn't he? He probably shouldn't, since he was trying to cut back. He was starting to show the lines of a rough road and he was certain he could handle it. But hitting it big at thirty-three had been rather unexpected. Now, two years later and climbing higher, he was determined to stick to his own style of writing songs and performing them. He'd been told that's what made him stand out from the rest.

It wasn't like he'd done it intentionally, blending the old classics with the trends of the past twenty years. He just did what his heart told him to do. He smiled and pushed the shot glass around with his forefinger, as the latest Keith Urban blasted loud and true and he thought of what his mom had told him more times than naught. *'I have no idea where you came from, must be the milkman's son.'*

Now that would be a scandal the Hudson empire would do everything to keep quiet. Especially since he was the last male heir to carry on the family name.

Chase dipped his finger in the whiskey and debated whether to lick the taste off. Maybe that's all he needed, but instead scrunched a napkin around his fingertips.

No, he wasn't an alcoholic

He'd seen enough alcoholics in his years to know the difference. But he also recognized that he was well on his way if he didn't make a change. He picked up the glass, leaned over the bar and put it back down on the other side. No booze tonight.

'Chase, Chase!' A familiar feminine voice yelled behind him. He smiled and turned around.

'Well, if it isn't Miss Daisy.' He looked at his friend as she bounced over. They'd grown up together, fast friends who got in all kinds of trouble in their youth. He knew she wanted more in their relationship. But to him, she was just a friend that he would treasure for the rest of his life. It couldn't be more. They tried it once when they were in their early twenties and, for him, it hadn't panned out. She'd been heartbroken but had come around and they hadn't talked about it since.

She was pretty, with curves in all the right places and a bust line that would pop out the solidest of buttons. She could have any man she wanted but, for some damn reason, whenever they were in the same place she started out her night by flirting with him. Even though he'd made it perfectly clear that he wasn't interested in reliving their greatest hits.

She slid on to the barstool next to him.

'Are you flying under the radar tonight?' Daisy leaned over and grabbed the glass he'd just put on the other side of the bar. Sitting back, she held it up and looked at him. 'Do you mind?'

'No, go to town.' He said, settling his butt back on the stool, hooking the heel of his boot on the lower rung. She shot the whiskey neatly, expertly, and dropped the glass back down on the bar. 'Now then, I asked you a question. Are you flying under the radar tonight?'

He nodded and gazed out, scanning the faces of the crowd on this level of the bar. 'Yep, I gotta find somebody and hand off some shit.'

'You're lucky no one has spotted you yet. You know, when they do, you'll be swarmed,' she said, winding her bright red hair up into a bun and tying it.

Daisy was the typical volatile redhead. He wasn't sure there was a bar on Broadway she hadn't been tossed out of at one time or another, not to mention the childhood tantrums he'd witnessed while they were growing up. Thanks to Daisy, he avoided redheaded women like the plague. Give him a curvy blonde or a cute brunette any day.

'Yeah, I suppose that comes with the territory.' Chase turned and looked at the masses of dancers.

She nodded and reached for his hand. 'Come on. They're playing my favorite song, and I need a dance partner.'

Chase grimaced and shook his head. 'I don't want to dance. That's one way to get spotted.'

'We'll just go to the back somewhere, find a line where nobody else can see you.' Daisy pulled at him, her stubborn streak making itself known.

'Can't you find somebody else to dance with? I gotta look for this woman.' He glanced around at the sea of people and just about groaned.

She shook her head, her pale blue eyes spearing him and her eyebrows furrowing into a line. He knew the look well. If he didn't do what she wanted, she would make his life absolutely miserable until he did. Another reason Chase avoided the reds.

He sighed and stepped off the stool. 'All right, then, come on.'

Daisy did a quick jump up and down, clapping her hands, and then he followed her on to the dark dance floor, illuminated only by strobing lights. The music was loud and sank into him. He let the thumping beat, guitar, drums, even that big old double bass, throb in his blood.

As she promised, Daisy set them up in a back corner with everyone lined up in front of them. It was a sea of cowboy hats, western shirts, jean-covered asses and, right in front of him, a woman with the most sparkly boots he'd ever seen. She was stumbling all over herself, trying to keep up with the music, and he smiled. This must be her first time line dancing.

Chase put his hands on his hips and swung into the steps like he'd been born to do. Which he supposed he had. But he couldn't drag his gaze away from the woman in front of him.

He watched her ass swing in the saucy dress she had on. The skirt, ending mid-thigh, swished as she moved. Her long legs disappeared into the boots. For the first time in a long time, he felt himself grow aroused.

The next steps had them turning around, and he hesitated, hoping to catch a glimpse of Sparkle Boots as she twirled around, but Daisy yanked hard.

'Hey, what the—' he grumbled at her.

'Concentrate, Chase. Come on.' Daisy gave him a fierce glare.

But it was like he could feel the woman behind him and, once facing back in the other direction, he couldn't pull his gaze away from her. He was amused at how badly she danced. She was with a bunch of friends and they were all laughing. Even *her*. It was obvious her friends knew what they were doing and were helping her learn the steps. He couldn't help giving a low chuckle as she nearly tripped over herself again.

He had to give her credit, though: she was trying. The song ended and he was about to make an escape back to the bar.

'Oh, no, you don't, mister.' Daisy grabbed his hand and held him in place. 'We've got a few more sets to do.'

Chase gave her an exaggerated groan. 'Seriously? You said one dance.'

'I lied.' She batted her eyelashes as she squeezed his hand. 'Oh, "Friends in Low Places". Don't you just love Garth? And, if I didn't know better, I'd say this was your song.' Daisy poked him playfully in the chest with her pointy nail.

'Oww, watch those claws.' Chase took her fingertips, lifted her hand high and twirled her around. 'Plus, I could easily take offense to you comparing me to the song. I've had my share of high-society girls and they're not my cup of tea. Give me a girl who can strip down a tractor or go fishing and not squirm taking her catch off the hook.'

'Music to my ears, my man,' Daisy told him.

The next dance step called for a reverse and shuffle

backwards. He was moving without having to think about it. His mind sorta wandered and, the next thing he knew, he smacked into somebody. It was like a freight train had hit him. Chase heard a clatter and feminine squeals from behind, then some raised voices. He spun around but hadn't let go of Daisy's hand quickly enough so he basically flung her on to the pile of women on the floor in front of him.

Had he mowed them all down? Good Lord. Chase leapt forward to try and help.

'What the hell, Chase!' Daisy reached up and grabbed his hand. He hauled her off the pile. 'What was that? You know how to dance.' She stared up at him, hands on her hips.

'I was doing the steps. They must have lost their feet.' He turned and looked at the ladies on the floor. They were killing themselves laughing. Clearly, they were drunk and having the time of their lives.

He leaned over and picked them all up, one by one, setting them on their feet until he saw the last woman at the bottom. Sparkle Boots. She laid on the scuffed hardwood floor, thick auburn hair covering her face, her skirt hiked up to her hips, allowing him a delicious peek of a pair of hot-pink panties, and he couldn't drag his gaze from her legs. He was poleaxed.

'Honey, are you okay?' The dark-haired woman went back down on her knees beside Boots and her other two friends were on the other side, fussing over her.

The woman moaned and reached her hand up to her face. Chase was worried she had a concussion and he'd have to take her for an MRI.

'Step away, ladies. Let me in,' he commanded, and brushed aside her friends. They fell back and stared up at him, mouths hanging open and their gazes darting to each other. Now he had full access to Boots, but first, though, he carefully took the hem of her skirt and pulled it over her thighs to protect her modesty, being extra careful to not let his gaze linger.

He glanced at her friends when one of them gasped, and briefly made eye contact with the woman who had a riot of wild, long curls cascading over her shoulders and down her back. He nodded at her and touched the tip of his hat with the side of his finger. 'Ma'am.'

'Holy shit,' she whispered, and looked at her friends. They seemed shocked into silence and he shook his head. Women.

Chase put his hands under Boots' arms and righted her. Gently, he held her as she got her feet under her and watched as she pushed her hair from her face. She was soft but lean and the warmth of her body scalded his fingers, sending flames racing up his arms and down his spine to settle low in his hips. It got worse when her balance wavered a little and she grabbed his arms to steady herself.

Fuck.

She tipped her head back and their eyes met. For the second time within a few minutes Chase felt like the breath had been knocked out of him. She was stunning and his mouth went dry. It took a moment for him to gather his thoughts as he stared down into her golden eyes.

'Uhm.' He gave himself a mental shake. 'Are you okay, miss? Are you hurt?'

She licked her lips and his gaze followed the movements. He had the strangest urge to pull her in his arms and kiss her until she was limp.

What the hell is wrong with me?

Chapter 5

Strong hands lifted Ava back on to her feet. She was still trying to sort out what had just happened. One minute, she was dancing up a storm and the next she was on her ass under a pile of people. Her hair stuck to her face and she couldn't see. She drew in a shaky breath and tried to get her bearings.

With her feet planted on the floor, she blinked behind the curtain of her hair, the flashing lights confusing her at first. The red-and-blue blinking looked like emergency vehicles and she wondered who'd called an ambulance or the cops. Then Ava remembered she was in the bar and the lights were from the show on the stage.

His strong hands didn't let her go, which was a good thing, since her knees were wobbling a bit. She reached out to steady herself and found a pair of very hard, muscled arms under her fingertips. The man said something. She tilted her head back and shook it to get her hair out of her face so she could see better. When she could, her heart nearly stopped.

Ava looked up into the most gorgeous set of chocolatey-brown eyes she'd ever seen. She drew in a soft gasp, her lips parted, but they were feeling so dry, so she licked them. His gaze dropped to her mouth, making her belly tumble with a sweet tightness. She'd never felt such an instant attraction to a man before.

'Steady.' His deep voice was magical and his hands continued to keep her upright.

Ava gazed at him, noticing how his beard and mustache were sun-streaked, as was his long hair, which curled around the base of his neck from underneath his cowboy hat.

He was huge, broad, tall, muscled, and Ava felt all trembly, like a tiny little butterfly, next to him. She stared at him, captivated, and tried to think of something to say.

'I am . . . who . . . w–what happened?' she murmured, close to being lost for words and unable to pull her gaze away from his hypnotizing eyes.

The grin behind his mustache and beard reached his eyes and they sparkled with humor. Ava was utterly and completely entranced 'Well, I think we had a crash,' he said in a low, intimate tone that gave her the shivers.

She swallowed and looked at him. 'A crash? We weren't in cars.' Ava inwardly cringed at how stupid she sounded. He was throwing her world off-kilter. She focused, not wanting to look like a complete idiot in front of this drop-dead-gorgeous sexy man.

The fast-paced song ended and now a slow ballad was playing. The line dancing broke up as couples gravitated together and began to sway on the dance floor. If this was a movie, Ava mused, this would be the initial precipitating incident. Of course, then there would be a script and she could sound impossibly witty instead of an idiot who stated the obvious.

'A dance floor can be just as dangerous as a highway.' His fingers lingered under her arms and then he gently released her. With their connection broken, the loss of his touch and the strength of his hand made her feel bereft. How silly was that? To feel like suddenly something was missing when he stepped away from her. Involuntarily, she moved closer to him in an effort to keep the resonance of his presence near. He smiled down at her and his teeth were even and white, his lips oh so kissable.

Yup, that was it, he had sealed his fate. Ava was determined that, before the night was out, kissing him was exactly what she'd be doing.

She flipped her hair over her shoulder as she lightly rubbed his arm, having to conceal a shiver of desire at the feel of his bicep. 'Oh yes, obviously. Both can be full of traffic.' Ava turned to look at the cluttered dance floor and saw her friends huddled like inquisitive Babushkas watching the interaction going on between her and this man. She gave them a stern look and they all raised their shoulders and shook their heads with the best innocent expressions they could muster. Ava turned her back to them and focused on her white knight.

'Well, thank you. Even if we did crash, I appreciate you help-ing me up,' she said, looking up at him through her eyelashes.

He was all gentleman, with a true Southern charm. She didn't really hear any accent in his voice and wondered if he was from around here or just visiting, like they were.

'It's my pleasure, miss. I'm just glad you weren't hurt. Are you sure you're okay? You didn't bump your head?' he ques-tioned, concern in his voice, leaning forward as if to look for a wound.

Ava angled her body a little closer. Gliding her hand up his arm, she then knocked her knuckles against her skull lightly.

'No, I'm pretty sure I'm fine. My friends are always complaining about my hard head. And you don't need to call me miss. Makes me sound like I'm a child, and I can assure you, I'm all grown up. My name is Ava, Ava Trent.' She held her hand out and he looked at her with a shocked expression.

He placed his hand in hers and the warmth of his fingers gave her back that lovely, tingly feeling she had had when he held her only moments before. 'Well, we were destined to meet. Although I didn't quite expect it this way. I was actually worried about being able to find you in here.'

Ava was perplexed and wrinkled her forehead. 'I'm sorry? I don't follow. We were destined to meet? You mean, like, cosmically?'

'Chase Hudson,' was all he said.

Ava's mouth rounded into a surprised O as the reality of his name sunk in. They *were* cosmically fated. Okay, so, yes, she had arranged to meet Chase here, but instead of an impersonal hand-off at the bar, they had had an epic meet-cute!

'Well, isn't this my lucky day? I'm glad to meet you, Chase. This certainly was a very interesting way to find each other.' Ava grinned, and he returned it.

'What's going on here?' Celia budged in, disrupting the illusion that Ava and Chase were the only people in the room. Music roared back in an astounding rush, and Ava blinked as if awakening from a dream, springing back from Chase. She had completely forgotten about her friends.

'Come now, Celia. Clearly, Ava's getting to know her knight in shining armor,' Fredi drawled as Bonni stood back, assessing the situation. You could take the woman out of uniform but you couldn't take the cop out of the woman.

'Ladies, this is the man I was supposed to meet,' Ava said, but blushed when she realized how it sounded. 'I mean, this is

Chase Hudson. He has the extra tickets for CMA Fest. It's why we're here, so he could give it – *them*, I mean, them – to me. Out of everyone in here, he's the one who swept – *knocked* – me off my feet. We just sort of collided together, I mean.'

'Well, then. Isn't this super-interesting.' Celia was looking between them and Ava could tell she was already thinking about matchmaking. She looked at Chase as he made charming small talk with her friends and they fluttered around him like busy little hens. But what she did notice is the way that they seemed to herd him closer to her.

'Well, come on, girls. Let Ava do her business with Mr Hudson and we'll go off and get us some drinks.' Bonni gave Ava an exaggerated wink, her elbows hooked in her two friends' as she dragged them away. Ava saw the reluctance on both Celia's and Fredi's faces. They wanted to see what would transpire between her and Chase. Ava wasn't sure exactly what she was feeling now that reality had shattered their little bubble, so she was glad she didn't have an audience while she figured it out

'Chase, who's this?' Ava turned to look at the redhead who came up to stand just behind him. The expression on the woman's face wasn't exactly friendly or welcoming. Were they a couple? She looked at Chase, but he didn't appear to be overly concerned about the woman's obvious jealousy. It fairly seeped off her, in thick, sticky, green waves.

Chapter 6

'Daisy, this is the woman I was looking for. Meet Ava Trent.'
Chase flashed Ava a glance over his shoulder.

Relief washed over Daisy's face and Ava felt a pang of sadness that settled in her chest, knowing he was likely already taken. Of course he was. A handsome, gentlemanly, charming guy like Chase? No way he was unattached. She'd have a better chance of finding a unicorn.

Looking for an escape, Ava said, 'Hi, Daisy, nice to meet you. I'd love to get to know you better, but I think I want to go sit on a stool. My feet aren't used to these boots.'

Both Chase and Daisy glanced down. 'New?' Daisy asked her.

Ava nodded and jolted a little when she felt Chase grab her hand. He pulled his hat a little lower over his eyes then shouldered his way through the crowd, using his body to block anyone from bumping into her. Chase led her over to a stool in a magically deserted corner by a nearby bar. Ava glanced around but couldn't see her friends. The Wildhorse had two different levels, with multiple bars scattered throughout. Fredi had been eyeing a hot bartender at a bar closer to the door; she bet they'd gone back there. Before she could figure out how to extricate herself Daisy was sliding between her and Chase, pulling out a stool.

'Here, sit. It's silly to wear new boots dancing, you're bound to get blisters.' Daisy pulled out a stool and Ava reluctantly sat, caught in a trap of her own making. Still, she let out a sigh of relief when she sat and stretched her legs out, before hooking the boot heels on the rung of the stool. She noticed that Daisy took the seat next to her. Chase would have to go a little further along if he wanted to sit, but instead he hovered behind Daisy, watching Ava's face.

Feeling self-conscious, her desire to kiss Chase tamped down with Daisy sitting there, she said, 'Well, it's been ages since I had a pair, so I wanted to get new boots to commemorate the first day of our vacation.'

'Oh, you're a tourist. Thought so.' Daisy looked satisfied and her body relaxed. She leaned back a little and started looking for a bartender. Clearly, she had dismissed Ava as a threat. 'You started things off with a bang, literally! What do you think made you fall?'

'I don't know, really. My heel slid out from under me and then it was like a train hit me.' A really sexy train. At the memory of his body colliding with hers she flicked a glance at Chase before turning her attention back to the bar. He was watching her with an intensity that she found breathtaking. Yup, it was time to go, before she embarrassed herself. Maybe she could fake a text from her friends.

'There coulda been some beer splashed on the floor.' Daisy indicated with her chin and Ava followed her gaze. 'See, all those out-of-towners are dancing with glasses and sloshing all over the floor. That's not right. You're lucky you didn't hurt yourself.'

Ava snuck another look over the woman's shoulder at Chase. She believed in love at first sight, but she hadn't thought her Mr Right would show up with another woman. Part of her wanted to flat out ask if they were together but she didn't think she could handle it if the answer was yes. Better to let Chase remain a 'what if'.

Before she could fish out her phone and start her exit a group of excited women approached them, waving papers and pens. Daisy rolled her eyes and Chase's shoulders slumped a little before he turned to face them. Ava looked at them curiously as they swarmed around Chase. The women asked for autographs and it suddenly it dawned on her that he must be famous. Given they were in Nashville, she laid odds he was a country star. She was just so out of touch with the current country-music trends.

'We love your music. Could you please sign my napkin?' a dark-haired woman asked him, jostled about by her friends.

He smiled and nodded then glanced briefly at Ava before taking the napkin from his fan's hand. 'What's your name?' he said as he put it on the bar, checking to make sure there was no moisture on the varnished wood.

Ava watched him sign his name in a nearly illegible scrawl for the woman and then repeat the process with the others. Daisy leaned forward and said in a low voice, 'The locals usually leave him alone – country musicians are a dime a dozen around here – but your little to-do on the dance floor must have caught the attention of the tourists. It drives his label crazy that he goes out without security.'

A bartender finally worked her way down to their corner and Daisy turned her attention to getting a drink. Ava declined, instead pulling out her phone. But rather than texting her friends, she googled Chase, drawing in a breath at the results.

She hadn't had any idea who he was before, and now she knew he was country music's newest crooner, desired by women across the country. Her heart fell. As she scrolled through the pages of results she was further dismayed. He had a bit of scandal attached to him and seemed to have created a bit of a bad-boy image for himself. Hmm, wonder what he'd gotten up to? He was probably bro-country, she thought. One of those guys who sang about women being faceless sex objects, shrews that held them back or window-dressing for their good times.

Ava glanced at him from under her brows, watching as he signed for the last woman. He seemed very respectful and engaging. Was it really right to judge him on blog posts and online tabloid articles, especially when she had never listened to his music herself? Just because there was smoke, did it mean there was fire?

There were other things to consider, too. So many famous musicians cheated. No way did Ava want to start anything with someone that had potential baggage like that. Plus, his roots were here, while hers were elsewhere, and it would mean a long-distance relationship. Those never worked, as Ava well knew. She stopped herself. What was she doing? She'd just met the man and here she was, thinking long term!

But maybe just a weekend fling?

Nope. Not happening, Ava knew her heart wouldn't be able to take it. She decided to nip this in the bud, before it grew legs and took her for a walk down the garden path.

Ava slipped off her stool when the last of the autograph-seekers had left. 'I'm going to go find my friends. Thanks for your help, but I'll take the tickets now.'

The expression on his face fell and she could tell he was disappointed. But she was not going to get herself involved. Even if her body had a different opinion than her brain.

'Why do you have to leave so soon?' he asked, and skirted around Daisy's stool to get closer to Ava. Daisy lifted a hand as if to reach out for him and then shrugged, letting it drop. She drained the remainder of her drink before sliding off her stool and disappearing into the crowds without a word. Ava was confused about what this meant.

She looked up at Chase and tried not to feel like this was going to be one of her biggest regrets.

'You're busy – you're really in demand.' She waved her hand in the direction of the departing women. 'And I should get back to my friends before they get into trouble.' Ava shrugged her shoulders. 'I'm sorry.'

He looked at her, perplexed, and she wished she could read his mind.

'I am, too,' was all he said, and Ava felt let down that he didn't argue with her decision. Then he said, 'Don't you like country music?' His question was direct and his expression genuine. 'I assume you do, since you are in Nashville, after all, and going to CMA Fest.'

'I know where I am. And yes I do. But, well, I don't think I've heard your music.'

He put his hand to his chest and faked being crushed. 'You're getting me. Oh man, I've never felt so gutted.'

Ava laughed at his theatrics. 'Sorry, but best to be honest, don't you think?'

He looked at her, suddenly serious, and her heart did a little tumble. 'Yes, it is always best to be honest.'

He reached into his pocket and pulled out a folded envelope, handing it to her. 'I think this is what you've been waiting for.' His deep voice sent ripples of delight along her spine and she second-guessed her decision for a clean break.

She looked at his big hand holding the white envelope and

reached for it. Their fingers brushed and she had another surge of pleasure. It only solidified her determination that she was doing the right thing. She was cutting her losses to protect her heart.

'Thank you. Well, then . . .' She hesitated a moment then took a step away. 'I'll get back to my friends now.'

He nodded his head and touched his finger to the peak of his cowboy hat. 'Perhaps we'll meet again sometime.'

Ava nodded and paused a beat. 'Yes, perhaps. Sometime.' She let her gaze linger on him for a fraction of a second longer. Before she could change her mind she whirled around and went off in search of her girls, leaving behind one of the most intriguing men she had ever met. The urge to look over her shoulder was great but Ava kept her eyes pinned forward, still feeling the weight of his gaze boring into her back.

Like the song said, these boots were made for walking.

Chapter 7

Chase watched Ava go. He frowned, bothered more than he cared to admit by her sudden change of heart. One minute, he's seeing interest in her eyes and the next it was gone, along with her. But he had learned a long time ago that, once a woman made up her mind, it was all over. He'd seen how his buddies had fared. Stump was a prime example. He'd loved Shelly-Jo so much he'd do anything for her, but when there'd been one too many Saturday nights with the boys she'd dumped him like a hot potato. It was as if a switch had been flipped. No matter how much Stump begged or cajoled, he couldn't bring her around. Chase shook his head and smiled, thinking how devastated he'd been when a similar thing had happened to him at the ripe old age of sixteen. Live and learn.

He figured she'd discovered who he was. How could she not when fans came up asking for autographs? That she still walked away was unlike anything he'd encountered before. He'd experienced women who wanted him for who he was in the music industry and all the trappings that came along with it.

They didn't want him for who he was . . . the man. For Ava to leave without a backward glance – it impressed the hell out of him.

He saw Daisy back out on the dance floor, glad she was off having a good time. Turning to leave, he spied a few of his buddies on the other side of the Wildhorse and decided to head over there for a bit. As he made his way through the crowd, he noticed people watching him and knew it wouldn't be long until word spread that he was here. He wouldn't be surprised if word wasn't already making its way through the Twitterverse and Insta.

He walked around the end of the horseshoe-shaped bar and approached his group of friends, who sent up a cheer when they saw him.

'Hey, Bulldog, what are you drinking?' The youngest member of their group leaned over to flag down the bartender.

'Nothing tonight, Stump.' They'd all pegged each other with nicknames when they were kids. 'I'll be on my way soon, just wanted to come over and say hey.'

They clapped him on the back as he moved into the group and they circled around him. His friends knew the drill. When in public, they used their bodies as a shield, closing ranks to keep the fans from seeing him. He'd grown up with this motley crew. They'd fished, hunted, rode horses and played Daniel Boone in the mountains when they were young. They knew him for who he was and never changed how they were with him. And that, he valued.

'You're performing this week?' Stump asked him.

'Yeah. I'm playing.' Chase scanned the crowd, hoping to see Ava again. It surprised him he was still so unsettled at the way she had left. Troubled and intrigued and . . . he had to admit it: he wanted to go and seek her out.

'Hey, Sal,' His other buddy, dubbed Magic for always doing card tricks as a kid, hollered at the bartender. 'Shots – Jack.' He held up seven fingers.

Sal tossed them a sexy smile. She was a rocking bartender and had a way with the boys, many of whom she'd let take her home.

'Hey, Chase.' She put coasters down on the bar and reached over to touch the back of his hand. He'd never been one who had fallen to her charms, and it wasn't for her lack of trying. 'No shots for you tonight?'

'Not me,' Chase told her and shook his head, carefully extricating his hand from under hers. Even though he'd only been here with them less than five minutes, that was his cue to leave. Once the shots started, it would be a late night of partying that he didn't need this weekend.

'Gotta run, guys. Catch ya later.' He was about to leave when his other friend, Krill, grabbed his arm.

'Listen, there's a dance at the Harper place tomorrow night. Not too many people know about it. Are you interested in coming?'

'I'll think about it. I'm not sure exactly what's happening this weekend. My publicist has a few things lined up. Maybe see you there, though.'

That was a lie, since his schedule for CMA Fest had been set in stone months ago and he knew tomorrow night was free. On second thoughts, it might be the perfect place to take Ava, so she could dip her toes in the world of country and country music. If that unflattering photo of her made one thing clear, she was a city girl, so she might need a little more Southern persuasion. The more he thought about it, the more he liked the idea of taking her to the Harpers'. He knew she was with friends, but he would invite them along if they wanted to come.

Now he was determined to find her. Search her out and try to woo her with his country-boy charm, which he'd been told made panties melt and albums fly off the shelf.

He slapped his hand on the bar. 'Later, boys.'

They all grunted their goodbyes and moved apart, making him a path to walk away.

Chase stuck to the perimeter of the room, keeping to the shadows and making sure his cowboy hat was low over his head. He did his best to keep a low profile and realized the crowd of women had likely been what had turned Ava off. If so, he didn't blame her. It was damn hard getting used to the fans. He still hadn't quite adjusted.

The Wildhorse was huge, with different levels and numerous bars to serve the crowd, so it was no wonder he had a hard time finding her in the crush of people. It was always a busy place, but tonight it seemed to be bursting at the seams. Lots of out-of-towners here for CMA Fest, no doubt.

After about fifteen minutes of searching the main floor from the shadows and ready to go upstairs to look in the lounge, he spotted her. Ava and her friends were seated at the circular bar in the middle of the room. The only drawback? It was surrounded by the dance floor. That meant he had to make his way through the gyrating, line-dancing throng of people to get to her and would probably be noticed.

He stood for a moment in a dark corner, watching her. It made him feel uncomfortably stalkerish. When she threw her head back and laughed, her auburn hair cascading over her shoulders and down her back, he froze. Watching her movements was like seeing perfection. She was perfection. The disco-ball lighting glittered off her boots, sending shards of light sparking into the air. It reminded him of her hot-pink panties.

Chase groaned at the memory. He pushed himself off the wall and decided that, in more ways than one, she was worth what he might have to face by going through the crowd.

Weaving his way through people, still keeping his head down and the rim of his hat over his face, he managed to avoid being recognized and, a few minutes later, he emerged from the crowd behind Ava.

It was the first time in his life he'd ever felt speechless. He didn't know what to say, and words were his living! She and her friends all had drinks and were chattering and laughing, looking like they were having a great time. Then the dark-haired one saw him. Her eyes widened and she seemed to be assessing him. He felt under scrutiny, but if gaining acceptance from her friends meant getting to the next step with Ava, he was fine with that.

The woman tapped Ava on the arm and pointed in his direction.

Ava spun around on the stool, and once again, he was snared by her spectacular eyes. A slow smile widened her lips and all he wanted to do was drag her into his arms and kiss, taste, consume her. He cleared his throat and took her smile as his cue to step forward.

'Ava,' Chase said in a low voice.

'Chase.' Her voice was lilting, beautiful. and he wanted to hear her talk, moan, whisper in his ear.

'Hi, I, ah, well. I was hoping you'd change your mind.'

Moments later, her other friends spun around on their stools and he was pinned by four sets of eyes. He looked at each one, acknowledging them, and was pleasantly surprised when each one responded in kind. Then he focused on Ava.

'What do you mean, "change my mind"?' She leaned back on the stool, resting her elbow on the bar, and gazed at him intently. Ava crossed her legs and his eyes were drawn to her trim thighs. She bopped the toe of her boot and it was all he could do to drag his gaze away and focus back on her face.

Her friends watched him, and it unnerved Chase. Clearly, these women traveled in a pack; they had each other's back, he was sure of it. If a man hurt one of them, the rest would take him down. He admired that kind of loyalty. He stepped closer to Ava, choosing to forget her friends were there beside her. It was Ava that he wanted to talk to.

'You said you didn't know my music. I was hoping to introduce you to it and maybe change your mind about spending time with me.' He tilted his head sideways and gave her a grin that he hoped didn't look like a shark's smile.

She laughed, and it was a deep, wonderfully throaty sound that echoed through him. He wanted to hear her laugh again – oh hell, he wanted a whole lot more from her. Namely, getting the chance to get to know her, and for her to know him.

'And just what did you have in mind, superstar?' She was teasing him, and he liked the way she played. There was a whole lot more to this woman than what you saw on the surface.

'First, I know you're going to be in town for a couple of days because of CMA Fest.' He lifted his shoulder and held out his hands. 'You can't hide that from me, so how would you like to spend some of your time with me this weekend and I'll do my level best to win you over.'

Her eyes widened and she reached the tip of her tongue to touch her upper lip. It was one of the sexiest moves he'd seen, pretty much ever. He realized he was holding his breath waiting for her to say yes.

'"Win me over"? Now let me think about that.' She glanced at her friends, who were silently watching their exchange. He had a feeling that, if they disapproved of him, he wouldn't stand a chance. Chase tried to draw her attention back to him.

'Now, don't take too long to come up with your answer, Boots. We don't have all night.'

'Boots, huh?' She stared at him and he forgot how to breathe. 'I've been called worse. Okay, sure. Dazzle me, superstar.'

Chapter 8

When Bonnie touched her arm a moment ago and Ava saw Chase standing there, looking all crazy sexy, gorgeous and yet with a vulnerability, it touched her heart.

She glanced around to see if Daisy was with him, but the redhead seemed to have disappeared. For Chase to come over and ask her out made her think that he wasn't already taken. She'd responded instinctively with her sultry answer and now it shocked the heck out of her that she'd said those words only a moment ago. *Dazzle me, superstar.*

Ava cringed inside a little and waited to see how he was going to respond. She held her breath and all her focus was on him. Her body hummed and desire settled with delicious heaviness between her thighs. Good Lord, he was definitely the kind of man she'd never, ever met before. She was unable to pull her gaze away from him. His deep brown eyes snagged her and she felt delectably wonderful. She'd never been so turned on by a simple look before.

'Dazzle you, Boots? I can definitely do that. These hands are magic.' Chase lifted his hands and did jazz hands, and Ava choked, lost between amusement and arousal.

'I'm sure you're a regular Criss Angel, but first I want to know if you have a lovely assistant waiting for you. As in, a girlfriend?' She asked point-blank, wanting that particular scenario cleared up right off the bat; there was no way she was going to beat around the bush when it came to the possibility of being the other woman. When she finally found her man, it would be just the two of them. For life. Ava shared almost everything, except food, but she definitely had no intention of sharing the man that she would spend the rest of her life with.

Which didn't mean that would be Chase. Because that would be crazy talk. She had just met the impossibly handsome, sexy and charming guy!

'Girlfriend?' He looked perplexed again and glanced around like there would be a clue to what she meant in the crowds. 'I don't have a girlfriend.'

'What about Daisy?' Ava almost held her breath, waiting for his answer. She wanted, so desperately, for him to deny that Daisy was his girlfriend.

'You got that all backwards.' Chase stepped closer to her and his presence seemed to vibrate in the air between them; it washed over her in a powerful wave. She inhaled a deep breath and held it when the scent of his soap, cologne, wildness filled her. Her eyelids fluttered as the feelings he roused in her did all sorts of good bad things to her, making her heart thump harder in her chest. If he could make her body respond so acutely with just a look, his voice, what he could do with his hands?

She had to think for a minute about what they'd been saying. *Oh yeah.* 'And how do I have that backwards?' Ava asked, tipping her head to the side and looking at him from under raised eyebrows, desperately trying to keep her equilibrium.

'I grew up with her.' Chase edged closer still and rested his hand on the back of her stool. His thumb brushed against her dress. Ava nearly sprang out of the seat at his touch but she saw the grin curving on his face. For a man with a beard and a mustache, something she was not normally attracted to, he had it all.

The urge to raise her hands and grab the bolo tie to pull him down to her so she could kiss him was nearly overwhelming, so instead she shifted to reach for her drink, and managed to tip it over. The contents of her glass spewed over the bar in the direction of Fredi and Celia. They both sprung from their seats with cries of alarm.

'Damn, Ava, we're not the ones who need a cold shower!' Fredi stood back with her hands out, looking down to make sure nothing had got on her clothes. Celia, on the other hand, had quickly grabbed a rag from the other side of the bar and was mopping up the mess.

Ava was mortified. She was behaving like a child: nervous, clumsy – and it so wasn't like her. Lord, she needed to get a grip, and fisted her hand when it began to tremble. She stared at it, not wanting to look up to see the humor that was probably shining in Chase's eyes.

From behind her, Bonni put a hand on her shoulder and Ava heard her whisper right next to her ear. 'Chill, Ava. This man has gotten you all aflutter. Just relax.'

Ava turned around enough to be able to look Bonni in the eyes. Her bestie nodded at her and squeezed her shoulder in reassurance. 'Thanks,' Ava said gratefully.

'You're welcome. Now, go with him. It's not like I can't track him down if I need to,' she said in a low voice, and gave Ava a little nudge.

Ava steadied her breathing then turned back to Chase.

'Have you met my friends?' She decided to avert her nerves by making introductions. 'That's Celia, cleaning up my mess – she's an amazing writer. Over there with the curly hair is Fredi; she's a wedding-dress designer.'

Ava turned to Bonni, not wanting Fredi to be her normal self and blurt out anything about how she had inundated Fredi with wedding-dress designs. Good Lord, could you imagine? 'This is Bonni. She's a cop – a detective, actually.'

Celia waved the rag in Chase's general direction and Fredi opened her mouth before snapping it shut at a killing look from Celia. Bonni leaned around Ava and put her hand out for Chase to shake. 'Pleased to meet you.'

'That explains it,' Chase said quietly as he shook hands with Bonni. As they let go, Bonni gave him a little nod combined with a warning look and Chase rested his fingers on the brim of his hat, as if tipping it.

'Explains what?' Ava asked, looking between the two of them.

'Ah, nothing. It's nice to meet you all. I know you're here for the festival and that you are spending time in one of the arena suites. But if you're free tomorrow night, after the last concert, I was wondering if you'd all like to come to a party.'

'Oh, I don't think so. It's going to be so late—' Ava started to answer.

'A party?' Fredi interjected, and smiled brightly at Chase. 'I'd love to go to a party.'

'Hmm, Celia, what's on the schedule for tomorrow night after the concerts?' Bonni inquired.

Ava was getting a little annoyed that this conversation was happening as if she didn't exist.

'Tomorrow – Thursday – is actually free during the day, and then the first performer goes on at the Nissan at—'

'Okay, guys, listen, I think I have some input here . . .' Ava said, giving them each dagger stares.

'Ava, you can think on the party and let me know. But I have another proposition for you.' Chase pushed up the brim of his cowboy hat with his fingertip. The shadow gone from his face and the bar light reflecting in his eyes, she realized even more how ruggedly handsome he was.

Her mouth went dry and now she desperately needed that drink she'd just knocked over. Ava craned her neck to see if she could flag down the bartender. If there was ever a time for two pina coladas, this was it!

Chapter 9

The bartender was not cooperating with Ava's need for alcoholic relief as she was helping customers on the other side of the bar. Ava ran her fingertips along the hem of her new dress. Best to keep her hands busy so she didn't flail again and send another drink flying. That had been so embarrassing, but it was really his fault for being so darn hot. Drawing in a steadying breath, she met Chase's gaze.

He was affecting her like crazy. A hint of his scent heated the air between them. It was spicy, leathery and fresh, like cotton sheets drying on a clothesline, worn saddles, and the slightest hint of jalapeños. Ava inhaled deeply, liking how it teased her nose and lingered in her senses. Years could go by and, if she ever caught a whiff of it again, it would bring her right back here. To this moment. She fought for words to say, but it was as if her voice had decided to do a vanishing act.

His hand was still behind her on the seat and she leaned back slightly, wanting to feel his touch again. He shifted on his feet and she got her wish as he brushed against her bare shoulders. Ava didn't even try to hold back the soft sigh that slipped from her lips.

It was like a flip had switched and now she could concentrate again. 'So, another proposition, huh? Careful, superstar, a woman could get the wrong idea about all the proposing you're doing.'

The corner of his mouth tipped up and Ava was distracted by the small movement, missing Chase pulling his phone out until he showed her the screen. She nearly screeched when she saw the godawful photo of her. She had been working with a dreadful but obscenely wealthy couple. The husband was a lech of epic proportions and the wife was insanely jealous of any woman she thought might cause him to stray. In order to keep both clients happy, Ava had deliberately made herself look as unattractive as possible. And now Chase had a picture of her like that.

She straightened up on the stool, as if her spine had solidified to steel, and made a fruitless grab for his phone. 'Where did you get that picture?'

'Your boss sent it to my guy, who sent it to me so that I would recognize you. Gotta say, Boots, not sure I would've.' Chase's gaze took another leisurely tour of her body and Ava was torn between dissolving into a puddle of lust and plotting the best way to murder David.

'So it's clear the Nashville air does you right. I'm proposing you spend time with me, let me show you how to live life, country-style, before you go back to your stressed-out city living.' He leaned in to her and spoke in a low, intimate tone that sent shivers of desire racing along her skin, through her blood, to pool in a sweet heat deep inside. It was all she could do not to moan. Then his words sank in. Was he for real?

'So you think I need a crash course in being country?' she

said, her tone sweet as sugar. There was an audible gasp from next to her and Ava suddenly remembered her friends. Celia had her elbow propped on the bar so she could rest her chin on her hand while watching the Chase and Ava show. Fredi raised her glass in Ava's direction and mouthed, 'Give him hell,' while Bonnie was looking down into her beer and shaking her head.

'It's like the Alabama song,' Chase said. 'In the city, you are rushing to get things done and life's no fun. In the country, we know how to slow down and enjoy life. Spend time with me and it'll be the most relaxing vacation you ever have.'

He slid his phone into his back pocket, before resting his hands on the arms of her stool, boxing her in. Ava should've felt trapped, but instead she just wanted to slide her hands up his chest until she could bury them in his hair and coax him down for a kiss. However, she was also appalled at his assumption that he knew what her life was like, based on one crappy photo.

'I'm not as unfamiliar with stereotypical country activities as you are *assuming* I am, you know. In fact, I'm a pretty damn good fisherman,' she announced, and Chase cast an amused glance at her. 'What's that expression for?'

'Where do you go fishing in the city? The local aquarium?' he replied. The bartender finally came over and started to ask them if they wanted any refills, but Celia was loudly shushing her and Ava could barely contain the eye roll.

'There's always good fishing around, even in a big city, if you know where to look. So what makes you think I can't fish?'

Chase gave her a knowing look. 'The woman in that pic definitely does not fish.' He nodded and absently stroked his beard.

'That is totally what I would call judging a book by its cover. Yes, indeed. After all, you really don't know anything about me, do you?' She crossed her arms and sat back in her seat, which nicely pushed her boobs a little higher over the neckline of her dress. She could tell that he tried not to let his gaze wander, but he failed.

'Okay, then,' he said. 'Prove it. Prove that you could be a country girl.' He leaned toward her and his cowboy hat shadowed them, sheltering them with an intimacy from the dance-floor lighting. He emanated a confidence that told her he was a powerful man. She'd been around enough men to tell weakness from power, arrogance from spirit. And most of the men didn't fall under the complimentary narrative.

'Really? You want to bet me that I can't be a country girl because I'm too city?' Ava knew that the right thing to do would be to confess she was country born and bred, but he needed to be taken down a peg.

'C'mon, Boots. Come explore the country side. I'm confident I can show you how.' *Confidence is not one of your weak points, my man.* Ava all but shivered and sat taller in her seat, which brought her face closer to his.

'Well . . .' She hesitated, and his even white teeth showed when he gave her a crooked smile. 'Deal. I bet you I can adapt to country life better than you could ever imagine. Shake on it?'

She gave him a sassy look. He straightened and laughed, a booming deep laugh that reached right inside and twisted her all up. Her lungs decided she no longer needed air and Ava had to force herself to breathe. Her attraction to this man was off the charts. He had some kind of country-boy charm, but she was going to show him the flaws in labeling women based on their appearance.

Bonni caught her eye and gestured to a restless-looking group of women that were whispering to each other and glancing over at Chase. They were beginning to realize who he was.

She turned back to him and wondered if he was aware of the rising buzz around them. He seemed unaffected and kept his focus tightly on her. It made her feel special that he could ignore his popularity and make her his priority.

Ava was about to suggest they leave before things got hectic when Celia said, 'I would suggest we start a pool, but we all know Ava is going to destroy him because—'

'She *is* a Cancer. And when Venus meets Mars in the fifth house – woo, boy, you better watch out,' Fredi said, nonchalantly running her finger around the top of her beer mug. Ava looked at her a little askance and Fredi winked at her. Fredi, who dismissed astrology as 'a load of bullshit designed to give people a false feeling of control over the chaos of life', was clearly on board with teaching Chase a lesson.

Bonni giggled behind her and added, 'Ain't that the truth.'

'Okay, enough cheap-seat comments.' Ava decided to take charge of what was happening here. 'I think Chase and I need to find a quiet place to discuss the terms of our bet, without the three of you chirping in the background.'

She slid off the stool and faced Chase. Ava took a moment to truly look at him. Lean and tight, his jeans hugged his hips and thighs and he had a huge silver belt buckle. His shirt looked like a soft denim and the buttons appeared to be mother of pearl, shining under the lights.

They weren't very far apart and the energy vibrating in the air between them was enough to make her knees weak. Ava tossed her hair back over her shoulder and reached for her purse, which was resting on the bar. She paused when Fredi called her name.

'Hey, Aves, see what happens when you stop looking?' Fredi smirked and toasted her again.

Ava couldn't say that she hadn't thought of it. The romantic in her already had them married, with a house with a white picket fence, a golden retriever and babies. But all the reasons she walked away the first time still applied. Chase lived his life under a magnifying glass, under constant scrutiny from fans and press alike. Any woman who entered his orbit would find herself equally exposed.

'Here we go again. Another weekend, another fling,' she heard Celia murmur behind her, and Ava shot her a glance. Then she looked at Bonni, who gave her a very secretive smile and nodded imperceptibly.

It could be a weekend fling if she wanted it to be. What was the harm in that? Really, who would pay attention to a nobody who blipped in and out of Chase's circle of fame? Just one weekend, and not even the whole time, since she had plans with her friends and she was sure he had CMA Fest things to do. Surely she could handle a single weekend. Then they'd go back to their separate lives.

Ava drew in a deep breath and grabbed her purse from the bar. 'Okay, then, shall we go find a quiet spot to talk about this wager?'

He nodded, grinned and held his hand out to her, palm up. She looked at it. If she placed her hand in his, then she was setting a whole new ballgame in motion.

He had a big hand, powerful, to go with the rest of him, she noticed, as he waited patiently for her. His sleeves were rolled up and it was the first time she noticed tattoos curling around his corded forearm and down to his inner wrist on his left arm. The images of his ink were unbelievably scintillating and now, on top of the rest of his yumminess, she was curious to find out if he had tattoos anywhere else on his body.

She placed her hand in his and loved the thrill that exploded inside her. 'Shall we?'

*

When Ava placed her hand in his, the emotion that raced through Chase shocked him. How could a simple touch create such a mighty response? One that excited him. Her fingers, warm and soft, gripped him tightly. He liked it and closed his hand over hers. Chase faced her friends.

'Ladies, do you have transportation back to your hotel? I can arrange it for you.' His heart kicked up a notch when Ava stepped closer to him. The heat from her body wasn't easy to ignore. Nor did he want to.

'Oh, we're good, don't you worry,' Celia replied, and clasped her hands together, watching them with the oddest expression on her face.

'Don't worry, ladies, I'll take care of Ava, and here . . .' He let go of Ava for a second to reach into his pocket. He had business cards in his wallet. Taking one out, he held it up and the dark-haired woman took it. Bonni, if he remembered correctly. The cop. He wasn't surprised in the least.

Bonni waved the card at him. 'Thank you. I appreciate this.'

Chase laughed. 'All my contact info is on the card. But you have no reason for concern.' He put his arm around Ava. 'She's in good hands. I'll make sure Ava gets back safely. It was nice to meet you all, and hopefully our paths will cross again.'

He liked them. They seemed quirky and obviously had a very special bond. He was close to his boys, but Ava and her friends were something else. Celia and Ava seemed to be conversing through facial expressions and eyebrow raises as Bonni entered his contact info into her phone. Fredi suddenly leaned in front of Celia, ending the silent conversation. She lifted her hand, mimicking a landline phone, and mouthed, 'Call me,' to Ava. Then she shot Chase a warning look.

He could tell that Bonni was the direct type. If she had an issue with you, then you knew your ass was grass right up front. Fredi, on the other hand, she seemed like someone who would pretend everything was fine and then jump you outside the bar at closing time. God help him if things didn't go well with Ava. He'd probably have to send out a search party for his balls once Fredi got through with him.

Fortunately for him and his anatomy, Ava had clearly had enough. 'I'll call you guys later. Have fun,' she said, blowing kisses to her friends.

Chase liked the feel of her body next to him and when she slipped her arm around his waist his blood heated. He did his best to keep chill.

He led Ava back through the crowd of people. It was unavoidable that they'd be stopped and greeted by many along the way. This was the only thing he'd had trouble getting used to. This weekend would be worse, too, with all the out-of-towners looking for celebs. He was polite, patient and signed a few autographs but he was very anxious to get Ava outside. He sensed a growing reluctance in her from the way she hung back from the crowd building around him. She clearly wasn't a groupie drawn to the light of fame but she didn't say a word and he appreciated her being a good sport. It wasn't really an ideal first date.

After dodging more fans and finally pushing the doors open, they escaped out into the night. Even though he found that fandom aspect difficult, it had seemed more manageable tonight, with Ava by his side.

They'd left just in time, too, as the buzz of him being at the Wildhorse was going almost viral. His phone was going off and he pulled it out of his pocket. Instagram and Twitter was blowing up with posts of where he was, as well as photos of him and

Ava and of them at the bar with her friends. He shook his head and frowned. Hopefully, the other girls would get out quick, or they'd be swamped.

'What's wrong?' Ava asked, concern edging her voice.

'Nothing if we can get out of here asap.' Chase escorted her quickly through the parking lot. He didn't want Ava scared off by this side of his life.

'What's happened?' she asked him as they made their way through the parked cars. The night was warm, sultry, and he inhaled deeply. He needed some nature; it always calmed the ruckus inside him.

'Paparazzi are going to be swarming soon and I try to avoid them.' He liked that she hadn't let go of his hand yet and he flexed his fingers on hers a little bit. She fell behind him as they squeezed through a couple of cars parked a little too close.

'It must be hard, the way they invade your privacy.' She took a couple of quick steps to catch up with him so they were side by side again.

'It is, but it's the trade-off for being successful. If I want people to hear my songs, I gotta get used to it. Anyway. Where you staying?' He fished the key fob out of his jeans pocket and unlocked the doors to his truck.

'Opryland Hotel.' He glanced down at her and liked how the streetlights shot fiery sparks off her hair. He smiled. Wouldn't you know it? Her hair was much redder than he'd first thought. Somehow, though, he couldn't see Ava getting up to the same antics as Daisy. Ava had more of an innocent quality to her, like she believed everything could be settled with earnest conversation and a long hug.

'Nice hotel.' He opened the passenger side door, deliberately crowding a little closer than necessary.

The June breeze, warm and soft, caught her scent and buffeted it around him. It was wonderfully fresh and seeped into his very pores, filling him with her.

'Well, this is a nice truck,' she said as she stepped on the running board and looked for a handhold above her.

'Here, let me help you.' Chase took her elbow and she rested her fingers on his arm to help steady her as she got into the passenger seat.

'Wow, it's so big and high. Fredi would have a heck of a time getting into it. She'd need a catapult.' He heard the humor in her voice. Another side to her he liked. He was sure that, if her friend was here, Ava would be gently teasing her to her face. His life had become far too serious since making it big, with lots of double-talking and schmoozing, and he was desperate for some chill time with someone who was honest and exactly who she appeared to be.

'Yeah, my mom has trouble, too.' He was reluctant to let her go, but he did, and shut the door to walk around the front of the truck, watching her through the windshield. He liked how she looked in his truck as she snapped on her seatbelt and settled into her spot.

He climbed into the driver's seat and started the truck. The throaty growl never got old.

'So, you've managed to coerce me away from my friends on our girls' weekend away, to talk about a bet that you're going to lose, by the way, even though you still haven't laid out the stakes.' Ava placed her purse on the console between them and he looked at it.

'Ladybugs, now I don't think I've ever seen a purse quite like that.' He glanced at her.

'I like whimsical things. And that little bag just caught my attention. It's a Kate Spade, I love her stuff. She was one of my favorite designers. It's so sad when we lose people too soon.' She twisted in her seat a bit and she faced him.

'Yes, it is.' He paused for a moment, thinking about his uncle for a second. His dad's younger brother, Uncle Trav, had always supported Chase's dream to pursue music, even buying him his first guitar and sneaking him out to guitar lessons. His death three years ago in a car accident was still gutting to think about. Wanting to shake off the heavy mood, he said, in a deliberately lighter tone, 'So, here we are.' He raised his eyebrows and gave an exaggerated wink.

Ava laughed and ran her fingers through her hair, pulling its length up and twirling it around her hands before letting it fall into a cascade of waves.

He. Was. Bewitched.

She looked at him and he knew he was being assessed. 'Hmm, I don't think you're a serial killer or kidnapper, am I right?'

He liked her teasing nature and laughed, shaking his head.

'We also have a professional connection through my boss and my friends know I'm with you. Plus, you gave them your card. So . . .' She shrugged her shoulders and her tongue was caught between her teeth when she gave him a cute smile. 'I believe I'm in relatively safe hands.'

'Even without that connection, I assure you, you have nothing to fear when you're with me.' Chase felt tongue-tied.

'Oh? You're not the same as other famous country-music stars, who have a bevy of groupies always around? Who are always looking for the next hook-up?' She continued to tease him, and it was refreshing. He was about to reply but she continued: 'I'm sure you're in hot demand.'

' "Hot demand." Well, I've been known to find a lady friend or two, but I value quality over quantity.' He backed out of the parking spot and kept his eye on traffic, really enjoying their banter.

'Oh, I don't know, I think it would be pretty hard for a guy to turn down a group of pretty young things shaking their money-makers at him.'

He tossed her a look to see the expression on her face but she was looking out the passenger window. There had been something in her tone, though. He could tell she was teasing because of the barest curve of a smile on her lips, but there had been something else, something deeper. Something that gave him pause. She'd been hurt. And he wondered just how hurt.

He decided to switch the subject.

'So then. About the bet.' He put on the indicator to get around a parked delivery truck on the narrow street.

'Yes, your whole reason for stealing me away. Let's hear it.' He saw her running her fingertip along the hem of her dress and it totally reminded him of the sight he'd caught earlier. Those hot-pink panties.

At a red light his gaze automatically sought her out again and he was pinned. She looked back at him, her eyes nearly translucent in the lighting, her skin flushed. The curve of her neck drew his eyes to the delicate collarbone and then the gentle rise of her breasts beneath the low neckline of her dress. He had no words for how beautiful she was.

Chase could look at her all day and still not see enough of her. But the challenge in her eyes was refreshing. He reached for the radio to find some background music and, when he found a tune that made him smile, he turned it up.

Ava laughed. '"Fishin' in the Dark"? I loved that song when I was younger.'

'You don't love it anymore?' It pleased him that she liked the same song he did. And it gave him an idea.

But before he could speak, she reached forward, turned the radio up louder and started to sing, coming in at the right time.

She faced him and sang her heart out. She knew every word by heart and Chase absolutely loved it.

Then she stopped and they stared at each other. Chase knew which words came next, just as much as she did. He turned back to the road and carried on with the words as if she hadn't stopped and she joined back in with him. The awkward moment passed and they finished the song.

'I bet that doesn't happen every day.' Ava was still tapping her fingers on the console between them.

'What doesn't?' Chase asked.

'That you get to do a sing-along with an up-and-coming country A-lister.'

He didn't answer because he had no idea what to say to that. After years of practising, putting in the work, playing in dive bars, being 'A-list' didn't feel comfortable yet, like a new pair of boots that needed to be broken in. He didn't think of himself as a super-star. 'Anyway,' she said, 'I think it's more of a kissing song than a fishing song anyhow.' Again, he heard the humor in her voice.

'You may be right about that,' he agreed. 'So then, how'd you like to go fishing?'

Ava giggled, reaching out to tap him on the arm. 'I'm on to you, buddy. I think you have more kissing than fishing on your mind.'

'I'm not opposed to either. But I still think your fishing skills are going to be as weak as your line dancing ability.' She gave an outraged gasp and shook her head, making her hair wave. God, what he wouldn't give to run his fingers through those silky strands.

'I'll have you know, sir, that I'm a classically trained dancer. And it was *you* that knocked me off my feet. So look into the mirror for the weak dancing skills.' Ava reached up to indicate the rear-view.

He was too distracted as the image of her ass swaying in the perky dress, her long legs and sparkly boots so out of step with the rest of the line, returned to his mind. And who could forget those hot-pink panties?

'Tell ya what, Boots, I think I know how we're gonna settle our bet,' he said, pressing down on the gas pedal, eager to reach their destination.

'Oh, I see. Don't keep me in suspense, superstar. What did you have in mind?' Ava moved her bug purse to the floorboard so she could lean a little closer.

'Three different activities. Best out of three wins. First up, fishing. Whoever lands the biggest fish takes the event.' They were finally out of the town proper and on the one-lane road toward his house.

'If you wanted to swap fishing whoppers, all you had to do was provide the water and the fishing rods. I'm pretty sure I have some stories that will blow your mind.' Ava made an explosion gesture with her hands, complete with sound effects, and Chase thought she was the cutest thing he ever saw.

'No whoppers – actual fish. In fact, I have all my fishing gear and tackle box in the back of the truck.'

'Well, now, isn't that handy?' she said. 'But we haven't talked stakes yet. *When* I win, what's my prize?'

What had started out a slightly inconvenient favor for a friend suddenly morphed into the best decision he'd ever made. Ava was matching him step for step, obviously not caring that he was rich or famous. She saw him as a regular guy and it was amazing.

'Well, as you have probably guessed, I'm doing a set on the last night of the Fest. So if I win, you have to stand in the pit

with a T-shirt on that says "Chase Hudson is Always Right."'
He lifted his forefinger and pointed at her. 'And you have to
take a photo of yourself wearing it and post it on social media
so I can share it. Deal?'

Chase reached his hand out, waiting for her to place hers in
his. He couldn't wait to see her in that shirt. He was already
designing it in his head and made a mental note to text his
assistant to get it made tomorrow.

He glanced at Ava and saw a look of confidence reflected
in her eyes. She wasn't going to go down easy. *Game on, Boots.*
Game on.

Chapter 10

Ava put her hand out to shake his in order to seal the deal but then quickly drew it back and curled her fingers into her palm.

He frowned. 'What's wrong?'

'Nothing, but I just had a thought. If I win, then what do you owe me?' She tapped her finger to her chin and thought about it.

'Uh, well. We can figure that out.' He didn't withdraw his hand and pushed it closer to her.

'I know! You have to sing, on stage, a song of my choosing. And it may not be a country song either, but it will definitely be a song written and played by a woman!' She giggled, thinking it just might be Shania Twain's 'I Feel Like a Woman'. That would be hilarious.

'What are you laughing at?' There was a wary tone in his voice.

'Can't tell you,' Ava said gaily, and did her best to stop giggling. 'But, I think I know the song you will sing.'

'Oh Lord, I don't think I wanna know,' Chase said with drama in his voice. 'But since I don't plan on losing, it won't be an issue. So, deal?'

He waggled his hand at her again. Placing her hand in his, they shook on the bet. Boy, was he going to be in for a big surprise. This would teach him to judge women based on one crappy photograph! She was country bred, through and through, thank you very much. Sure, she may not look like it now and had become rather citified, but you can't take the country out of the girl.

At least she hoped so!

Truthfully, while she wanted to cream him on principle, it didn't really matter to her whether they had a bet or not. It was what had brought them together and that was good enough for her. She was with him in his pick-up truck, driving to who knows where, and she felt fine. Fantastic, in fact. She cast a quick look at him and tingles rushed through her. She hadn't had tingles since she was a teenager.

She saw the corner of his eyes crinkle and his teeth showed as he smiled. He turned to look at her and the dashboard lights made him look so dangerously sexy that those tingles turned into a whole body shiver. Ava found herself returning his smile. He was just so easy to be with and it eased her mind about whatever might come later. What she *hoped* came later.

He poked his cowboy hat higher on his head and Ava couldn't believe how such a simple movement could hold her so captivated.

'Okey-dokey, then. How about we get this bet off to a rousing start?' He rested his wrist on the top of the steering wheel.

She was torn between being amused or being turned on by the confidence in his voice. 'Oh? Sounds like you have an idea?'

'What song did we just hear?' he asked, and tapped the radio on the dashboard of his truck.

She thought for a moment, a little bit thrown off by the switch in conversation. And then she opened her mouth to a little surprised O. 'You were serious, then? You want to go fishing tonight?' She stared at him.

'I most certainly do. Like I said, I've already got the gear we need. And there's no time like the present.'

'Does that gear include bug spray? I go out in this skirt and the skeeters will eat me alive. And it's really dark out. Do you have a fishing spot that's going to be safe?' A little niggle of uncertainty settled in her belly.

''Course, I do. I'm a local boy and I know this land like the back of my hand. Maybe because I have the perfect fishing hole I've been going to since I was a little kid.' He turned to look at her, slowing the truck down and, all of a sudden, his teasing became serious. 'I completely understand if you don't want to go. We can go tomorrow if you feel nervous. It's important you feel safe. But I can assure you, you're safe with me and I'll take care of you.'

She couldn't read his eyes in the reflective dash lights; the depth of their color almost black. Ava wanted to see beyond his eyes and deeper into who he was. The urge to get to know him better suddenly became an insatiable desire. Yes, there was so much more to Chase and she wanted to peel back his layers and find out who he really was.

'Okay, you're on. Prepare to have your butt kicked,' she replied.

He gave her a sideways look and raised his eyebrows before focusing back on the road. 'Oh, I don't know about that, Boots. I don't think it'll be my ass that needs tending when we're done.'

'Is that right? You just might be a bit overly confident there, superstar.' He shook his head and she liked how his long hair brushed against the collar of his shirt. Her fingers twitched with her desire to reach out and touch him.

Ava peered out the window of the truck into the dark forest that edged the side of the dirt road they'd turned on to a while back. She chewed her lower lip, wondering if agreeing to go fishing was the right thing to do. After all, where the heck were they? The moon was high and lit their way with an ethereal glow, shooting rays between the leaves overhead and casting shadows on the road.

It was so pretty it made her eyes hurt and Ava realized just how much she missed the country. She was excited about this bet, although she wasn't entirely sure why. Maybe it was the simple fact it meant they'd spend more time together over the weekend. Their underlying current of sexual tension had her primed.

Her competitive nature was also clamoring for her to win. He clearly thought he was going to but this first competition would be like taking candy from a baby. Her daddy had said she was the Fish Whisperer.

They had fallen into an easy silence and she took the opportunity to really look at him. Ava had never dated a man like him – rough, raw and so delectably shiver-inducing; it almost made her breathless. Men like him were few and far between back home. In her quest for Mr Right, she had gone on many a disastrous date, suffered through mediocre first kisses and, on a few occasions, experienced adequate sex. It had been so long since she'd had really good, explosive sex.

Her last real relationship had been long distance. She'd met Bill at a convention out in Texas and they had immediately clicked. They'd fallen into bed almost right away and it had been urgent, passionate. With Bill based in London, and her in middle America, they couldn't come to an agreement on how to make their relationship work. She had become invested, really quickly. It had felt like a fairy tale come to life, complete with the handsome British prince. But in the end, she couldn't let him sweep her away. With neither of them quite willing to bend and uproot their lives and move, it had ended before it had even really begun.

Ava didn't regret it, not exactly. She liked to tell herself that, if it was meant to be, they would've found a way, but sometimes when she was lying awake at night she admitted that she could've made more of an effort for it to work. Dreams are well and good, but real relationships take effort, communication. Castles in the air fade away soon enough. It was a hard lesson to learn. Ava hadn't even told her friends until she shared the story with Bonni in Vegas.

Still, she stayed positive. Mr Right would come eventually and sweep her off her feet. Like Fredi said, maybe it was time to stop actively looking and let the universe work its mysterious ways. After all, it had led her to Chase, hadn't it?

She drew in a deep breath and the darkening night swept by as they drove down a country road. For her, tonight was just the beginning of a fling. Provided that the sex was better than adequate. Ava snuck another look at Chase and was hit by another wave of desire. She was willing to bet her retirement fund that he was incapable of delivering anything but knock-your-socks-off sex.

Ava leaned forward to adjust the vent so that the fan was blowing more directly on her. Lord, she was hot. They'd fallen silent but the air crackled between them. He shot her a heated look before the truck sped up a little more. Clearly, he was just as eager as she was.

She laced her fingers together on her lap and told herself again that this weekend was just going to be fun. She would enjoy herself and let what may happen . . . happen. A financial manager like her and a musician like him could never be anything but a fling and she was okay with that.

But then why did she feel so crappy about it?

Chapter 11

Ava settled on a stump underneath a stand of trees. Chase had placed a blanket over it to protect her dress, which was very thoughtful of him. She'd kicked off her boots and pushed her toes into the dewy grass with a happy sigh, after liberally spraying her legs with the bug spray. The leaves in the treetops rattled against each other on the soft night-time breeze and she tipped her head back to look up at the night sky.

There was pale moonlight, all silvery and dappling the water where the creek turned back, making it looked like someone had flung diamonds over the surface. It was just so pretty here. How long had it been since she'd enjoyed the quiet solitude of nature?

Too long.

The creek was a wide pool at this point and the water here was smooth and silent, but downstream she could hear the faint sound of ripples as it passed over river rocks. Some twinkly lights in the bushes caught her attention

'Oh, fireflies! I love fireflies. This is a lovely spot.' Ava sighed and let the feeling of freedom and happiness push out any worry or concern. She was here, sitting here under the moon, next to a river with a very sexy cowboy crooner.

'It's one of my favorite places. I grew up here, learned to swim and fish here.' He reached into his tackle box and held his penlight between his teeth to light up the inside as he searched for whatever he was looking for. He stood from the crouch he'd been in and carried the rods to the edge of the creek.

She watched Chase set the hooks. He was using jigs under a bopper, which told her he could be looking for crappie. Now, if he'd put on crankbait or spinnerbait, then he'd likely be fishing for bass in this Tennessee creek.

'And I bet you did more in this spot than land some catfish.' Ava couldn't help herself asking. Then she cringed a little, wishing she hadn't said anything at all. She didn't think she really want to know the answer.

'A lot has happened at this fishing hole. But never any kissing in the dark, if that's what you're beating around the bush to ask.' He looked at her and then back at the hook between his fingers.

Ava didn't answer and watched him silently. The swell of relief she felt surprised her. It wouldn't have changed anything if this had been his regular make-out spot but the fact that it wasn't made her feel like he was sharing something special with her. A new, warmer sensation began to grow deep inside her.

He handed her a rod and she rose from the stump and let her gaze roam over him. The woman that hooked him was going to be a very happy lady indeed.

Chase was surprised how easily she took to fishing. She handled the rod well and didn't say one word about getting muddy. Somehow, she looked right at home standing creek side in her short, sassy dress. He wouldn't have thought a city girl would be so at ease. The more time he spent with Ava, the more he wanted to be with her.

Ava cast her rod back then snapped it so the jig sailed across the water to plop quite nicely out in the center of the pool, near a copse of tulip trees. 'So this is our first competition. To see who can land the biggest fish.'

Chase nodded. 'Impressive beginners' luck. Now, isn't this so much more relaxing than sitting in traffic to get home or working late in some stuffy ole office?'

He saw her smile and couldn't look away from her, she was so serene and beautiful under the moon. The moon's rays glinted off the curve of her cheek and sparked along the strands of her hair. It was as if the moon bathed her in silver and turned the night to shades of grey. She was magical, like some kind of woodland fairy that could flit away on the evening breeze at any moment.

'Well, I think you're discounting the ability to get pad thai at 8 p.m. and the joy of not having to drive thirty minutes to the nearest movie theater.' She gave her rod a little tug and a couple of turns on the reel. 'Anyway, I know my way around a fishing rod. My dad took me fishing a lot when I was a kid.'

'I see. So I got a ringer on my hands, do I? Now I'm wondering what else you're hiding from me.' Chase snapped his wrist and his line sailed out beside hers.

'I think everybody hides something.' She looked up at him and her eyes were almost translucent under the moonlight. 'Don't you agree?'

He stared down at her. He'd had his fair share of girlfriends while growing up, and casual hook-ups since he started playing, but Ava was unique. She wasn't swooning over him or hinting at expensive dates or putting on an act to impress him.

She was the real thing. If he wasn't careful, it wasn't only the fish that were gonna get hooked. He cleared his throat and focused on his fishing rod. 'Maybe. Especially when people are just starting to get to know each other, maybe some people don't intentionally keep things from the other person, they simply don't share everything right away.'

She let out a squeal and jerked her rod up. 'Oh, I have a bite!'

Chase put his rod down and went to stand beside her. He watched her handle the fishing rod, teasing and turning the reel, playing with the fish on the other end of the line.

'I think I have it.' She was excited and that excited him. The last thing he'd figured he'd be doing tonight was fishing in the dark with a beautiful woman he'd just met.

'Easy, easy now. You don't want to lose it.' He inched a bit closer to her side.

Her tongue poked out and touched her upper lip as she concentrated on the water.

'Do I detect a competitive side to you?' He wanted to reach out and help her as she continued to play her line. Mainly because he wanted to touch her.

'Oh, definitely.' She nodded.

Chase took the opportunity and rested his hand on her shoulder. She didn't flinch away, she didn't even look at him. He wondered if she'd even noticed; all her attention was on the line she was swiftly reeling in.

'Okay! Here, I've got it. Hold this a sec so I can reach out for the line.' She handed him her rod and leaned over the river bank, her fingers reaching, and she wiggled them as if it would magically make the line come to her. He moved the rod so she could catch it.

The fish was fighting and he reeled in more, but when Chase glanced at her, stretched out, balancing on the bank and trying her damndest to reach the line, he forgot about fishing. Her dress had hiked up her thighs, tight across her ass, and he was poleaxed.

He couldn't pull his gaze from her. Then, in the blink of an eye, she slipped. Ava let out a shriek as her feet went out from under her and she slid down the shallow bank to land on her butt in the grass. Her feet splashed into the water, sending up a spray of droplets all over her. She kept sliding and grappled at the grass with her hands.

'Hey now!' Chase tossed the rod aside and quickly grabbed her arm before she tumbled all the way in to the river. With swift hands, he lifted her back up and into his arms, against his chest.

'Damn good thing you took off those sparkly boots,' he said as she gazed up at him, shock etched on her face.

She slung her arms around his neck and he caught her by the waist, keeping her next to him, and he realized just how wet she was. They froze like that, at eye level, her legs dangling against his, staring into each other's eyes.

'Yes,' she whispered. 'Damn good thing.'

His gaze dropped to her lips, shining in the moonlight, and her eyelids seemed to droop, giving her the sexiest pair of bedroom eyes he'd ever seen. All this sensory overload made his belly clinch with desire that rushed down into his balls.

He nodded, knowing he had nothing creative to say. Words weren't necessary; only the two of them silent and holding each other under the night sky were what mattered. He wanted to stay this way for ever.

Chase lowered his head, keeping eye contact with her. She gazed up at him and he raised his eyebrows, hoping she was giving him the consent he was looking for.

Ava nodded her head ever so slightly and her tongue poked out to wet her lips.

Chase didn't waste any time and dove in for the kiss he'd been dying for all night. It promised to be a kiss he knew would rock his world.

Her lips were soft and expressive under his. They were slightly parted and he took the opportunity to delve deeper and find the inner warmth of her mouth. Her arms tightened around his neck and she pressed against his body, thrilling him and arousing him to the point where it would be very evident to her.

She moaned, and it was practically his undoing. He cradled her head and let his hand wander down her back, enjoying the curve of her waist and the gentle swell of her hip that led him to the firm roundness of her bottom. He was drowning in her and he never wanted rescuing.

Splashing vaguely registered in his passion-filled mind. Reluctantly, he lifted his head from her with a last long look into her eyes before glancing at the creek.

He struggled to steady his breathing, and the sound of her own quick breath told him that she was just affected as he was by their first kiss.

'Fish,' was all he said, and set her back on her feet. Letting his hand run down her arm, he took her fingers in his. Bending, he retrieved the rod. A fish floundered at the end of the line, trying to make its escape.

'My fish,' she said, and reached for her rod, her fingers brushing next to his as he let go and she took it.

'Yes, your fish.' He stepped back and picked up his own from where it had fallen when he'd tossed it aside during the rescue effort. He reeled in, but the whole time he was watching her pull in the line and take hold of the fish at the end. Quickly, she unhooked it, stuck her finger through the gills and held it up.

'I think I won.' She struck a pose, her hand on one hip.

They both looked at his hook devoid of worm and a fish. Chase tossed back his head and let out a quick laugh.

'I concede. You win this round. That's a nice black crappie. Good eats. But I think I've got a bigger win.'

'You do?' she said as he took the fish from her and put it in the chill bag.

Chase pulled her back into his arms. 'The biggest prize is right in front of me. You, here, in my arms.'

Chapter 12

Ava had never been kissed like this in all her life. It was full of passion, tenderness and edged with something deeper. He had a way with his lips and his tongue that had her melting in his arms. He teased her. Tasted her. Drew out her own hunger that had been locked so deeply inside her.

It was just a kiss. But it was also so much more. Ava couldn't get close enough to him. Even though she was completely molded to his body, she ached to feel more. It astounded her that they'd met only a few hours ago. This had to be what Juliet felt when she met her Romeo. What Sleeping Beauty felt when she met Prince Phillip.

An instant, unexplainable connection.

Ava drifted into him. His tongue was deep in her mouth, playing with hers, and she let these new and welcome sensations play through her body. It was like every nerve and fiber was connected, lighting up and bringing her new life. She hooked her ankle around his leg, never wanting to let go of him or the emotions he roused in her.

Chase squeezed her tighter, as if making sure she couldn't escape, but that was the last thing she wanted to do. Ava was in heaven. This is how she always wanted to feel. She'd always wanted a man to bring this level of emotion, sensation, passion out of her, and no one ever had.

When Chase did lift away she tried not to let him go and slowly opened her eyes to meet his. When he looked down at her from under his cowboy hat, his eyes stormy with passion, a contented sigh slipped from her.

Ava was sure she could live out here with a man like him, under the stars, with the fireflies twinkling around her. She drew in a deep breath and savored the night air. It reminded her of her childhood and teenage years. Those wonderful country nights spent outside with her friends, camping under the stars, jumping into the swimming hole on those hot, long dog days of summer. But never, ever had she been in the arms of such a man as Chase.

Her instincts told her this man was extremely dangerous. Dangerous in the passionate, attentive, kill-me-with-pleasure, shivery kind of way. Dangerous as in she was beginning to think he'd be so easy to fall for. Her track record had proved that she wasn't good when it came to placing bets on winners, not to mention their incompatible lives.

She looked up at him. 'Where did you learn to kiss like that?' she whispered, and tried to stop her legs from wobbling.

'I guess you must bring out the best in me,' he said, his voice deep and husky.

'Aren't I a lucky girl.' Ava's heart swelled and restricted her ability to breathe.

'We have a fish here – our fish.' One side of his mouth lifted in a crooked grin. He let her slide down his body, a delicious tease as they bumped against each other until her toes touched the grass.

'My fish,' she said, raising her eyebrows and nodding.

'Okay, yes, *your* fish. So, do you want to head back to your hotel or do you have somewhere else to be tonight?' he asked.

She shook her head. 'Here. I want to be here, with you.' Ava knew her friends didn't likely expect her back tonight, but she would check in with them a little later. Right now, her choice was to be here, in this moment, so she could remember it for ever.

'Then we're in agreement. So what do you say we cook that bad boy up?' Chase let go of her hand and picked up the chill bag and his tackle box.

'Here?' Ava glanced around. 'It doesn't look like you have any supplies.'

He raised his finger up and waggled it 'A country boy is always prepared.' Ava smiled, liking this new development.

'Does this mean another one of my tests is to clean this fish?' She gave him a cheeky grin.

'Well, that would be fitting, since it's your fish and all, but I've got something else in mind for the other competitions. Remember, this is my favorite fishing hole, so I have a little stash of necessities just over there.' He pointed to a small wooden structure she hadn't noticed before, tucked away between two trees set back from the river's edge.

She followed Chase over to the small building and was surprised to see what was inside when he opened the door and tapped a small light stuck high on the wall. It was neatly organized with chairs, blankets sealed up in plastic bags, canned food, lanterns, wood tidily stacked, shelves with all sorts of stuff on them, and the list went on.

'What is this? Your Y2K survivor bunker? Are you in a militia?' Ava asked him, intrigued by the well-stocked little space.

He laughed loudly and it echoed off the canopy of trees

above them. Yes, she really did love the deep, warm tones of his voice. They made her shiver nicely.

'Y2K – I haven't heard that term in years. Like eighteen or more.' He reached for a lantern.

She shrugged her shoulders. 'Well, we were old enough to understand all the fuss and worry. Daddy wasn't too bothered, though. He said humans had survived hundreds of years without computers, so if Y2K destroyed everything, we'd continue to survive. I wasn't so sure. I would've been really pissed off I couldn't watch *Buffy the Vampire Slayer* anymore.'

He chuckled, and Ava did as well. 'It all went well and we're still here to talk about it.' He handed her the lantern. 'Can you hold this, please? But you know, I really did think something bad was going to happen.' He picked up a couple of pieces of wood, a handful of kindling and took some matches off the shelf. 'Yeah, I was totally freaked out. And it was right around the movie *The Matrix*, too. The combination of worrying we lived in a real-live *Matrix*, along with the dawning of a new millennium, it really messed with my head. My mom and dad dealt with me pretty good, though, by making me watch the televised New Year celebration at the International Date Line. Just to prove it would all be fine. And here we are today, eighteen years later, and no worse for wear.'

'Yup. But, if we had been in the *Matrix*, I would've been a bad-ass Trinity,' Ava said, making wild karate chopping motions as she followed him over to a spot by the edge of the river. There was a bare patch of dirt set with a ring of round, smooth stones, likely pulled from the water.

'You know, this is quite a nice little set-up you have here. Doesn't the property owner mind?' She watched him set the kindling and the wood, and in no time he had a fire going.

'Nope, the owner doesn't mind.' He rose from the crouched

position and gave her a wink. She reached up, unable to resist the urge, and touched the side of his cheek, his beard tickling her palm.

'I'm glad. It's nice here.' Her voice sounded all breathy.

She felt a bit transfixed at that moment, the fire crackling beside them, tendrils of smoke rising up into the night air and a ghostly mist rising off the water. The moon shining overhead made everything shimmer. 'It's magical.'

'I have to agree with you there.' He took her hand and kissed the delicate flesh of her inner wrist. 'You're magical.'

Ava trembled and got the feels all over again. She watched his face as he glanced at her, the brim of his hat cocooning them with surprising intimacy.

'Now, what do you say we get that fish ready for cooking?' His voice was warm against her flesh.

She nodded, unable to find any coherent words. She didn't even bother to try and come up with any, because that fish was the last thing on her mind. Instead, Ava was desperately trying to remind herself that this wasn't *Brigadoon* and she wasn't about to be swept away from her life. When the sun rose, her life, and all the reasons it would be a bad idea to fall in love with Chase, would be waiting.

Chapter 13

This night certainly had taken a swift detour. While he cooked the fish over the fire Chase glanced at Ava, sitting on a chair he'd pulled out from the shed. She didn't seem uncomfortable or disappointed that they were here. Quite the opposite, she seemed amazingly content. He was pleasantly surprised, since he had originally been dubious she would be able to relax and enjoy herself so easily. He was thrilled it had turned out this way. Sitting out here was one of his favorite ways to decompress.

'The fish is ready.' He set the mesh grill, another item he had stashed in the shed for occasions such as these, with the sizzling fish on the stump she'd been sitting on earlier. 'It's hot, so let it cool a bit and we can move the chairs.'

'Oh, like a makeshift table. Perfect.' She stood and went to grab her chair, but he nudged her aside. His mom would never let him hear the end of it if he let Ava do the heavy lifting. He brought both chairs over to the stump and held one for Ava while she sat down. He tested the temperature of the fish with a quick touch before breaking it up with a fork.

'Thank you for bringing me here,' Ava said. 'I never thought my night would wind up like this.' She reached for a piece of fish, holding it between her fingertips. She nibbled on it for a temperature test before taking a real bite.

'I was just thinking the same.' He also took a piece and popped it into his mouth. 'There's nothing like fresh-caught fish cooked on an open fire.' He smacked his lips and made an exaggerated *mmhm* sound.

'I definitely agree. I didn't realize I was this hungry.' She took another piece and swallowed, closing her eyes and enjoying the flavor bursting in her mouth. '*Mmhm* is right.'

They ate in silence for a little while then Chase started to clean up and Ava began to help. This was a first for him. He'd gone camping with a woman or two in the past, but they'd been content to let him take care of everything. Yet Ava pitched in without question. She didn't seem to mind getting her fingers dirty. Plus, she still hadn't put her boots back on. He glanced at her toes and they were painted a bright green with some kind of sparkly jewels on them. He smiled.

As he went about dousing the fire and putting everything away in the shed, with Ava's help, he knew he wanted to suggest that she come back to his house. He was just mulling over the right way to bring it up.

She raised her hands to her nose and sniffed. 'While I do like fishing and all, now I kind of smell fishy. And my butt's wet.' She looked at him and laughed. 'You know what I could use right now?'

The way she tilted her head, her hair tumbling down over her shoulder and a sweet smile curving her lips, got his heart racing. 'Actually, I don't think I can guess,' Chase answered her as he lifted his tackle box on to the stump.

'A shower.' She reached her hand up into her hair, bundled

it like she had in the truck, before arching her back and shaking it out. He could watch her all night. Demanding a shower? It certainly appeared so.

'A shower? I didn't expect you to say that.' Chase put his hands on his hips and thought about it. 'There's only one place to get a shower around here, unless you want to take a dip in the creek . . .'

She bent to pick up her boots, which she'd placed earlier at the base of a massive, old tree, and looked at him from behind the fall of her hair. Her eyes were sparkling and her lips were shining and Chase knew his life would never be the same after this chance meeting tonight.

'As much as I'd love to jump in the creek, I could use soap, I think. I feel kind of grotty and my hands smell fishy.' She held up her hands and wiggled her fingers.

'Soap, huh? You have two choices, then.' He paused, really wanting to just sweep her off to his house.

'And they are?' She stepped closer to him.

'I can either take you back to your hotel . . . or . . . we can go to my place, which isn't far from here.' Chase was holding his breath as he waited for her answer. He knew what he wanted her to say.

She was considering her options and it disappointed him that she didn't immediately pick his house.

'If I go back to the hotel, I'll face a barrage of questions from my friends. And, additionally, I know they will be highly disappointed I did not stay overnight with you. So, I choose your house,' she whispered, and stepped into him, placing her hand on his chest before sliding it up to slip her fingers under his hair and caress the back of his neck.

Boom. There it was. This wonderful woman who had fallen into his world, quite literally, had decided to stay with him.

Chase was transfixed. He took ahold of her shoulders and pulled her closer. She let out a tiny little whimper and her lips parted as if waiting for his kiss.

Happiness and desire surged through Chase. He was surprised to realize how devastated he would have been if she had chosen to leave.

'Well, we certainly don't want to disappoint your friends . . .' They stared at each other for a few beats and he leaned over her, drawing her closer still until her body was flush to his.

'No, don't take it like that. I didn't mean—'

He heard a little bit of worry in her tone and wanted to put her at ease. He sensed she was the kind that usually put others' feelings ahead of her own and would never intentionally hurt anyone, so he was quick to reassure her. 'I'm only teasing you. You haven't hurt my feelings.'

'Oh, good. I didn't want to do that. But trust me, my main reason for staying at your house is purely selfish.' She tipped her face up to him.

He brushed a soft kiss over her lips but it quickly shifted. The kiss was different this time. It ignited a fire, an intensity, an urgency that he had to hold back from bursting out of him. This new, raw emotion that played through them when their mouths met, tongues touched and the sigh that came from her nearly brought him to his knees. She clung to him and he cradled her in his arms, almost unable to breathe. When he thought he would explode, he gently stepped back, held her, his breathing rough. She was the same.

'Let's go.' He grabbed his tackle box and reached for her hand with his free one. Entwining their fingers, he led her back to his truck and swung his tackle box into the bed.

They stood for a moment beside the truck.

He didn't imagine that she leaned a little closer to him. Nor did he imagine the desire in her eyes. And he most certainly didn't imagine the way her tongue swept around her lips in a tantalizing tease.

In a perfect world Chase would kiss her, lay her on the soft grass and make love to her here, surrounded by the nature he loved, but a chill was creeping through the forest and he noticed goose-bumps on her arms as he ran his palms down them. 'You are a siren, Boots. And Lord help me but your song is hypnotizing.' He held the truck door open for her and then helped her in.

'How far to your house?' She settled her skirt over her knees and put on her seatbelt as he slammed the door shut and walked to his side. Climbing in, he told her, pointing, 'Just down that track there.' She peered in that direction, narrowing her eyes.

'But that's not a road. That's practically a game trail.' She leaned forward in her seat and then looked at him. 'Are you sure you know where you're going?'

He chuckled and started the truck, punching the seat warmer for her. 'Trust me, yes. You are full of surprises. How would a city girl know about game trails?'

She shrugged her shoulders. 'Wildlife television shows. Plus, my daddy made sure I had a well-rounded education.' Her voice held a teasing lilt to it again and he realized, once again, that this woman ran deep. He was going to enjoy diving through those depths to find out who she was beneath all the layers.

The growl of the truck's engine broke the serene silence of the forest. The headlights pierced the night gloom and he drove carefully down the two lines of tire tracks. It was a tight fit under a canopy of trees that created a tunnel through the foliage, and the branches almost brushed the sides of his truck. 'Keep your eyes peeled. You never know what animal might decide to give us a showing.'

'Really? It's been a while since I've seen a whitetail.' She trained her eyes out the front window.

'They live around here, but I can't guarantee any'll make an appearance.'

After about fifteen minutes through the trees they emerged at the beginning of the driveway up to his house.

Chase felt nerves kick in. Which was ridiculous. But suddenly he wanted to impress Ava. He wanted her to love his house and feel comfortable in it. It was really too early to tell, but he was starting to think that one night wouldn't be enough.

Ava was looking out the passenger window, fiddling with her bag, as the moonlight spilled across her hair and skin. It gave her a mystical glow, like a magical forest fairy had danced her way into his truck. One who could fish with the best of them and laughed off getting muddy. Now he wanted to see if she could be more than that. Chase had started falling under her spell the moment he laid eyes on her in the Wildhorse but he knew now, with each passing minute, there was no turning back.

It was like a fairy tale. The small paved road wound through some lovely rolling meadows with miles of white fences that glowed in the moonshine. It was ethereal and she saw darker shapes of horses in the fields, which she'd like to imagine were unicorns.

When they rounded the last stand of trees, a house on the far side of an oval loop appeared between the trees. Ava drew in a sharp breath.

'Is this your house?' she asked in awe.

'Yup. It's mine.' She heard the pride in his voice.

'It's stunning. And all those fields we just passed . . .' She hitched her thumb behind them.

'Those are mine, too.' He pulled up to the grand portico, its columns a combination of stone and wood. Strategic lighting on the house, in the gardens and in the trees beyond made it all seem so surreal.

'Wow.' It was the only thing she could say. Never in million years would she have expected him to have such a house. She would've expected a rustic bachelor pad, not this gorgeous mansion, and the beautiful gardens were just that . . . beautiful. It just didn't seem to match up with his burly cowboy persona.

She wasn't one to be starry-eyed over someone's wealth or possessions – people were just people at the root of it – but this was beyond anything she'd ever encountered. Ava wondered where it had all come from. Sure, she could just google him again, but it would mean more when he chose to share. Something told her there was a bigger story to Chase.

Physical attraction was important but she wanted to learn more. To find out more about just who this man was. And, boy, she was eager to do that. Not because of all these trappings but because he had an aura to him that hinted at something so much deeper and she wanted to know the man. *Him*.

He came around and helped her down from the truck. She inhaled the scent of the night.

'It's beautiful. Peaceful and serene. Do you live here all alone?'

'This is my haven. I much prefer to be here, working on my ranch and doing business in my home office. Of course, I have a foreman to oversee the day-to-day, but I like to keep my hand in. I also built a home recording studio. It's not much, but it lets me get music down when the inspiration strikes.'

He led her up the wide stairs to a door that looked like it was made out of a tree. Beautiful leaded windows framing either side let her peek inside to the foyer.

Chase pushed the door open. 'Welcome to my home.'

She glanced up at him and the look on his face touched her heart. It wouldn't matter if he was leading her into a double wide. She was with him. And that's what counted.

He reached out his hand. 'Shall we go inside?'

Ava stared up at him as she took his hand. She was here, with this man who did all kinds of wonderful things to her with just a look.

Now it was time to find out what kind of things he could do to her with his body. It seemed like days ago when Fredi had asked her to picture her dream man. She didn't think she would have ever pictured Chase, and yet he seemed to be everything she'd ever dreamed of. He gave her a slow wink.

Oh my god.

The moment felt heavy; as if, when she crossed his threshold, everything in her life would change. Squeezing his hand, she stepped forward.

Chapter 14

Her boots clicked on the hardwood floor as she entered the house, Chase a step behind her. Their fingers remained lightly hooked together and she smiled, looking at them. How she loved seeing their connection like that. So light, so fragile and yet so powerful. She couldn't believe she was here right now. The path she'd stepped on at the start of her vacation certainly had sent her to a very unexpected destination.

Chase dropped his keys into a bowl next to the door then tugged her forward. She let her gaze roam over his wide shoulders, his powerful back and down to the trim hips encased in nicely molded jeans that hugged his rather tantalizing ass and showcased the strength of his thighs. His cowboy boots might be well broken in, but they were lovingly cared for. She could tell by the soft buttery luster of the leather.

Ava knew it. She was in trouble. Her romantic nature was definitely finding perfection in him. He was the full package. Sweet. Sexy. Mysterious. A gentleman. And an amazing kisser.

Ava's attention was so focused on Chase she barely noticed

the room he'd led her into. The cool silence of his home cocooned her as she noticed they were in a great room. A floor-to-ceiling fieldstone fireplace was positioned on a full double-story wall with stacked windows that looked over a portion of a stunning pool area. There were more fireflies twinkling on the night air in the branches of trees that appeared to ring the pool and patio, contrasting with the dark of the country night.

'This is quite a house. I feel like I just walked into a magazine editorial.'

'Thank you. It's my place to escape.' He leaned a hip against what looked like a tree trunk that was stained and highly polished. It rose up to the roof and supported the cathedral ceiling, which was complete with skylights that would bathe the room in sunlight during the day.

'And a wonderful haven it is.' The decor was spectacular as well. Ava loved the combination of country and mountain and how it blended effortlessly together with an element of modern. It was a warm, welcoming place that she could easily imagine as a family home full of love, laughter, meals, and kids, and . . . Ava stopped. What the heck was she doing to herself?

She knew she'd have to be very cautious and not let her romantic nature carry her away. Which she was wont to do.

But that was exactly who she was. Ava wasn't fooling herself. She knew she saw love and romance and happily ever afters around almost every corner. She sighed. *I could find something romantic about a tree stump.* She wore her heart on her sleeve.

Ava had so many questions. She wondered if he had designed it or had had help. Why did he live way out here alone? And why such a massive home? What were his likes, dislikes? How did he spent his days when he wasn't working? How did he take his coffee? Did he even drink coffee? Did he sleep on his back, or his belly, or—

She had to stop her rambling thoughts.

'Would you like anything before we . . . go upstairs?' Chase asked her, and his hesitancy was sweet, one more thing to make her swoon.

'Oh, uhm, maybe just some water, thank you.'

He went into the kitchen, which was just off the great room. It was all open-concept and flowed wonderfully together.

'Have you been living here long?' Ava watched him take two heavy tumblers from a glass-fronted cabinet and place them on a counter that also looked like it was made from a slab of a tree. She twisted her hands together and got another whiff of fish stink. She wrinkled her nose and went over to the sink. Pumping out a generous portion of cherry-scented soap from the bottle, she scrubbed her hands. Chase took a dish towel from a drawer and handed it to her so she could dry her hands.

'I've owned the property all my life.'

'All your life, huh? As a child as well? That's odd—' Then it dawned on Ava. 'The fishing hole . . .'

'Mine, too.' He took a jug of water from a monstrous-sized, very professional-looking fridge, filled the glasses and then slid one toward her over the counter. She sipped at the water as he explained.

'My grandfather transferred the title to me when I was born. He brainwashed me to love the land from as far back as I can remember. Care for the land and treasure it. He drilled into me "*They don't make any more land, son.*" I've never forgotten it.' Chase grinned at her and she could see how he felt about his grandfather and the land by the look in his eye. He took a long drink and placed his glass beside hers on the counter.

'Smart man. Real estate can be a sensible long-term investment, so long as you can afford the taxes and the upkeep,' Ava answered. Chase's grandfather sounded like her kind of person.

'Is he still alive?' As soon as she said the words she wished she could pull them back. 'I'm sorry, that was indelicate.'

'No, it's fine. He is alive, a ripe old ninety-five. He no longer rides but he does drive his Morgan horse around the trails.'

'That's amazing. I bet he's quite a character.' Ava picked up her purse from the counter as Chase came around the far end and placed his arm around her shoulder. Her heart did a little dance in her chest and a strong feeling of contentment washed over her.

'He is. One day I'll tell you more about him. Gramps and me got into all kinds of scrapes. Drove my mom up the wall.' Chase led her back through the great room.

'I'd like that.' His words echoed in her ears. *One day I'll tell you more about him.*

One day ... oh, the possibilities those two little words opened up.

So far, the night had been full of surprises. No one had taken her fishing on a date since she was thirteen. Now, here she stood, in a fabulous house, smelling like fish and mud and easing into sex with a man who was lusted over by thousands of women. Chase's fame was the last thing on her mind, though, she was so ready to be with him. She reached up to touch his hair. He hadn't taken his hat off when they arrived.

She got up the nerve to gently lift it from his head. 'May I?'

'Of course.' He nodded, and his mischievous grin made her smile.

She removed it and set it on a low table beside them. He had thick, wavy, wild hair. With an intake of a soft breath, Ava ran her fingers through it. It was just as sun-streaked as his beard and mustache. She dated a lot of businessmen, because that's who she was surrounded by all the time. Chase was so different from those guys, hard where city life had made them soft.

'All good?' he asked her with a grin 'Did you think I was bald or something before I took my hat off?'

She shook her head, unable to respond. He was just too damn gorgeous to be legal.

'So, Boots, do I pass the no-hat test?' He placed his hands on her shoulders and Ava didn't resist when he pulled her closer. It felt like the entire night had been foreplay and she was eager to continue their kisses.

She couldn't deny that the closer they were to each other, the more powerful the fire of her attraction to him burned and the more her body craved him. Even though they barely touched, the air between them seemed energized. Ava knew what she wanted to do tonight, and it was to be with him. The butterflies in her belly told her it was the right decision.

'Mmhm, yes, I think you do past the test.' She reached up and fingered his long strands, tucking one around his ear, noticing that it was pierced. Well, well, wasn't that intriguing?

'Now, about that shower?' He took her hand.

'Yes, about that shower.' Ava let him guide her.

He stopped at a wide set of incredible stone stairs that led to the second level. Ava glanced up at Chase and her belly did a little flutter. She was so ready for what was coming next.

His eyes searched hers, deep, brown and questioning. Instinctively, she knew the question and her decision hadn't changed since the fishing hole. Reaching out, she took his hand and stepped up on to the first step, turning to face him. They were at eye level now. 'The stairs are magnificent. They match the fireplace on the wall there.' She raised her finger to point and was unable to drag her gaze away from him.

She was happy to see the look in his eyes soften and the etchings of concern on his forehead relax. *He was nervous.*

Ava's heart swelled and she hoped he could see the eagerness and desire she felt reflected in her gaze.

'I built it myself,' he told her in a low voice. Chase slid his arm around her waist and stepped up beside her. Ava heard Chase's deep breathing and then his words sunk in.

'Y–you what?' She tried to process what he'd just said and looked up at him. 'You built the stairs and that fireplace?' She was incredulous. The stonework looked very complex and she tried to picture him with a trowel or whatever, painstakingly putting everything together.

He looked at her and pride filled his features. 'Yeah. As a kid, I used to imagine what I'd want my home to be like when I grew up. Back then, there was just a small log fishing shack on the property and a few hunting lean-tos. I've been working on the fields, barns, outbuildings for years. This house was more recent, and I finished it last year.' He looked around, his gaze far-off. 'I had to go on tour a coupla times, but whenever I was back in Nashville I was here, helping to build my house. You know, whenever possible, I reclaimed wood from the original structures on the property and used it in this building. See there, the mantle on the fireplace is one spot.'

Ava gasped and stared in wonder at the majestic fireplace, the high beamed ceilings, the beautiful log and stone that accented the room. The floors were a blend of wide board oak and what appeared to be slate as well as some very scarred wooden patches in front of the fireplace and various other places in the room. She bet those were from the original structure.

'Those spots on the floor are reclaimed?'

'Yes, from the floors of the old cabin.' She heard pride in his voice and couldn't say she was surprised.

This wasn't just a building, it was historical and held the essence of his ancestors. It would have been very easy for him to have someone else build the house, overseeing from a distance while he went on tour, making more money, until the house was completely done and he could move in. But that didn't seem to be Chase's style. He wanted to be part of building the home he had dreamed of for so long, a home that incorporated his family's past. It gave her a whole new appreciation for the house, and for Chase.

'It's like a living history and I'd love to know more. I'm just blown away by this. I can't believe you were that involved in the construction. Didn't your label worry about your hands? '

They slowly climbed the stairs as he replied, 'Well, it wasn't like I was out hang-gliding or racing motorcycles, but you gotta live life. I have some awesome back-up with a group of guys that I've been touring with for ages, so as long as I can sing, the fans will get their money's worth.'

Ava was the one with him now and she leaned into him, slipping her arm around his waist. 'I'm absolutely stunned. To know that you helped build this, that makes it even more special.'

'My hand touched pretty much everything in this house. I had help designing it, I'm not that creative.' He chuckled. 'But I knew what I wanted. Brought Gramps out to see it, too, and he was almost moved to tears.'

'What an accomplishment. You should be proud of yourself.'

As they reached the top of the stairs Ava glanced up at him and was concerned to see sadness now in his eyes. He had been bursting with pride a minute ago – what had changed? Was he thinking about his grandfather or maybe something from his past? This house had been made for a family. Even though he said he'd been designing it since he was a kid, maybe he had planned to share it with another woman? That thought gave her a little spark of jealousy, which she firmly tamped down.

She wasn't one of those people who judged others on their pasts. It didn't matter if he used to date a supermodel, he was here with her now, and she only planned to keep him for a little while.

After this weekend he could go back to dating drop-dead-beautiful celebrities, but, at the moment, he was all hers.

Chase's presence was reassuring as he led her along the balcony that overlooked the great room below to a hallway that ran off into another wing. It was a wide hall and also very striking. Beautiful paintings hung on the walls, and she paused.

'These are old.' Ava said. The first one was of a military man wearing a pith helmet on a stunning white horse. The background looked like desert, complete with Bedouin-style tents. The horse was magnificent and had a beautiful face with tassels hanging from the bridle and a tail held high. She bet it was an Arabian and the tack looked luxurious. Clearly, he had been a wealthy man.

'That there is a very distant relation of my mother's. It's a mystery who he is. We just call him old Uncle Jed.'

Ava giggled. 'That's funny. I'm fascinated by stories like that. And he doesn't really look like a Jed, he looks more like a Nigel. The horse is beautiful.'

Chase laughed. 'Nigel – I think you're right. Rumor has it is the stallion was one of the original sires of today's thoroughbreds.' Chase looked up at the artwork and nodded. 'Yup, there's definitely a story in that painting. I just wish we knew it.'

'You mean you don't know anything? There's not one clue about the horse and Nigel? That's just tragic.' Ava felt suddenly sad that the subject of this painting was a mystery. To think, someone who looked as proud as Old Jed seemed to be, who had a horse as magnificent as that stallion, had lost their place in the family history book.

'Back then, I don't think people had the same desire to know their roots. So many records were lost in wars, emigration, and in a lot of cases it was just plain denial. People wanting a fresh start. And lots of skeletons in closets.' Chase led her along the hall, and she was interested in all the other paintings, too.

'I'd really like to open some of those closet doors and rattle the skeletons,' she mused, pausing in front of another one, of a woman on a chair under a rose arbor, a dog on her lap and others lying at her feet. 'Who's this?'

'My great, great, great, great, and a few more greats, I think, grandmother Thirza. She came over on the *Mayflower*.'

'Oh my God! You are kidding me, right?' Ava blurted, and looked at him wide-eyed. The *Mayflower* had existed only in the history books for her until this moment.

Chase chuckled. 'Nope, she did.'

'Wow, I'm so impressed. My history doesn't go back as spectacularly. My grandparents immigrated in the 1950s and, like you said, due to the war, many records have been lost. I really don't know anything about any family I have left in Europe.'

'Really? I'd like to know more about where you came from,' Chase told her, interest in his voice.

'It's long and complex story in the Second World War, but my grandfather was Polish, forced to fight for the Germans until he escaped, and my grandmother was English. She was evacuated from the south of England to north of London.'

'Now that is a story I would like to hear.' They continued on down the hall and she looked at the other paintings with interest. 'How did they meet?' Chase asked her.

'My grandparents? After the war, he went to England and was decommissioned there. They met at a dance.' Ava looked up at him and smiled.

'Now is that a fact. I wonder if he knocked her over?' Chase smiled and Ava giggled, liking the humor in his voice.

'I wonder. He obviously swept her off her feet. They were married sixty years.'

'I like the sound of that.' The look on his face was unreadable. She bet Bonni's fiancé Quinn would love to play poker with him. But it was super-easy for Ava to speculate about what was going on behind the expression and to conjure up all sorts of things he might be thinking. Like, did he want a love like that? Was he thinking the same thing she was? About how her grandparents met and the way they met earlier tonight was eerily similar?

He carried on down the hall, not letting her go, his arm around her waist. Knowing what was coming next, the anticipation built in her until she thought she might burst from it. He stopped in front of one door and opened it.

'You're welcome to stay in this room. There's a shower that I think you would enjoy. And a lock on the other side of the door.'

She peered into his eyes and saw honesty shining there. She appreciated his offer and it further cemented her idea about the kind of man he was. She knew it was up to her which way the night ended. And she knew darn well which way she wanted it to go.

'Or?' She said the word so softly that Chase leaned in slightly to hear.

'Or?' Ava could see behind his beard and mustache a slow and very sexy smile that reached his eyes. She couldn't deny it. It was so sweetly evident to her now. In this short period of time, she was falling for this man.

She nodded and repeated the word. 'Or?'

Chase let her hand go and gathered her in his arms. His

cradling touch was exciting and powerful and made her want to know what his *or* would be. She waited.

'I'd love for you to come down the hall. And shower in my room.'

She looped her arms around his neck and it was as if their surroundings faded. She no longer had a sense of place or time. She was floating, floating along on a magical current that he created. In a wonderful world that belonged just to them. And she loved it.

Ava let out a sigh she'd been holding in, her words tumbling out along the way. 'Does that shower have room for two?'

The look in his eyes told her what she needed to know and he tightened his arms around her.

This whole evening had been the most romantic, albeit somewhat quirky, evening she'd ever experienced. He was romantic. His house was romantic. The food was romantic – well, for being fish on an open fire. The fireflies. The creek. It was as if the concept of romance had been conjured up especially for them. Ava was beguiled and in such sensory overload she could barely stand it.

'I would love to use your shower.' She stared up at him and pulled her lower lip between her teeth.

Chase seemed to grow in size after she whispered the words, almost like her answer made him swell with happiness, and the smile on his face conveyed so many things. She was unable to resist him and felt her own lips curving happily. The biggest surprise, though, was when he swept her up into his arms.

'Oh! No one's ever carried me before.' She linked an arm around his neck and rested her head on his shoulder, gazing up at him.

'Then I'm glad I can be the first.' He strode down the hall with sure steps and she felt very much like Scarlett O'Hara being carried up the grand staircase by Rhett Butler. Chase was romancing the heck out of her and she loved every minute of it.

'I'm not too heavy?' Ava asked hesitantly.

He chuckled. 'Far from it. Here we are.'

He stopped before the double set of doors and used his foot to nudge the door open, then kicked it shut behind them. He held her for a moment longer before letting her legs drop so she could stand. Part of her wished he just carried her right over to the bed and tossed her on it.

But no matter.

They'd be there together soon enough.

Chapter 15

Ava rested a hand on his shoulder while she got her balance then moved away a little as she examined his bedroom, leaving her purse on the window seat. Chase couldn't tear his gaze away from her. Her dress looked the worse for wear, as it was rumpled with a few random streaks of dirt. Her red boots were still sparkly, though, as she walked over to the fireplace to run her fingers along the oak slab mantle. 'Look at the fireplace. Is that the same one from downstairs? Is that even possible?'

He had never brought a woman into his home before. This had always been his sanctuary, a private place for just him and his family. Watching her, here, now, it felt right. Like this was always where she was meant to end up.

'Yes, the chimney was incorporated as a support structure. It runs up through the two floors of the house and connects both hearths,' he replied as she continued to investigate. She peered out the windows that now only showed a sheet of black but would reveal a glorious sunrise in the morning. She trailed her fingertips along his thick feather duvet and the heels of her boots sunk into the deep carpet.

'It's magnificent. Too bad it isn't chilly enough to light it.' She looked over her shoulder at him. 'Where's this shower, then?'

Her words spurred him to move, to pull his feet from the floor and walk toward her. Chase placed his hands on her hips and she softened into his touch, leaning back against him. He closed his eyes and held her, felt her, inhaled her. She filled him so completely.

It was as if she was a long-lost part of him. A piece he'd been missing all his life. It was baffling and intriguing and he wasn't quite sure how to deal with it. There would be time enough in the morning to think about it but, for now, he had more immediate concerns.

'Boots,' he whispered in her ear, 'I'm glad you're here.'

She turned in his embrace, his hands sliding perfectly over her as she faced him. She opened her mouth to say something but, before she could speak, he gathered her in for a deep kiss. He wanted to clutch her fiercely, to claim her as his, and a deep raw side to him wanted to make her his, but the overpowering urge to romance and woo her made him check himself.

'Oh, Chase,' she murmured against his lips and he watched her eyelids flutter shut before closing his eyes, too.

Kissing her now, here, was just as extraordinary as the first time under the trees. Their previous kisses were merely a tease, a prelude to how she could make him feel. Her intensity and passion drove him to a near-mindless state. She pressed her fingers into his neck and up to the base of his skull, holding him as if she never wanted to let him go. She held every inch of herself against him; he felt all her feminine curves that his body was desperate to map.

The material of her dress was thin and light, no match for

him if he chose to rip it off her. But he wouldn't. At least not yet. As Chase shifted a bit, the movements of her breasts against his chest made her moan and she stepped tighter into him. He wrapped her in his arms while he deepened their kiss, feeling the intoxication of her body against him, her thighs, and god-damn . . . the way she hooked her ankle around his leg.

Chase didn't hold back his groan. Even if he tried to, it wouldn't have been possible.

'Oh, woman, that you're here with me.' He uttered the words next to her lips when he briefly lifted his mouth from hers then let himself fall back into her.

He slid one hand up to the base of her neck and the other over her ass. He couldn't get enough of the feel of her. She was perfection, ripe, curved, soft and firm . . . and hot. The urge to see her naked seared through him.

'S–shower.' Ava said the words against his lips.

With their mouths sealed, Chase lifted her and strode across the floor into the bathroom. In front of the shower, he let her down, holding her until the last possible second. Ava took a cursory glance around at the large shower with multiple shower heads, gleaming mirrors and hand-painted tile walls before returning her attention to him.

Her fingers played with the hem of her dress and he knew that, in a matter of minutes, he'd be seeing those hot-pink underpants again. Chase's gaze traveled down her body. He licked his lips at the way the edge of her dress rode up on her thighs as she scrunched it between her fingers. He'd never seen a more stunning sight. Not even the joy he got while perform-ing and seeing his sea of fans fanning out from the stage could be better.

Nope, that didn't even hold a candle to this.

But it was the look on her face, more than anything else, that drilled down deep into the heart of him. A soft smile curved her lips, her face relaxed into a mixture of joy and desire.

'You are the most beautiful woman I have ever seen.' Chase couldn't believe all the words that threatened to spill out of him. It was like a song that wanted to be written. There was no effort, just a story he needed to tell. Words filled his brain and the tune was not far behind. And he knew, right then and there, she was the inspiration for his next song.

'You say the most wonderful things.' Ava's voice was low, husky, and she lifted her arms, holding her hands out to him. 'Chase, come to me.'

The sensation that exploded inside him at her simple words astounded him. He took her hands, vaguely knowing that he had his song title.

'I can't get enough of looking at you.' He stepped toward her.

'Me either. But I do think it's time for that shower.' She turned around and gestured to her back. Slowly, carefully, he unzipped her dress. 'I had no idea that a casual bump on the dance floor would lead to this.'

Her flesh was soft and warm when he trailed his fingers down her back and she shivered delicately. 'I'm not sure I would call that a casual bump. We were always fated to meet, remember?' Chase slid his hands up her sides to unclip her bra.

'It's at the front.' Ava leaned back on him and let go of her dress. It dropped to the floor and she stood only in her hot-pink panties and matching lacy bra. She reached behind her to take hold of his hands and steer them where they needed to go. In a flash, he had the clasp undone, her bra off and his hands holding her breasts. His cock nearly exploded and his jeans became way too tight.

Desire ripped through him when he rubbed his thumbs over her nipples. He looked over her shoulder to see her breasts, beautiful and full, as if carved from ivory, and the nipples stiffened as he cradled them in his large, tanned hands. She drew in an excited breath. He turned her around.

'You are a vision.' Ava met Chase's gaze. Desire cleaved down his spine and settled in his hips.

'You and your words.' Her breath hitched.

Chase reached down and hooked his thumbs into the sides of her panties, leisurely peeling them off, pressing gentle kisses on her legs as he went. She arched her back and sucked in a surprised breath before pinning him with a seductively tantalizing look.

'Off with your clothes, superstar.'

She helped him shed his shirt while he kicked off his boots, shoved his boxers down and then they were naked.

Except for her boots.

'Oh.' Ava whispered as she reached out and touched the tattoo that fanned out from his left pec. 'I saw the one on your wrist and wondered if you had more.'

His nipple rose up and he groaned when her fingertip ran across it, along the arc up to his shoulder and then down his arm.

'Ava—'

She toed off her boots and stepped into the stone-walled shower. Her hair tumbled down her lean, curved back. For a willowy-looking woman, she had a strength and muscle that was surprising.

'Coming?' Ava turned on the water and gave him a come-hither smile over her shoulder. He was mesmerized, watching the water stream down her body. Her soaked hair, hanging over her shoulders, draping her breasts, gave him only a shadowed peek of her nipples. Water slipped over her hips, glistened off her taut belly and ran in rivulets down to the juncture of her legs, where her neatly trimmed hair drew his attention before he followed the water's path down her thighs and calves, then back up to her face.

Chase pulled out a drawer on the vanity, never taking his gaze off her. He came in to the shower and placed the package from the drawer on a shelf, then pulled her into his arms and pressed a kiss to her temple.

'Can anyone see in?' Her words came out on a breathy sigh.

She placed the palm of her hand against the floor-to-ceiling window that spanned a wall in the shower. All dark right now, except for the flittering of fireflies. During the day, it was one of his favorite views, of the meadows below with his horses grazing on the green grass.

'Nope, one-way glass, Boots.' He tapped his forehead. 'I thought of everything.'

He shook his head and his long hair sent droplets of water flying from his lion's mane.

'Oh my God, you could not be any more delicious-looking,' Ava said, and wound her arms around his neck, their bodies slipping against each other in the steaming water.

The water from the rain shower streamed over him. Ava could've sworn she was with Aquaman. She'd seen the trailers for the new movie but only now realized just how much Chase resembled Jason Momoa. If Celia wasn't so happy with Landon, she would probably be pushing Ava in front of a bus to get a shot at Chase. But he was all hers, hers, hers. At least for now. And after letting her hungry gaze roam over Chase, she was very okay with that.

She'd known he was muscled and ripped but, until he stood naked, water flowing over him and highlighting all his rock-hard muscles, she hadn't realized just how much. She dipped her gaze and fought the blush that threatened to rush up her checks when she saw how hard and ready he was for her.

He gazed at her and a look softened in his eyes. His lips turned into a smile and she could've sworn she read something in his gaze. But then that was her, right? She was a romantic. She saw the love and passion and happily ever afters all the time.

As he swooped in for a kiss, she reached between them and held his cock, stroking and moaning as he hardened in her hand.

His hands slid down her back and gripped her ass, lifting her as she wrapped her legs around him and tipped her hips so his erection slid teasingly between her legs. It would be very easy to shift just a little bit and they would be making love. His tongue found hers, and they locked together. She rocked her hips and tightened her hold around his neck. Her nipples rubbed against his chest hair and the sensations were electric.

He lifted from the kiss and she was about to say something but the words vanished from her mind.

'No talkin'. Just lovin'.' His breath was hot on her neck.

'Y–yes, no talking.' She was on fire. 'Hurry, you're driving me crazy.' She let her legs drop and had to steady herself by leaning against the shower wall.

'Yes, ma'am,' Chase said. He reached for the package, tore it open, and Ava watched him slide the condom over his cock. She couldn't believe how erotic it was to watch him handle himself.

'Quit calling me ma'am.' She clutched his shoulders when he lifted her and she guided him to her opening.

'Whatever you say, darlin',' he groaned, and found her mouth; at the same time, he thrust in deep, and slow.

Chase knocked her world off its axis. She tumbled through the building tension and let out a cry of delight with each deep thrust. He filled her, and it was as if all the pieces of her that had been scattered suddenly clicked back into place. Ava wrapped her legs around him, locking her ankles to meet his powerful thrusts.

He carried her to a place she'd never been before. A place she *knew* existed but feared she'd never find. When that place exploded into wondrous glory, she clung to him, shower water mingling with her tears of joy. She had promised herself that she'd stop looking and then encountered this amazing and wonderful man who seemed to be exactly what she'd been seeking so long.

He roared out his release on the heels of hers. She felt him inside her. They were perfect together. Meant for each other. Slowly, her body calmed. He held her tightly as his body trembled. She unwrapped her legs, one at a time, and her toes touched the shower's pebbled floor but she kept her arms around him, not wanting to break their embrace. If she did that, then this moment would be over. Ava couldn't bear that thought and clung to him.

'Aw, Boots, why are you crying?' He scooped her up, grabbed a couple of thick towels from the warming rack and took her back out to the bedroom.

'I–I don't know. Happy tears.' She started to shiver and he put a towel around her shoulders, rubbing her until she stopped shaking.

He pulled back the covers. 'Get in and warm up.' She wound her hair up and slipped between the sheets.

'You, too.' Ava watched him walk around the foot of the bed. He climbed in beside her and she rolled over to snuggle against him. 'This night.' She sighed and relished the heat from his body.

'I know,' was all he said. But those simple few words made her wonder if he was just as moved as she was by everything that had happened so far.

Chapter 16

Ava heard the chime coming from her bag and sat up, confused for a moment about where she was. Then she saw Chase beside her, on his back with his arms stretched out. He was fast asleep. Ava smiled and, careful not to wake him, slid out of bed to find her purse.

It was on the window seat and she picked it up, taking out her phone.

'What's up, Boots?' His deep voice filled the darkened room and Ava nearly jumped out of her skin.

'Holy shit, you scared me. I thought you were still asleep.' She walked back to the bed and crawled in beside him.

'I was. Your friends?' he asked.

'I'm surprised I hadn't heard from them sooner.' Ava unlocked her phone and turned it, holding the face of her phone toward him. 'See.'

'And what do they have to say?' He stretched out on the bed, the sheet draped enticingly over his hips, his legs tangled in the blankets. He put his hands behind his head, which only accentuated the size of his chest and bulging muscles. Chase's movements oozed sexuality that made Ava draw in a quick breath. She was hard pressed not to put the phone down and give him all her attention. Forcing herself to look away, she did her best to focus on her phone.

Celia: *So can you still walk?*

Ava saw that it was a group chat and waited for a barrage of texts to come in.

Fredi: *Did you propose yet?*

Ava laughed and glanced at Chase, who was looking at her. 'What's so funny?'

She shook her head. No way would she tell him that. 'They're just being funny.'

Ava: *Stop being silly. But I will tell you this, I think he's the Peter Kavinsky to my Lara Jean! <3 He's such a gentleman, sooooo sexy, and he can cook! Over an open fire, no less!*

Bons: *An open fire? Like a fireplace? Or a firepit? A bonfire? Where are you exactly?*

Celia: *Ava's in lurrrvvve #NoSurprise #WeddingBells Are you ready, Fredi? Dress time.*

Fredi: *Oh Lord save me. Thank God we have the JD distillery tour tomorrow. Mama's gonna need to stock up.*

Ava snorted and laughed, and she heard Chase chuckle beside her. Eyeing him suspiciously, she leaned a little more to the right to block his view. No boys allowed in this conversation.

Ava: *We're at his place! It's a huge ranch, and so so so gorg! There were fireflies!*

Fredi: *Just what every girl dreams of. Glowing insects . . .*

Bons: *I still wanna know more about him cooking over a fire. Didn't we leave that behind in the Stone Age?*

Ava: *Hello, BBQ!!! But it was a firepit. Seriously, though, it's been a great night. How are you guys?*

Celia: *Not so fast, deets, beeyotch! #tellus*

Ava: *He took me fishing, at his favorite spot! He used to go there all the time as a kid! I caught one and almost fell into the creek! O_O*

Fredi: *What kind of date is that? #notforme*

Ava: *The best kind! But what about you?????*

Bons: *Back at the hotel, having a drink in the bar. Fredi's pregaming for the tour tomorrow.*

Fredi: *Did you at least get some nookie to make up for the nature?*

'So, Ava, the distillery tour you're going on tomorrow. You know how they always say that people who live in an area never do the touristy stuff that's around? Like, say, going to the Jack Daniels distillery tour?' Chase said, clearly aiming for winsome. 'I have a free day tomorrow. I'd love to tag along with you and your friends . . .'

Ava was torn. On the one hand, yay, more time with Chase! On the other hand, Fredi took her JD pretty darn seriously. She said, pouting a bit, 'I knew you were reading my texts! I'm not sure. We try to keep our vacation outings pretty testosterone-free, but I'll ask.'

He swept her hair to the side so he could nuzzle at her shoulder and Ava nearly fumbled the phone before she could send out the text.

Ava: *Chase wants to know if he can come tomorrow . . . Totes up to you guys, you can say no!*

Celia: *Hmm, let's think, going whiskey tasting with a famous country superstar. They will probably break out the GOOD stuff! Hell ya, he can come.*

Bons: *Is he willing to be the DD?*

Fredi: *And purchase carrier? There will be a loooooottttttt of purchases.*

She loved her friends. Twisting to drop her legs over Chase's, she delivered the verdict. 'You are permitted to come so long as you are willing to be the designated driver and carry stuff.'

Running his hand down her leg, he replied, 'I accept those terms.'

Ava gave herself a mental shake, trying not to melt at his casual caresses, and looked at the screen on her phone, trying to process words. 'This will work out well. Your truck would fit us all so much better than the red bug.'

'Red bug?' he inquired, brushing a finger experimentally against the sole of her foot. Slightly ticklish, she kicked out and tried to pull her legs back, but he caught them before she could go far.

'Fredi's car. She drove up from Florida in her VW bug. It's candy-apple red and we call it the red bug. We'd have to squish in there between the four of us and all Fredi's new alcohol.'

'Yup, a lot more room in my truck. Tell 'em to be ready at 10 a.m. and I'll have a car come around and bring them here.'

He leaned back and linked his fingers behind his head, a very satisfied grin on his face. The move was simple enough but was also wonderfully dangerous to her libido. Arousal flowed through Ava in heavy, thick waves. Unable to pull her gaze from his chiseled features or keep herself from staring at this wide and muscled chest, she had to catch herself from almost letting her tongue loll out. He was just too distracting for words.

He mouthed, *Text them*.

Ava snapped herself out of her daydream and texted them back with instructions.

Celia: *I'm requesting a stretch, stocked with a hunky guitarist or 2.*

Bons: *What would Landon say if he could see you now?*

Celia: *There's the hot babe I'm madly in love with? He would say that. #iyamwhoiyam*

Fredi: *Am I the only one who realizes our darling lil Ava is spending the night with Chase the rock star?*

Ava stared at the words and realized the way this conversation had just gone. Spending the night with Chase. Truthfully, her thoughts had been pretty centered on getting down and dirty with Chase. She hadn't thought much about what would happen after. But it made sense.

Before she had time respond or check with Chase, more texts chimed on her phone.

Celia: *OMG! I AM SO PROUD! #saveahorse #rideacowboy*

Bons: *I hope you have condoms. And that you use allll of them . . .*

Ava rolled her eyes and heard Chase chuckle again. She swatted him with her free hand. 'Stop reading my texts!'

'I can't help it, they're so entertaining. That Celia seems like quite the character.' Before she could blink, he flipped her legs around so that he could lift her between his legs, resting his chin on her shoulder. 'There, now I have a better view.'

Shaking her head and taking delight in hearing him sputter as her hair drifted across his face, Ava quickly texted back.

Ava: *No, I do not have any because I never thought anything like this would happen. But, trust me, he has some.*

Celia: *yeeeeeaaaaaahhhhh babbbbyyyy! Deets deets deets!*

Fredi: *Is that where the shower came in?*

Bons: *Oh, we're so gonna ditch him at some point tomorrow. It's your turn to face the inquisition, hahaha!!!*

Ava: *Okay, byeeeeee.*

She locked her phone and stretched to put it on the bedside table beside her. Chase had his arms wrapped around her and his hands felt so warm against her stomach.

'You guys have a really special relationship.'

Placing her hands over his, she leaned back a little. 'Definitely. We met in college and there's been no stopping us since. We all live in different parts of the country, but we've managed to stay really close.'

He started pressing small kisses against her throat and she tilted her head to give him better access. 'I got my boys here in town, but I don't think it works the same for men. It's more like I go out on tour, we exchange a few texts, then I come back and it's like I never left.'

Her voice was breathless as she tried to focus on the conversation. 'That's nice, too, though. Comforting. Like there's a piece of home always waiting for you.'

'How can it be possible that you are here in my bed? I've imagined you, sung about you . . . all these years and never figured I'd find you.' He spoke in a low voice as his arms tightened around her. Chase gazed at her and knew his mother would fall in love with Ava. She'd been making noises for years that he should give up his music dreams and settle down and give her grandbabies. It wasn't like he needed the money. But Chase was determined to prove himself. There'd never been a woman that meant more to him than his music but, with Ava, it felt like he could have the best of both worlds. She was open, honest and didn't play games. She was exactly the slice of heaven she appeared to be.

Ava twisted in his arms so that she could straddle his legs. 'If I'd known I'd find you here, I would've been here even sooner.'

Chase reached up to cup her cheeks, brushing her lips with a tender kiss. Ava suddenly felt a wave of sentiment for all the awful first days, disappointing crushes and nights of loneliness she had experienced, because it had all brought her here.

Bless that broken road.

Chapter 17

They were in tune. Chase couldn't have written a better song than the one that was playing between them. He slid his hand down her back, over the tightness of muscles, the rounded globes of her ass. There was still much more he wanted to discover about her. He pressed his palm into the curve of her side, wanting the imprint of her on him and to explore her further.

This was so hot, so new and so surprising that Chase was still trying to process it all. He sensed something special was developing between them. Something that he needed to cultivate and treasure.

She was full of soft sighs, moans, as she molded her body to his. This would be the third time they'd made love tonight and he already knew it would only quench the flame of desire, not satiate it.

Ava grabbed his chin with her hand, holding him and, in the gloom of his bedroom, they moved against each other. The clutch she had on him was possessive and he felt a tremble in her touch. He wanted to believe that she was just as overcome as he and it was almost like she was holding on so he couldn't leave. But he had no intention of going anywhere.

Her eyes were luminous, deep and sucked him into their depths. He saw desire and something else in them. 'Oh, Chase, I love the way you have with words. I really need to start listening to your music,' she murmured in a husky tone.

'Just say the word and I'd be happy to give you a private concert.' He ran his thumb against her nipple, enjoying the way she gasped at the sensation.

'I bet you say that to all the girls.' She pressed a kiss to his chest.

'Only the sexy ones with sparkly boots,' he teased.

'You're a sweet-talker, superstar, but let's stop talking for a while.' Ava pressed more kisses on his chest then reached between them. She opened a condom they'd put under the pillows earlier, slid it on to him and stroked his cock.

Thunder rumbled over his house and lightning flashed out the window. In the explosion of light, he saw her as clearly as if it were day. He took her hand that was holding him and together they positioned him against her and she sank back down, his cock filling her, with a deep groan that matched his.

More thunder crashed overhead and flashes of lightning gave him staccato images of this wild angel as she rode him, her hair in a beautiful, tumbled disarray, her breasts bouncing and nipples firm and hard like cherries. The curve of her waist bloomed into her hips, where he placed his hands and held her tight. He watched where they were joined, unable to look away.

Gliding his hand up her side to cradle the back of her head, the thick strands of her hair tangled around his fingers, soft and sensuous. Chase pulled her down, touched his tongue to her lips and she fell on him. Their mouths sealed, her hips working him, and he met her with every beat.

Then she cried out, the sound resonating into him, as she came. Her eyes opened and he felt like a hot poker had twisted his gut and trails of smoking desire had settled in his balls. Yes, Chase knew for sure now that she'd cast some kind of witchy spell over him. And he didn't give a shit in the least.

She gazed down at him, lifting her head slightly, and he swallowed heavily at the passion-clouded look in her golden eyes. There was a longing in them that pinched at his heart. Instinct told him to be gentle with her. While she was absolutely alive above him, there was a fragile edge to her that needed special care.

He flipped her over, pressing her into the pillows and tumbled sheets. She wrapped herself around him. He pressed his mouth to the base of her neck, his tongue followed the rapid beat of the vein there and the smell of her skin enveloped him.

'Come for me, Chase,' she whispered into his ear as he ground into her.

Her words, her response to him and her kisses on his cheek were more than he could bear. Chase was lost as he was overtaken by his orgasm. It crashed inside him, he was mindless and lost his sense of space and time, the tight embrace of Ava's arms the only thing anchoring him to reality. She tightened around his cock in sweet, pulsing waves and he knew she'd climaxed again, in time with him.

Moments later, his body came down from the orgasmic high. He had left his teenaged years behind a long, long time ago, but he felt like, with a ten-minute nap and a couple of glasses of water, he would be ready to go again. Chase gathered her to him like she was something delicate and touched his lips to hers. She responded as he knew she would. Then she rested her head on his shoulder and drew in a deep breath.

She draped her arm over his hips and tucked her foot around his leg. The lost puzzle piece had just clicked into its place.

Chase's mind began to shut down. The last fleeting thought he had was, there wasn't much he hadn't experienced these days, but being here, with Ava, felt brand new.

Chapter 18

Ava rolled on to her side, propping her head on her hand, and snuggled down into the cozy bed. Judging by the sunlight peeking through the window, it was morning, and she was *starving*. She wasn't entirely comfortable going to raid Chase's kitchen for breakfast but he looked so peaceful and beautiful sleeping that she didn't want to wake him. Stopping herself from reaching out to brush the hair that fell over his forehead, she settled for simply watching this wonderful man who she'd spent the most amazing night with . . . sleep.

She listened to his deep, even breathing. Their night of sweet love left her with a satiated and exquisite feeling she was unable to fully describe. All she knew was he'd made her feel unlike she could ever have imagined. It had never been explosive like that, a clash of energies demanding satisfaction. And every time she thought they were done, he would find a second, third, fourth wind and bring her to climax all over again.

And it was only the beginning. They potentially had three more nights together.

Her stomach growled and she knew it was time to get Chase moving before Hangry Ava made an appearance. Remembering how talented his mouth was on her body, the magic of his hands as he caressed her, Ava grew warm and turned on. Unable to stop herself, she slid down in the bed. She placed her hands on his hip and lightly ran her fingertips over the ridge that ran from his hip down his flank to the prize she sought. Cradling his cock in her hands, she took him in her mouth and was pleasantly surprised by his swift response as he hardened.

He shifted from his side on to his back and his hand touched the back of her head. Ava touched him lightly and loved how he grew firm in her mouth. Stroking and caressing, his hips finally started to pulse. Meeting her cadence, he groaned, fisting his hands into her hair.

He spread his legs and she shifted between them. He tensed his thighs against her and that simple move made her feel protected and her arousal grew. The reaction in his body made her realize that she was responsible for it. He was succumbing to her, and she was thrilled to know it was her that made him feel so good. He was such a wonderful lover, and Ava wanted to give him all that pleasure back.

She ran her tongue from the base of him along the underside to the tip of his cock and then took him wholly into her mouth. He thrust up his hips to meet her. She circled her fingers around him and moistened her lips so her hand and mouth could work in unison.

His great body tensed, he held her head tight to him and his groan as he orgasmed brought Ava such satisfactory pleasure.

Chase pushed the covers off her head and she gazed up at him. 'Now that's a way to be woken up.'

He had a lazy, satisfied smile on his face as he reached for her. 'That's not a sight you see every day, but one I could definitely get used to. Come here.'

He hooked his hands under her arms and gently pulled her up his body.

'Mmm.' Ava was at a loss for words. Waking a man up with oral sex wasn't part of her normal repertoire, but it felt right in that moment. She let him tuck her into his side and draped her hand over his belly. He pulled the sheet up over them, sighing comfortably.

'Are you hungry?' he asked her as he swirled his fingers over her shoulder.

Ava shivered at his touch, loving it, and shifted slightly so he could reach more of her back. Having her back tickled was the best thing . . . well, except for sex and food. 'Yes, and I could definitely use a coffee.'

'I could eat like a bear. I think the housekeeper stocked up yesterday. But I feel way too lazy to get up.'

Ava nodded. 'Me, too. Yet my stomach will not be contained!' Then a thought occurred to her and she began groping for her phone on the bedside table.

'What are you looking for?' Chase asked her.

'My phone. I want to make sure I'm ready to go before the girls get here. Fredi will not welcome any delays in her day-drinking.' She rolled over and swung her legs over the side of the bed, grabbing her phone from the table. She walked over to her dress, which was in a scrunched-up pile on the bathroom floor.

'Well, shit, I forgot to arrange the car. *Someone* was a little too distracting last night.' Chase moved and reached for his own phone.

After checking the time, Ava stretched a little, feeling a pleasant ache in her muscles. She was naked and felt not the least bit self-conscious. Years spent performing ballet had stripped her of whatever modesty she had and it seemed perfectly natural to walk around nude in front of Chase.

'I could definitely get used to these kinds of mornings,' he said, and she glanced over at him to discover he was watching her over his phone.

'I think I could, too.' She gave him a happy look as she bent down to grab her dress. Shaking it out, she frowned, it wasn't even suitable for a walk of shame. 'I have to tell my friends to bring me a change of clothes.' After sending off a quick text, she said, 'Now I'm going to rustle up some coffee and grub, not necessarily in that order.'

'Grab one of my shirts,' he told her as he typed on his phone.

She went into his walk-in closet, which was a huge room in itself, with all manner of drawers, mirrors and hooks to keep things organized. His clothes were all neatly hung up, shoes and boots perfectly in line, sweaters and T-shirts folded precisely. She took down a plaid cotton shirt and pulled it on. Lifting the collar of the shirt to her nose, she inhaled. It smelled like him.

Before exiting the closet, Ava noticed a vacant portion where there were no hangers, no shoes on the racks, nothing folded neatly on the shelves. She realized it was where the lady of the house would have her clothes. For half a second she pictured her sparkly boots sitting there before she waved her hand, chasing the image away.

'Hurry back, and we can conserve some shower water again.' Chase winked at her and Ava melted inside as she left the room

She dashed down the hall and the stairs to the kitchen. Investigating the cabinets, she scored the jackpot when she found a box of peanut-butter granola bars. Ripping one open, she looked for coffee fixings. The man had an entire cabinet devoted to coffee. There were pods and whole beans and insta and ground, along with varying syrups and sugars. It was slightly overwhelming to someone who liked to eat and drink things but wasn't particularly patient enough to make the things.

Ava poked around a little more in the bottom cabinets until she found a pod coffee maker and picked a flavor at random to make. This had proved more complicated than she assumed it would be so she ate a second granola bar while she waited for the coffee to brew. Her brain required additional sustenance after all that thinking this early in the morning. She checked her phone. There were a bunch of messages from her friends.

Ava: *I need clothes. My poor dress is not fit for the light of day. Bring me jeans, undies, my makeup kit, sneakers and a top, sandals.*

Celia: *You're alive! Can you walk? #sexnite*

Fredi: *Really Cee, you have to ask that? Of course she can't.*

Bons: *Guys, we have about an hour to get ready before being picked up.*

Fredi: *Speak for yourself, Jack loves me the way I am.*

Ava: *I think it's a good thing Chase is coming because I don't think we'd be able to carry you out of the distillery.*

Celia: *I, for one, am super looking forward to hanging out with your man. My insta is going to blow up.*

Ava: *He's not my man. I'm just ... borrowing him for a little bit.*

Celia: *You know what they say, possession is nine tenths of the law! #keeper*

Bons: *Criminals say that, Cee. Criminals.*

The coffee maker began to gurgle out the coffee but Ava wandered over to the sliding glass doors separating the kitchen from the patio. She snapped a pic and forwarded it to the group.

Ava: *#mycurrent view*

Ava: *Now I'm going back upstairs to an even better one!*

Before anyone could reply she locked her phone. Taking a sip of the steaming coffee, she wrinkled her nose a little at the taste (*coconut vanilla, really?*), before popping in another pod to make Chase a cup, too. She agonized a bit about which flavor he'd prefer before rationalizing that it was his house and surely he wouldn't stock anything he hated. While it brewed, she checked out the remaining cabinets and found a tray. When the coffee was ready she put the mugs on the tray, along with the box of granola bars, a couple packets of chocolate pop-tarts she found hidden behind some Ziploc bags and a little pitcher of cream and sugar.

Carefully climbing up the stairs, Ava took a moment to reflect that she couldn't quite believe all this was happening to her. Girls like her did not pick up famous country superstars in bars and then go home with them to have amazingly passionate sex. Girls like her debated if *Enchanted* or *Ever After* was a better movie while balancing her checkbook and then going to bed at a reasonable hour. Guess she really was taking a vacation from real life right now.

When Ava entered Chase's bedroom her gaze was immediately drawn to his bed. He was stretched out, propped up against the headboard, his phone resting on his knee. She could smell his cologne and their passion on the air. A shiver raced through her.

'There's my girl,' said Chase's deep voice. The dim lighting was a complete opposite to sun streaming into the windows in the rest of the house and it took a moment for her eyes to adjust.

'I come bearing coffee.' She carefully picked her way over to the bed and set the tray on the side table.

She sat on the edge of the bed and handed him a mug. 'I don't know how you take it.'

'Thank you, just a bit of cream.' He accepted it then reached for a remote. He pressed a button and the blinds opened, letting the daylight in.

'How did you sleep?' she asked, and lifted a knee to sit sideways on the bed so she could look at him. Taking in his sleep- and sex-rumpled hair, she thought he was just too charming for his own good.

'Not bad. For those brief moments that you actually did allow me to sleep.' He smiled and reached out to circle his fingers around her ankle that she rested on the bed.

She was relieved by his response. It wasn't going to be awkward; it was going to be okay. And as much as she tried to hold it back, she couldn't stop a soft moan of happiness at his touch.

'Excuse me, I seem to remember a certain someone else being the instigator, thank you very much. And do you really have any complaints?' She sipped at her coffee, giving him a look of mock-outrage.

He shook his head, shaggy hair swinging around his shoulders. 'Nope, no complaints here.' He lifted his mug to drink and kept his eyes pinned to hers. 'I had no idea my forest fairy would turn into a nymph once we got going, baby.'

'I guess I'm full of surprises.'

His cell phone rang and he lowered his mug to check the display. 'I do need to get that.'

She leaned over to kiss his cheek then went into the bathroom to give him some privacy. Closing the door behind her, she took the opportunity to freshen up and, even though she didn't have any of her toiletries, she jumped into the shower. This time, she really looked around and, of course, the view out the window was mind-blowing. The house definitely showed how much time and thought Chase had put into it. Ava thought back to her cozy apartment and sighed a little. How the heck was she ever going to go back to her normal life after being with Chase?

Shaking away the sad thought, Ava chose to focus on how unique the shower was – seriously, it was like something out of a luxury spa – and what a great day they were going to have. The minute she suggested coming to Nashville, Fredi had been insistent on the distillery tour and it was going to be so awesome to watch her friend in hog heaven. Plus, with Chase coming, it should be even more fun.

It was really important to her that he and her friends got along. She wanted all the people she lo—was very fond of to be friends, too. Ava sat on one of the shower benches and dropped her head into her hands. It was getting harder and harder to remind herself of all the reasons she and Chase were a bad idea.

She really needed a pop-tart.

Chapter 19

Chase was surprised how nervous he felt. Waiting for Ava's friends to arrive was almost more nerve-wracking than his debut at the Grand Ole Opry. It was obvious they were very close friends, and close friends like that could have a significant impact on how his relationship with Ava played out.

Relationship.

He pondered that a moment. The fact that he'd only met her last night and was already thinking about them in terms of a relationship was pretty significant. Chase reminded himself Ava and her friends were only here for the weekend. To enjoy CMA Fest and then go home.

He glanced over at Ava, who was standing at the window, looking out over the paddocks. She was barefoot and the dampness of her hair turned the color to a deep auburn. His shirt hid all his favorite places on her body but she didn't seem self-conscious about standing half naked by the window. She fit so well with his house, it was like he built it for her. That rocked him deeply.

His phone vibrated. He glanced at the display to see an update from the limo driver then slid it back into his pocket. Walking over to Ava, he put his arm around her shoulder and liked how she leaned into him.

'They'll be here soon, Boots.'

Her nose crinkled as she gave him a pleased smile. Reaching up, she played with his fingers, as she said, 'So, is that my official nickname?'

Chase was powerless against the cuteness, ducking in for a quick kiss. 'I think it suits you, considering. Why, don't you like it?'

Ava shook her head. 'I don't mind it at all. In fact, I kinda like that you've given me a pet name already.' She turned in his arms and linked her arms around his neck.

Chase looked down at her and the happiness radiating from her. He wanted to tell her he felt like he'd known her for so much longer than a day. But he didn't. The timing wasn't right yet.

Too soon.

'When I see something I want, I don't drag my ass. I make it happen.' He dropped his hands to her waist and shifted so that one of his legs was between hers. The little minx cuddled closer so that he could feel her warmth against his leg.

'Well, based on last night, I can definitely attest to that, superstar.' She deliberately brushed her breasts against his chest and it was something he definitely couldn't ignore.

'Moss doesn't grow on you either, Boots. Let's hope your friends hit traffic or they're going to be waiting on the front porch for a while.' Chase snaked an arm around her and dragged her closer. She let out a little sigh that was so much like the sounds she'd made last night and he was a goner. Time to see how Ava felt about wall sex.

*

After another extraordinary bout of sex where Ava met him step for step, they were sitting in the kitchen having a quick game of Snap when the doorbell rang.

'Yay! They're here!' Ava said, and jumped to her feet. 'Do you mind if I let them in?'

'Of course not,' he said, shuffling the cards into a neat pile. She dashed off when there was a pounding on the door and a faint feminine voice hollering on the other side. Chase stood and followed her to the foyer.

The door opened and her three friends piled inside, bringing with them a cacophony of excitement and hellos and hugs all around. Lord almighty, it hadn't even been twelve hours since they last saw each other and they were acting like it had been days. It was a special bond that had taken years to develop and build into what he was witnessing.

Chance watched them. God help him if any of them decided that they hated him.

'Now this is a house,' Fredi said as she walked deeper into the great room. 'Wow.'

She dug a sketchbook and pencil out of her bag and crouched in a corner to get a better look at the light falling through the skylight. Celia was close behind, her phone clutched in her hands. Unlike Fredi, who was content to absorb what she was seeing, Celia flitted from place to place, depending on what caught her eye. Right now, she was making a dirty joke about the size of his couch.

Bonni was the one who closed the front door and locked it. A tote was slung over her shoulder and she quickly surveyed the room before giving Chase a nod. Ava bounced over to her friend, giving her a sloppy hug. Bonni returned the hug and handed her the bag. She leaned in to whisper something to Ava and Chase caught the quick looks they darted at him. A blush staining her cheeks, Ava nodded and Bonni made her high-five.

Chance tried not to smile, but he was pretty sure they were talking about last night. And goddamn if he didn't feel a little nervous. After all, he'd banged their best friend.

Holding the tote by its straps, Ava said, 'I'm going to go get changed. Chase, you want to show them around a little?'

'Oh yes! A tour!' Celia was nearly jumping up and down. 'I'd love to – we'd love to.'

Bonni checked the time. 'We don't have a lot of time to play with here. To be honest, I don't know how we'll all fit in.'

'Okay, so Ava goes to get changed and we'll see what we can.' Celia was already at the patio doors and very impatient for the house tour to begin.

Fredi finally stood and shook out her legs as she put her sketchpad away. 'Be quick like a bunny, Ava, my beloved's waiting for me.'

'I won't be long, then.' Ava dashed up the stairs, leaving the woman gaping after her. Chase bit back a cheesy grin, pleased about how comfortable Ava was in his home.

'Well, ladies? Shall we?' Chase led the women into the kitchen and gave them the nickel tour of the first floor, but he couldn't get the image of Ava upstairs in his room out of his mind.

She didn't take long and then he had the job of herding them all to his truck. Celia kept insisting on taking selfies and nearly fell into the paddock trying to get a picture of a foal frolicking next to one of his prize mares. He had all four doors to the truck open when a bee passed through, leading to an immediate evacuation and Chase being used as a human shield. Finally, he got them in and they set off. Chase had to admit he was pretty damn happy. He and Ava had had such a great night together and now

he was able to spend more time with her. Her friends were turning out to be damn entertaining icing on the cake.

'What do you guys have planned for later today?' he asked
as he steered the truck around a slow-moving vehicle.

'We have a suite at the Nissan Center, as you know. I suppose a lot of time will be spent there. Bonni and Celia have us
pretty much planned out,' Ava replied.

He didn't like hearing that bit of news. He wanted to spend
more time with Ava. Private time.

'True, but you never know, sometimes people ditch plans. If
something better comes along.' He looked at her and winked.

'Is he suggesting there's something better than us? If he
wasn't chauffeuring us to the promised land, I'd vote we ditch
him,' Fredi snarked.

'I'd like to pack in as much touristy stuff as possible,' Celia
said, ignoring her friend. 'The Country Music Hall of Fame,
the Bluebird Café – anywhere else you can suggest, Chase?'

'Guys, let's just take the day as it comes,' Bonni intervened.
'For all we know, Fredi will manage to get rip-roaring drunk in
a dry county and that'll be that.'

'Wait. Dry county? What do you mean, dry county?' Celia
demanded.

'Ha,' Fredi said. 'Now look who didn't read the emails.'

As they bantered as only old friends could do, Chase took a
quick glance at Ava, next to him the passenger seat. She was
craning around so she could look at her friends in the back seat
but, when she caught his eye, she gave him a secret smile full of
promise and he felt better about his chances for one-on-one
time. He reached over and took her hand, squeezing her fingers.

Chase couldn't remember the last time he'd chauffeured
around a bunch of women. These days, he was the one being
chauffeured. He thought back and figured the last time he'd

had this many women in his car was back in high school, but he'd also had the guys, too, as they all drove down to the fishing hole. His truck was filled with a sudden riotous burst of laughter and Ava was hysterical, clutching her stomach. She was just as animated as the rest of them and he couldn't stop himself from glancing over at her frequently. He loved discovering all these sides to her personality.

The Jack Daniels distillery was a little over an hour away depending on traffic. He'd been there so many times, since everybody always wanted to see it when they came to Nashville. Chase was thoroughly enjoying himself as the drive continued. Fredi was sharply sarcastic and Bonni had a fine dry wit, while Celia just put it all out there. Ava chimed in with an aside or two but was mostly content to enjoy the others.

'This is nice.' Ava reached up and touched the pocket watch hanging from the rear-view mirror. 'It looks very old.'

'It is, from the early 1800s, as far as we can tell.' He briefly looked at the watch swinging gently with the motion of the truck.

'Oh my, it's over two hundred years old? That is really old. Is it a family heirloom?' She leaned forward and cradled it in the palm of her hand to look at it more closely.

'Yes, my six-time removed great-grandfather's. It's been passed down through the years. To the first son.'

'I love that kind of history. Genealogy fascinates me. But don't you worry that something may happen to it if you keep it here?' She sat back in her seat, letting the watch slip from her fingers. He could only shake his head. His mom was going to love her.

'We're almost there,' Chase announced when he turned on to Lynchburg Highway. 'Cave Spring Hollow is just up that way.'

Bonni said, 'It's supposed to be cool, sweet water . . . mmm. I could go for a glass of it right now. Jack Daniels bought the acreage for about $2,500 way back then. Imagine what it's worth now.'

'A fortune,' Fredi said. 'But whatever water it is, it sure turns into something delicious.'

'I wonder if it's highly commercialized,' Bonni mused. 'Over time, that's usually what happens, and it's a damn shame to taint all the significant places. And the true flavor of the location is lost.'

'Everything is so commercialized now,' Fredi said. 'Look at the wedding industry. Getting married used to actually mean something and now it's just an excuse to have a party. The only thing that hasn't changed is the taste of that wonderful whiskey.'

'I'm looking it up. I'll let you know in a second.' Chase looked in his rear-view mirror and saw Celia hunched over her phone, tapping and swiping. She glanced up and they made eye contact in the mirror. She smiled at him then held up her phone.

Ava chose that moment to lean toward Chase to tell him something and Celia called her name. Ava glanced to the back and Celia quickly snapped a photo.

'Oh, that'll be awesome. I got a couple of great shots of you guys. You'll thank me for it later,' she said, looking at the photos. 'Oh yeah, priceless. Chase, do you mind if I Instagram some?'

Chase tipped his hat back. It wasn't an issue for him, but if she tagged him and Ava both, he was sure the press would pick it up. It didn't bother him much as he liked the idea of Ava being linked to him. 'My PR people run my account, but it's cool with me if it's cool with Ava.'

Celia and Ava had one of those magical silent women

conversations, and then Celia pivoted back to the Jack Daniels conversation like nothing had happened.

'Okay, here's some info on the Jack Daniels' website, about their distilling process. They take, like, 800 gallons a minute out of Cave Spring Hollow. Wow, that's a lot. Wonder where all the water comes from,' Celia said.

'I'm going to guess . . . a spring in a cave,' Bonni remarked. Celia flipped Bonni off over her head, still focusing on her phone.

'I don't care how much water it takes,' Fredi said. 'It makes my favorite beverage, baby.'

'This site has so much on it, but I bet they cover a lot of it on the tour. I think I have to use this for a book. A hunky distiller – is that a word? – who falls for . . . someone. It'll come to me,' Celia muttered as she tapped notes to herself.

Chase said, 'It's quite a process for Jack and they'll tell you all about it. And you can also get samples. This tour, they do different flights so you can taste a variety.'

'I wouldn't have expected anything less,' Fredi said. 'I am gonna buy sooo many "commemorative bottles". Take that, dry county!'

It was hard to focus on the road when he wanted to bust a gut laughing. Not once had his fame come up and the women all treated him like he was an average guy. He couldn't remember the last time he had this much uncomplicated fun.

And he wanted more.

Chapter 20

The distillery tour had been a blast. The tour guide was awesome, full of interesting facts, and it had felt a little like walking in history's footsteps, especially because they had to turn off their cell phones and weren't allowed to take pictures. Fredi had asked a million questions and, true to form, had gone a little overboard in the gift shop. They engraved the commemorative bottles so Fredi had bought six bottles and had them engraved with the days of the week, Monday through Saturday. The cute cashier had asked about Sunday and, in her best Southern drawl, Fredi replied, 'Sunday's the day of rest, sugar. I drink wine on Sundays.'

Celia had practically gone into withdrawal, not being able to use her camera. When it came time for the sampling portion of the tour, she had shot the first glass on the whiskey flight, rather than sip and savor. Then, after a sharp inhale of breath, she'd grabbed her second glass and shot that, too. The distillery employee had just handed Celia a glass of water and moved on.

Ava had bought herself a cute tee and was incredibly touched when Chase handed her a bottle of Tennessee Honey engraved with her nickname. 'Sweetness for the sweet one,' he said. She had to pull him into a corner and kiss him to say thank you.

Chase had been amazing the entire morning. She'd watched him and couldn't detect an ounce of frustration. He fit in so well with her friends and didn't seem at all fazed by any of their craziness. He was one hell of a special man and she thanked her lucky stars she met him.

Now, back at the hotel, it was time to part ways. At least for now. He had to head to the studio and the girls were going to take a short break before heading out to lunch. But she didn't want to say goodbye. It made her heart hurt.

It felt too real.

Her friends swung their doors open and Chase jumped out to grab their purchases from the back while Ava waited in the passenger seat. Bonni helped Fredi carry her whiskey and they all told Chase goodbye, Fredi even deigning to kiss him on the cheek. Celia popped her head back into the truck. 'Ava, you coming, babe?'

'I'll be right in, just give me a second,' Ava said. Celia gave her a searching look before reaching forward to pat her on the shoulder.

'Take all the time you need, honey. We won't be far.' And she was out of the truck.

Chase slid back into the driver's seat and Ava stared at the dashboard rather than meet his eyes. They were cocooned in silence after a morning of being with her friends.

'That was fun,' he said as he reached up to tilt his hat back. 'I've done the tours a bunch of times but you guys made it seem like the first time.'

He looked quite content and happy, which made Ava feel wonderful. 'We do bring the magic. I had a good time.' She wanted to reach to take his hand but knew they couldn't stay parked for ever. He was already getting curious looks from the valet guys but he didn't seem in much of a hurry.

'So you all have the evening planned?' he asked.

'We're going to the concert in the stadium tonight. We have that suite so if you find yourself kicking around the area, come on up and see us. I'm sure a hotshot like you can get through security.' Ava began to reach for her purse, knowing that the time was coming when she was going to have to rip the Band-Aid off and get out of the truck.

'I'll do my best to try and pop by, but I have some engagements later as well. I'm doing a stand-up interview for CMT at one of the smaller venues and I promised a buddy I'd catch his set. Oh, did I tell you about the party tonight?' Chase asked her, draping his left arm over the steering wheel as he faced her.

'I think so. It's not until much later, right?' She furrowed her brows, trying to remember what he told her last night.

'Yep, it won't really get underway until the Fest is over. Did you want to come? It'll be fun.' The earnest look in his velvety brown eyes made her catch her breath.

'Yes, I'd very much like to come, but I'm not sure what we're doing later. Our days of being able to stay up all night partying are far behind us.' Ava was torn. She wanted to be with him so badly but she also had about three hours of sleep last night, thanks to his insatiable desire, and walked all over creation this morning in pursuit of Fredi's one true love. A quiet night in close proximity to a bed sounded just a little more appealing than a party with strangers.

'Your friends are welcome, too. My buddy won't mind. I think Fredi would have a blast.' Well, that settled that. Love me, love my friends, she always said. Not that she was implying Chase was in love with her. Or that she was in love with him.

The latter might be getting more and more likely, except Celia's picture of the two of them had started to spread. Celia hadn't tagged either of them but one of her followers had liked it and tagged Chase in a comment. The initial comments about Ava were . . . not incredibly kind. Would she really want to expose herself to that twenty-four/seven? Not to mention, she dealt with many conservative types in her job. There was the possibility her professional reputation could take a hit if her face and name was blasted all over social media and online gossip sites.

'I could ask them.'

'Yes. Do that and let me know.' Chase glanced out the front window.

The valet guys were starting to get braver and edging closer to the truck. Chase finally noticed them so he opened his door and exited the truck. Ava reached for the handle on her door so she could get out.

'No, wait there,' he told her as he walked around to the back of the vehicle. She turned and watched him lift the tonneau cover and take out her bags before coming to her. Opening the door, he reached in for her so he could help her down from the high truck.

'Really looking forward to seeing you tonight, Boots.'

She searched his eyes and smiled when she saw the emotion she'd hoped to see reflected in them. 'Me too, superstar.'

He pulled her into an embrace, the bag bumping gently against her butt, and she tightened her arms around his waist. She looked up at him and he lowered his head for a kiss. He didn't seem the least bit concerned that they were standing in the lobby driveway of the Opryland Hotel and that everyone could see them.

'Okay then.' He lifted from the kiss. 'Keep in touch before tonight?'

Ava nodded her head, still recovering from their passionate kiss. He handed her the bags and she reluctantly walked across the driveway to the front doors of the hotel. Chase raised a hand in farewell before getting back in the truck and driving off. Ava stared after him until there was a discreet cough and she startled. A doorman was waiting on her to enter the hotel. Fumbling with her purse, she gave him a tip – how long had he been holding that door? – and finally went inside.

Feeling oddly bereft, she went up to the room, uncharacteristically oblivious to the gorgeous hotel. When she opened the door her friends were in the living area waiting for her.

'There she is!' Celia cheered, waving around a bottle of beer. 'I'm kinda surprised he didn't just kidnap you and whisk you away.'

'Oh, guys!' She broke down into tears and they swarmed in on her for a group hug.

'I knew it,' Fredi said, but she hugged Ava the hardest.

Chapter 21

Ava didn't mind crying the way some people did. Crying was a healthy way to release emotions and it was never something she avoided. Heck, she had *The Notebook* and *Casablanca* on her Blu-ray keeper shelf. Still, after this latest crying jag, she felt a little raw, so she was grateful when her friends didn't plunge right into the inquisition. Instead, they speculated on the party, about what celebrities they might see, and ripped apart their luggage to find acceptable outfits.

Bonni, sprawled out in an armchair, was currently wearing one of Celia's longer skirts, paired with a shirt of Ava's while she texted her fiancé, Quinn.

'I'm kind of beat,' Ava said, and flopped down on the couch in their hotel room. She was just going to go back to the store where she bought the pink dress. There had been this little black dress that she had considered, and if ever there was a time to dive into the mad-money fund, this was it. She rested her head back on the cushion and closed her eyes with a big sigh. Her actions seemed to signal to her friends that she was feeling better.

'I'm not surprised. You had quite the active night,' Fredi called from the balcony, where she'd been standing. 'You have much to tell, young lady.'

'I know, I know. I'm just reliving it all in my mind.'

'That good, huh?' Celia sank on to the couch next to her and nudged her shoulder.

'Holy shit, look at that grin on her face.' Fredi came into the room and pointed at her before dropping into the armchair beside Bonni's.

Ava laughed and pushed herself up on the sofa. She gave her friends a recap, holding back certain parts as precious, to be shared only between her and Chase.

They were all open-mouthed and sighing with delight for her as she told them about first kisses, fireflies, the cozy bed and what a workout wall sex was. When she'd finished they fell silent and looked at each other.

'It sounds like it was an amazing night. I can only imagine what tonight is going to hold,' Bonni said. She leaned forward and put her elbows on her knees, resting her chin in her left hand, which made her engagement ring shoot sparks of light from its perfection.

'Your ring is so gorgeous,' Ava said with a wistful tone in her voice.

'Hey, with the way this weekend is shaping up, odds are pretty good that one of those is in your future,' Celia advised with great authority.

'Oh Lord, you guys are just awful. Don't wish that kind of horror on her,' Fredi said with a groan.

'Just because you are a marriage hater doesn't mean other

people have to believe the same thing. Look at me and Quinn. Celia and Landon. And now, here's Ava and she's met Chase.' Bonni raised her eyebrows and gave Fredi the sternest cop stare she could muster.

Ava raised a hand. 'While we all know I don't agree with Fredi, let's not jump the gun here. I just met Chase and there's a lot more that goes into a relationship besides amazing, phenomenal, passionate, unbelievable sex . . .'

Celia said, 'Oh, I think we've lost her again. Earth to Ava. Look, sometimes you meet someone and you just know.'

'Really? Did you just know when you met your ex?' Fredi snapped.

'Low blow, Fredi, low blow,' Celia replied. She crossed her arms against her chest and leaned back, retreating into the couch.

Fredi rubbed her forehead. 'Celia, I'm sorry. You're right, that was going too far. But you're different from Ava.' She shifted so that she could put a hand on Ava's knee. 'You wear your heart on their sleeve. You've been hurt in the past. You let everybody in without guarding yourself. So I'm worried for you, babe. How much can you give before you empty yourself out? Just don't let this whirlwind love affair happen too fast. I don't want you to get your heart broken,' Fredi said, with some very uncharacteristic emotion in her voice.

Ava curled her fingers around Fredi's hand and squeezed. 'Don't worry about me, hon. Even if I do wind up with a broken heart, last night alone would have been worth it. Because if Chase turns out not to be my Mr Right, then, when the real one shows up, he's going to be straight out of a fairy tale.' She softened her voice with love for her friend.

Fredi shook her head, vehemently tossing her long curls in a riot around her head. 'Why do you never listen to reason? Fine, then, just don't come crying to me and expect me to share some of my Green Label Jack with you.'

Bonni snorted and Celia said, 'Fredi, who are you fooling?' but Ava replied, 'I promise.'

There was a beat of silence then Celia remarked, 'Guess we know who's going to be Ava's maid-of-honor.'

It was really hard to keep from building castles in the air when her friends insisted on providing the clouds.

Chapter 22

Chase was at the label's preferred studio and his concentration was definitely shot. All he could think of was Ava and their time together. Even his band sensed he was off. But they only had the studio for four hours so they needed to get recording.

She'd permeated his soul. She'd seeped into every piece of him and snared him to the point that he couldn't focus. The time he spent with her, and with her friends, it had reconnected him with his love for life. There was so much to explore, so much to experience. When had he gotten so jaded? Ava made him think of new possibilities.

The song was still formulating in his head and he had put some words down after dropping the girls off at the hotel. Now he just had to follow the tune, let it come out. But he needed help from his band. It felt important that the song be finished before his set on Saturday night. So the pressure was on. If he nailed it, then he might just sing it for her, depending how everything played out.

He had to slow down his thoughts because knowing he'd be

seeing her tonight was having a physical effect on him. He shook his head and, regrettably, pushed Ava out of his mind.

'Chase, bro, you hung over? What's the deal, dude?' Chip, his producer, said through the headphones.

'Yeah, buddy, what's up with you today? You do smell of whiskey. You been visiting with Uncle Jack?' his drummer and long-time friend, Stone, asked him, then did a quick shuffle on his snare.

'Took some friends on the distillery tour this morning. I'm okay, just got a lot on my mind. I'll shape up.' He wasn't going to mention Ava yet. Chase was very private about his life, even with friends. It was just how he was, and the situation with Ava felt like it needed to be protected, nurtured, like a delicate seed. Picking up his guitar, he finger-strummed a riff that had been rattling around in his brain to warm up his fingers and to snap him out of his distracted state.

'Yo, man. What's that?' Chip asked him.

'Just a little something I've been working on. Still in the beginning stages and doesn't have any traction yet,' Chase replied, but continued to play it. He almost had it.

'Keep playing,' Chip told him, and gestured to the other band members. Their bass player, Tim, jumped in, finding the melody with the ease of years of practice. Stone picked up the groove and soon they were jamming to Chase's chords and then, just like that, he saw the song.

He started over again, playing the music from the top, the sound deep and rich on his vintage Martin. As he played the notes he fell into that strange state of surrealism that happened when he wrote something he knew was good. The words found his mind and he saw them like a painting on a canvas. Chase forgot the band was there as he went deeper into the song.

This song for Ava came from his fingertips and his lips, as if he was touching and kissing her now, bringing her out through the strings of his guitar and the words from his heart.

He finished and placed his fingers flat over the guitar strings, the last vibrations muted. His eyes still closed, he slowly came back from the creative place that had drawn him in. The guys were quiet, but he heard the chairs creak as they shifted on them. He opened his eyes.

'So.' It wasn't a question, it was simply a word, and he looked at each one of them. He could tell by their eyes and expressions that what he had just done was magical.

'Where did that one come from?' Tim stood up and hitched his bass from front to back.

'Dude. That's a number-one hit if I've ever heard one,' Stone said as he twirled his sticks.

'Where does any song come from?' Chase said, and turned to the control window. 'Were you recording?'

His producer nodded and leaned forward, opening the mic to the booth. 'Got it all. Do you want to hear playback?'

Part of Chase wanted to hear it again immediately but this song was special and he was wary about sharing it too soon. 'No. If you can burn it for me, I'll take it. I know it still needs some work.'

'You know, I don't think it needs any work,' Stone told him. 'Why don't we mess around with it a little bit?' The rest of the band was nodding in agreement as Stone continued, 'Let's play it back, then we'll see where we can layer.'

Chase wrestled with his instinctive desire to keep the song private before acknowledging that maybe it wasn't such a bad idea. The only potential drawback was that it would bring Ava full-blown into his world if anyone found out she had inspired the song. But, he admitted to himself, there was nothing about that he did not like. Nodding, he looked up at Chip.

'Okay then, we'll do it. You do your producer magic as we're settling in here. If we can make it work, I want to play it at my set on Saturday night.'

'You wanna introduce it at the Fest? Does Dozer know? Or did you want to see if we can slip into the Bluebird?'

'How about we just see how we make out today? I doubt we'll be able to get into the Bluebird but, if I do take it somewhere before the Fest, I might go to Sugars instead.'

'Who are you kidding? You'll get into the Bluebird, you just have to say the word, hotshot,' Stone said as he settled on his throne behind his kit, stomping his bass a few times.

'Anyway, let's just see what we can do with this now.' Chase felt an urgency to get this song perfect. It would be his gift for Ava and, possibly, be enough to win her over, bet or no bet.

Chapter 23

'Are they bringing us food, too?' Celia asked when they arrived in their prime suite at the Nissan Center. Security had been a bit of a pain, but they were finally ready to get their party on.

'Yes, they're supposed to. I checked because, otherwise, I was going to need serious snackage.' Ava found a menu on a sideboard and waved it at Celia. Handing it over to her friend when she came over, Ava continued to explore. 'This is really cool,' she said, walking out to the row of seats that overlooked the stadium below.

'This is the best ever. I'm so glad you were able to make this happen,' Bonni told her, and gave her a quick hug. The crowds were filling the seats below them. 'This place is massive.'

'I'm impressed,' Fredi announced, dumping her bag on one of the seats by the window.

'Oh, thank God,' Bonni said dryly. 'We were worried we'd have to leave.'

Ava snickered as she shrugged off her jacket. You never knew when stadiums like this overdid the AC inside to compensate for the open floor plan, but it was warm right now. She placed it on one of the barstools and began to investigate the refrigerator, having already noticed all the beer bottles sitting in ice in a big tin tub that sat on the counter. 'I wonder what we have in here. I'm going to have something – anybody else?'

'That's the dumbest question that you've ever asked.' Celia nudged up beside her and reached for one of the beers. 'I've never been much of a beer drinker, but I'm really liking these small brewery finds. Look, this one is a strawberry-flavored beer. Who would've ever thought?'

Before heading to the stadium, they had grabbed dinner at a local pub that specialized in local beers. It had been quite an education. Celia wiped her mouth with a cocktail napkin. 'It's pretty good – have a try.'

'Nope. It's bad enough I'm cheating on Jack on his turf. If I drink beer, I wanna taste the hops.' Fredi curled her lip and took a different bottle.

Ava closed the fridge and selected the same flavor as Celia but poured it into a glass.

She held the glass out for Fredi, who stepped back, shaking her head. 'Come on, don't be a diva. You won't be able to talk smack about the Bridezillas if you're a hypocrite.'

Pouting because Ava had backed her into a metaphorical corner, Fredi accepted the glass and took a tentative sip. Her eyebrows shot up. 'Wow, that *is* good. I think I'll have one, then. Sorry, Jack.'

'Is there a non-fruity beer?' Bonni asked, stepping in behind her friends.

Ava watched the three of them discuss beer, and she felt such a sense of gratitude. She loved being with her friends and was so happy they made the conscious effort to keep their friendships healthy, despite everything else going in their lives. These little getaways were just the sprinkles on the sundae.

Her phone buzzed and she pulled it from her back pocket.

Chase: *How's the suite?*

Ava: *Awesome. How are you? Did you have a good day after you dropped us off?*

Chase: *Yup. Went into the studio and put down a new track. Did a little work on the next album, too, before I had to go meet my PR rep for the interview.*

Ava: *Such a busy life you have, superstar.*

To Ava, Chase was just a guy, one she might be a little too emotionally invested in maybe, but then something would remind her, like his text, that he really was a country-music star. It was easy to forget that during their time together.

Chase: *Yeah, but the music makes it worth it. I'm happy with new song. Can't wait for you to hear it.*

Her heart warmed up. Once again, he was making plans for the future and it made Ava feel like she wasn't the only one who was dreaming a little bigger than she should. Maybe a long-distance relationship would be different this time.

Ava: *I'd love to hear it. When?*

Chase: *Soon. Listen, gotta go. Will check in with you later. Still game for the party after your concert?*

Ava glanced at her friends, who were now sampling all the beers.

Ava: *Yup! Wardrobe took a little doing, but we're looking forward to it.*

Chase: *I'm looking forward to seeing you. Text when you're ready to head out and I'll either come get you, if I can, or send another car.*

Ava: *Will do :*)*

She put her phone back into her jeans pocket as Bonni sidled up next to her.

'Was that your sexy cowboy?'

'It certainly was. He was confirming we're going to the party later.' Ava held out her hand and Bonni put a glass of beer in it.

'We've had such a good time so far and we've only been here a day. It was really nice of Chase to take us out today. And this party tonight . . . wow. Do you know who'll be there?'

'I have no idea, but he's been doing work stuff since he dropped us off, so I expect industry people.' Ava sipped from the beer.

'Ooo, maybe Faith Hill or Chris Stapleton. I just love his song "Tennessee Whiskey".' Celia sounded super-excited. 'Are they performing at the Fest?' She fished out her phone to check the event schedule.

'Your guess is as good as mine. But you know who I'd love to see? Dolly Parton.' Ava leaned her hip against the railing and looked out over the crowds below.

'Dolly Parton?' her three friends chorused.

'Yes. I have great respect for that woman. I would love to meet her. It's too bad we didn't have more time because then we could go down to Dollywood.'

'She's so old-school, though,' Celia said over the rim of her beer glass.

'Dolly is the iconic female country star. Not only has she given us classic songs – hello, "Jolene", "Nine to Five", "I Will Always Love You" – she has a huge heart. Her Imagination Library foundation has mailed out over a hundred million books to kids. She's never forgotten her roots. She's amazing,' Ava said fiercely. There weren't many things Ava was willing to throw down on, but the awesomeness of Dolly Parton was near the top of the list.

For a minute there was just the faint ambient noise from the stadium crowd and then Bonni said, 'I thought Whitney Houston sang "I Will Always Love You". In that Kevin Bacon movie.'

Ava felt her eyes bug out. 'Okay, there are so many things wrong with what you just said. First of all, it was Kevin *Costner* and the movie was called *The Bodyguard*. Second of all, I think Dolly's version of that song is a million times better than Whitney's version, which, don't get me wrong, was quite lovely. But haven't you heard Dolly sing it in *The Best Little Whorehouse in Texas*?'

Celia said cautiously, 'Was that a place or—'

'It's a movie! Well, it was a musical first, but it was a movie! Dolly plays a madam and Burt Reynolds, RIP, plays her love interest, the sheriff!' Ava exclaimed.

'Y'know, if you squint a little, that could basically be Bonni's and Quinn's love story,' Fredi remarked teasingly.

'Hey! That is not remotely factual. A sheriff is an elected position and I am a regular cop!' Bonni said.

Leaving Bonni and Fredi to bicker, Ava went over to top up her drink. She picked through the bottles of beer and decided on a Bud.

'Ms Trent?'

Ava looked up at the hostess that approached her. 'Yes, hello. I'm Ava.'

'I'm Karen, and I'll be your hostess for tonight. If there's anything you need at all, please just let me know. The food will be up shortly. It had already been pre-ordered, so I hope you're okay with the selections but, if you have any concerns, let me know. I'm here to ensure that you and your friends have a great time.'

'Thank you very much, Karen, we really appreciate it.' Ava smiled at her and said another silent thank you to her boss for making this great weekend happen and, by extension, for meeting Chase.

She turned to lean her back against the counter. Her friends had moved away from the beer to stand down by the railing overlooking the stadium, their drinks in hand. The only thing missing was Chase, but she was determined to enjoy herself with her friends, knowing she would be seeing him later. A sudden aching heat flared low in her belly as she remembered their night together. The sex had been amazing, she couldn't deny that, but she was also quite thrilled that they seemed to be developing something beyond the sex. She couldn't wait for what came later.

And maybe beyond this weekend, too . . .

Chapter 24

The first set was nearly over and Ava was starting to hope that they might end up with the suite to themselves. She knew that David had chipped in for it and that someone else was arranging things, but it was getting late and, if there were others coming, they were cutting it pretty close.

Right on cue, she heard boisterous voices at the doorway and her heart sank. Three couples blew into the suite like a hurricane, clearly already having done a bit of pre-drinking. They were laughing and talking loudly, practically drowning out the music being piped in.

Ava glanced at her friends, who were down in the front-row seats of the suite. They had turned around to see what all the ruckus was about. Ava shrugged her shoulders. Fredi frowned at the unruly bunch, Celia turned back to look at the stage, while Bonni rose, coming up to stand beside Ava.

'Somehow, I don't think they're here solely for the music,' Bonni said in a quiet voice. Ava shook her head in agreement and they watched as the new arrivals got settled in.

Ava thought she should go over and say hello. It was the polite thing to do, especially since she didn't know how these people were connected to David.

'Hi, I am Ava. I'm with Enbridge?' She held out her hand to shake but no one took it so she let it drop.

One of the guests, a tall red-headed man, looked disinterestedly over his shoulder. 'Never heard of the company. Are you based in Nashville?'

Holding on to her civility with an iron grip, Ava replied, 'No, we're not. My friends and I are just in town for CMA Fest.'

The brunette woman with a pixie cut sneered, 'Oh, tourists. Do have a delightful time. Over there.'

She made a little shooing motion and Ava counted her blessings that Fredi or Celia weren't standing here because, otherwise, she was sure security would be escorting them out after an epic brawl. The food arrived at the perfect time, proof that there was a deity and he/she was quite fond of Ava.

'Celia, Fredi, food's here.' Ava was starving and filled up half her plate before her friends could even stand up.

Fredi and Celia strolled back to the lounge area as if they didn't have a care in the world. They grabbed plates and got in line behind Ava.

'There you go, Aves, you shouldn't go hungry now,' Celia joked. 'Oh, that looks yummy. Let me try a bite.' Celia reached out as if to pick something off Ava's plate and she turned her shoulder to her.

'Back off my food. You know the deal.' Ava continued to shield her plate from Celia as she loaded it up with more food.

Celia laughed. 'Just bugging you, chickie. We know how you are about your food. I'm surprised you don't mantle over it like an eagle.'

'Mantle over it?' Fredi asked, popping a spring roll into her mouth. 'That sounds like a kinky sex position.'

'Eagles, especially the eaglets defending their food, spread their wings out and hunch over their meal so nobody else can get it. If you watch those live eagle cameras, you'll see. Anyway, that's like Ava. She has food issues.'

'I do not. I just don't like people picking off my plate.' She took a step back from the girls, out of arm's reach.

Fredi burst out laughing. 'What's that, then? Look how you're backing away. We've got our own food. Why would we take yours?'

'Because you always do.' Ava looked down at her plate, trying to decide which tasty morsel she would eat first.

Big mistake. She dropped her guard for a second and Celia swooped in to snatch a meatball from right under her nose.

'Hey!' Ava reached out to try and grab the meatball back, knocked Celia's hand and the meatball went sailing. They all watched it bounce off the seat backs like a freaking golf ball, heading straight for Bonni. She ducked and it landed with a splat against the wall.

Silence filled the suite and they all looked at each other. From over to their left, a snide voice drawled, 'Are we having food fights now? Did we wind up back in middle school again?'

'It was an accident,' Ava burst out, even though she knew she was playing right into his mean-boy narrative. The ever-efficient Karen was already cleaning off the wall, the scent of cleaner filling the air as Ava fought against a wave of embarrassment.

'Okay, guys, just ignore them and eat. We came here for some awesome country music performers, not second-rate extras from *Gossip Girl*.' Fredi nudged Ava toward a seat. 'Here, we need to feed the beast. Eat, Ava. And you,' Fredi said, pointing her finger at Celia. 'Behave yourself.'

'Wow, are you going to put her in time-out?' Pixie Haircut said.

Well, that just took the cake. Mess with her all you want, but go after her friends and the gloves were off. 'I didn't get your name.' Her voice was sweet but held a don't-mess-with-me edge. Fredi let out a low whistle.

The woman sized her up again then gave a small shrug, turning her attention to the food on the buffet. 'It's quaint that you don't know who I am. Donna Evans. The E of E&R Records.' Nodding toward the stage, she said, 'That's one of our acts on stage. Perhaps you've heard of him?'

The condescension was so thick in her voice, Ava could've cut it with a knife. Before she could up with a suitably scathing response, Donna the E put two pieces of lettuce and a slice of tomato on her plate before flouncing away. God, what a bunch of stuck-up snobs.

Before she could shake off her anger, her phone vibrated in her back pocket. As she pulled it out, she was anxiously hoping it would be Chase, but it wasn't. It was David.

David: *Checking in. I hope you're enjoying yourself with your friends, Ava. I'm glad you were able to use the tickets.*

She quickly typed back to him: *We are and it's amazing. Thank you so much. See you when I get back.*

'Who is that? Loverboy?' Fredi asked around the mushroom she'd just stuffed into her mouth.

Ava shook head. 'No, it was David, you know, my boss, the man responsible for getting us into this suite.' Sending a final glare to the awful people on the other side of the room, she resolved to take the high road. She didn't want to do anything that would reflect badly on David or the company.

Settling back into her seat, she rescued her plate and started eating. Halfway through the first headliner, and right as she was finishing a delectable chocolate mousse, her phone vibrated in the pattern she had set for incoming Facetime calls. This time, it had to be Chase.

'Here, hold this.' She shoved her plate at Fredi, who didn't have time to juggle hers and Ava's properly so the plates tilted precariously, nearly spilling all the food down the front of her top. Bonni came to her rescue as Ava answered the call.

'Hey, superstar. How are tricks?'

'Exhausting, that's what they are. I tell ya, Boots, I'm looking forward to chilling at the party with you. I swear that last interviewer would have been all over me if I'd given the slightest hint I'd be open to it.' Chase looked so adorable when he was this grumpy.

'Aww, is that why you Facetimed instead of texted? You wanted to remind yourself you were taken?' The words just fell out of Ava's mouth. Celia gave her big eyes as Ava's brain began to scramble for ways to deflect.

Fortunately, Chase didn't even seem to notice that Ava had staked a claim on him after less than forty-eight hours. 'Yeah. And to see when you wanted to be picked up.'

She breathed a sigh of relief over her narrow escape. 'Well, Luke Coombs is finishing up now, so Little Big Town is up next. Another hour, maybe? We can meet you downstairs?'

Chase stared off into the distance for a moment, like he was checking the time, before he looked into the camera and nodded. 'Sounds like a plan, Boots. Ask the suite's hostess to show you where. See ya soon.'

Ava said goodbye and clicked off the phone with a silly grin on her face. The grin died quickly when a voice said from behind her. 'Was that Chase Hudson? *You* know Chase Hudson?'

Folding her arms across her chest, Ava stared down Donna

the E and her band of misfits, who were gathered in behind her with curious expressions on their faces.

'I do know Chase, rather well, actually. I also know CEOs of Fortune 500 companies, a couple of A-list entertainers, a best-selling novelist or two, and many, many members of the idle rich. But why should that matter to you now? You didn't give a rat's ass a minute ago.'

Donna the E gave her the brightest, fakest smile Ava had ever seen. 'Oh, well, it was all in good fun. Perhaps we can arrange—'

'Why don't you go have your "good fun" over there?' Ava echoed the insulting brush-off gesture the snobs had made earlier then turned back to her friends, completely ignoring the other group.

'Where did that lioness come from?' Celia asked her.

'I knew you had that roar in you,' Fredi said as they did a round of high-fives.

'I guess it takes a certain kind of something for that roar to come out loud and proud,' Ava said, feeling wonderful. Chase was eager to see her and she had put those arrogant jerks in their places! She was flying higher than a kite right now.

The lights dimmed and the music from the stage got louder. Cheers echoed around the stadium and the crowd surged to their feet, heralding the beginning of the final set of the night, Little Big Town.

'Oh my God!' Celia screamed, her voice mixing in with the rest of the thousands of concert-goers. 'It's Miranda Lambert! She's crashing into their set!'

Ava quickly tapped out a text to Chase: *OMG, Miranda Lambert is performing with Little Big Town!!! I love LBT! Will text you when set is almost over. XO*

He replied back almost instantaneously: *I'll introduce you to them someday.* ☺ *enjoy the show and c u later.*

She pumped her fist in the air and did the loudest 'Yeehaw!' she could muster. If only Chase could hear that. How could he ever say she wasn't country when she could holler with the best of 'em?

She trembled with anticipation of what was going to come after the concert: time spent with her superstar and likely between his sheets. Now how could a night end up any better than that?

Chapter 25

Once again, Chase had a truckload of women. 'I'm kind of getting used to chauffeuring you ladies around,' he said as he put the truck in gear.

'So what kind of party is this?' Celia inquired.

'A bunch of old buddies, some industry people, their womenfolk—'

'"Womenfolk". Can you believe he just said "womenfolk"?' Fredi said, and rolled her eyes.

'No offence meant. It's not a long drive, so we should be there soon.' Chase's phone rang – he'd tossed it in the tray under the dash – and quickly picked it up. As he answered the phone, he heard the women begin to talk among each other, and tuned them out.

'It's Chase,' he said into the phone.

'Hey, bro, it's Dozer. Are you heading to Astro's?' His agent always wanted to know where Chase was; his reasoning was that you could never know when an opportunity would present itself.

'No, Harper's. Why, what's up?' He glanced in the rearview and smiled at seeing the women in his back seat having a laughing fit. He looked at Ava. She had turned and had her arm slung over the back of the seat and her knees pulled up so she was sitting sideways.

'What's all that racket?' Dozer demanded to know, but before Chase replied he bulldozed right over him (hence his nickname, Dozer). 'Listen, Warrington's agent is going to be at Astro's, maybe even Warrington himself. I want you to go and schmooze him up a bit, because they're talking about you coming on stage with Lance.'

'Is that right? Exactly how do you want me to schmooze him? You know me, I am who I am and a schmoozer ain't it.' Chase knew that would irritate the hell out of Dozer, and he loved to yank his chain whenever he could. But Chase was a little pissed he was throwing this at him at such late notice. He had plans, and the biggest one was sitting right beside him.

'Enough of the bullshit, Chase, this could be big. You know he's on top right now. You're not there yet, but you're on your way, and if Lance Warrington wants to play with you, then dammit, you're gonna play.' Chase could hear the tone in Dozer's voice change. He'd hit a nerve and now was the time to bring Dozer back down.

'Okay, boss, I'll go and schmooze, but I'll be taking people with me and I'm not staying long. When was he thinking for this performance?' Chase was running through his schedule in his head, he wanted to make sure he could fit in Ava as much as possible, but, at the same time, ensure he did all he could for his career.

'I don't care if you take Santa Claus, just go. And he's thinking during his set on Saturday, since you're performing before him,' Dozer said with great emphasis.

'Are you kidding me? Huh, that's a pretty big deal.' Chase was a little surprised to be invited – correction: potentially invited – to play with the closing headliner on the last night of CMA Fest.

'And why you need to talk the talk,' Dozer said. 'Okay, then, I can count on you? I've done my bit, now it's up to you.'

'Yep, it's all good. Don't you worry.' Chase ended the call and, while he was glad this opportunity had presented itself, he was a little annoyed it happened when he had Ava with him. He didn't want to have to split his time between her and industry talk, but now he was going to have to.

He hardly noticed Ava had put her hand on his forearm until she squeezed it and he turned to look at her. 'Everything okay?' she asked him. The sincerity in her eyes told him she really did care.

'Yes, that was my agent. We have to make a little detour before Harper's.' He shifted his hand so he could close his fingers around hers.

'Does he have some good news for you?' She shifted in her seat a bit so she wasn't facing her friends as much. They were carrying on a rather rowdy conversation in the back seat.

'It could be. Apparently, I have to do some schmoozing for a while.'

'If it's good for your career, then you should definitely do it. What's the schmoozing for?'

Chase debated how much detail to go into, since they'd not really talked jobs or careers yet in their relationship. The fact that he even used the word 'relationship' again made him realize she'd become more important to him than he'd ever anticipated. And in such a short space of time!

'It could be very good for my career. Lance Warrington's agent is going to be at our first stop tonight. Lance might be there, too, and there's talk he might want me to join him on stage during his set on Saturday night.'

'Oh my God!' Celia squealed from the back. 'Lance Warrington is going to be at this party tonight? If I wasn't in a committed relationship, man, I would be all over that sexy boy.'

Chase chuckled. 'You and about a million other women.'

'I know.' He watched the expression on Celia's face turn to a pout in the rear-view mirror. 'Anyhow, a little bit of harmless flirting, if I get the chance, will give me the thrill of a lifetime. Even though I have my man waiting for me back home and he's even watching my children so I could come out and have shenanigans with my girls. Definitely, *that* man's a keeper.'

'Well, I don't have any man back home,' Fredi announced. 'Perhaps you can make an introduction for me?'

'Fredi, don't put pressure on Chase like that. This is business for him and he doesn't need to worry about you,' Ava reprimanded her gently.

'Ava, hon, I am a good Southern girl. One whiff of my magnolia blossoms and he will come to me,' Fredi said, fluttering her eyelashes exaggeratingly.

'Unfortunately, Lance tends to be a bad Southern boy, so I don't know if he'll stick around long enough to smell your, uh, blossoms,' Chase said.

'Well, now,' Fredi said, with a cat-ate-the-canary smile. 'Now he really sounds interesting.'

In response to that remark the women spoke over each other and Chase was hard-pressed to figure what the hell they were saying. All he could make out was that Fredi could be very, very bad indeed. And for her to call herself a good girl was an oxymoron.

He broke out laughing, which halted their conversation as they all stared at him. 'I'm sorry, but you guys are too much.

Hilarious. And, by the way, Fredi, Lance is a *very* bad boy, so if you're a very bad girl, y'all probably get along just fine. I'm happy to make an introduction.'

'Fantastic!' She clapped her hands and stuck her tongue out to her friends. Which made him laugh even more.

He turned to Ava and shook his head. 'I'm really getting to like your friends.'

The bright smile that broke out on her face was all he needed.

Chapter 26

The event at Astro's wasn't a small and intimate gathering, it was a huge affair. It was catered, with waiters walking around holding silver trays with all manner of hors d'œuvres, and others with trays of champagne flutes. People dressed up or down, but there was bling, and sparkle, and big hair, and fancy instruments all lined up along one wall. Platinum records were showcased above the instruments and they were all for country music. Music played from the speakers at a carefully selected decibel in order to facilitate conversation. It was absolutely mind-blowing.

'Can you believe this?' Celia linked her arm through Ava's and whispered into her ear.

'No, actually I can't. I was expecting, like, well, I don't know what I was expecting.' Ava was feeling a little out of place in this crowd of industry folk.

'Aw, honey, it's just people. You're good with people. In fact, you're an amazing businesswoman so this shouldn't faze you one little bit. Don't fret about it. It's all good.' Celia shook her arm in encouragement.

'Where did Fredi and Bonni go?' Ava asked as she looked around, trying to find them in the crowd.

'No idea, both of them seemed to vanish the minute we got inside the door. Listen, are you feeling a little weirded out by this? Because if you are, you shouldn't be. Look at how it all turned out for Landon and me, and I was truly weirded out. Being with him was so much more than I'd anticipated, and I kinda get the same feeling about you and Chase.'

Ava nodded. 'Yeah, I think you're right. It's really strange because I feel like I've connected with him so well, and yet I see all this and I feel like a fish out of water.' She waved her hand around and raised her eyes to the ceiling, stunned by the beautiful crystal chandeliers sending prisms of sparkling light across the cathedral ceiling.

'This doesn't seem like him at all. Remember, we've been in his house, seen his truck and spent time with him. He's way different than all this. He's a down-to-earth guy.'

Ava knew Celia was doing her best to reassure her and she appreciated it. 'I know, even though I've known him for such a short period of time.' She turned to look at Celia. 'Not even two days – barely one! Yet I feel like it's been a lifetime. I can't even imagine life before him or, dare I say it . . . without him.'

'Wow, you've been bitten by the love bug, haven't you?' Celia wrapped her arm around Ava's waist and gave her a squeeze. 'Just don't get yourself hurt.'

Movement caught their eye and they turned to find Chase maneuvering through the crowd of people with ease and charm, a total gentleman.

'He's just so effortless in how he works the crowd,' Ava said as she watched him, starting to get annoyed with herself for beginning to feel a little bit left out.

'Ava, need I remind you, you are a very successful business-woman. Where is this insecurity coming from? This isn't like you,' Celia pointed out. 'You've schmoozed CEOs, CFOs, board presidents, just like you pointed out to those dicks in the suite earlier. You don't need a hug or mollycoddling here, you need a kick in the ass.'

Ava looked at her friend in surprise. Celia rarely got this serious unless she was in her so-called 'Mommy mode'. So her loving, chastising words really made Ava sit up and take notice. 'You're right.'

'Of course I am. Moms are always right.' Celia flicked her long blonde hair over her shoulder then gave Ava a big hug. 'Come on, you know you can do it.' Then she looked intensely at Ava and tipped her head to the side. She narrowed her eyes. 'Unless there's something else bothering you.'

Ava smiled at her friend and shook her head. 'You can see right through me.'

'Of course. We can all see through each other. We've known each other far too long.'

'This is only a weekend fling. But if it were to be more—' Ava started to say.

'Which it looks like to me,' Celia interrupted.

Ava raised her hand, knowing Celia was about to go off on a tangent. 'Hold on, think about it. If this was to be more, how would it work? I am stuck in a contract for the minimum of another year and based way in the middle of nowhere. He's here in Tennessee, while also traveling around the world doing concerts, cutting records and having all kinds of demands placed on him. Look at what happened tonight with this event overshadowing the party. And my career demands time as well. Where do I fit in? How does he fit in? How do we make it work?'

'Where there's a will, there's a way. Like trying to make it work long distance. Like Landon and me. Sorta. It can be done. And Chase's star is rapidly climbing. He can afford his own jet.' Ava saw the determination in Celia's eyes and felt deflated. She let out a sigh and shook her head.

'No, I've been down that road once before. It was an abysmal disaster.'

Celia cocked her head back and gave her an inquisitive look. 'What? Why don't I know about this?'

Ava didn't really want to get into it with Celia, but her friend would be relentless if she didn't give her something. 'Oh, a few years ago I met this guy at a conference and we were hot and heavy, but in the end we couldn't figure out how to make it last longer than a weekend. Plus, he was from London.' Ava shrugged her shoulders.

Celia gripped Ava's arm and shook it. 'That was London. As in the UK. As in flying across the Atlantic Ocean. This is America. You can practically walk to each other's state.'

Ava laughed. 'Walk? You're the one who's a dreamer, Celia.'

'I'm being facetious. But, Ava, we *will* talk about this later. If you feel that much for him, you ought to treasure it.' Celia gave her a little nudge and pushed her in the direction of Chase. 'Now, go get 'em, tiger. That's your man standing over there.'

Ava watched Chase: he was magnificent, there was no doubt about that. Just looking at him gave her all the feels, made her breath quicken, and something intimately deeper, more heartfelt, blossomed inside her.

Love?

There was no doubt he caused her to have a barrage of naughty thoughts and all sorts of other physical responses when she remembered their passion. But love? Insta love or insta lust? She pulled her bottom lip between her teeth. She owed it to herself to find out, but Cupid sat on her shoulder and Ava was pretty sure he had already shot his arrows.

She squared her shoulders and made a decision. Love or no love, she wanted to be with Chase and she didn't want any regrets. Perhaps she should just see how it all played out and not try to control the future. Let come what may and she would enjoy herself in the meantime. Still, the romantic that lived within her wondered, could he be the one to not break her heart?

The first step toward him led to a second, then another, until he turned to face her with a big smile on his face and reached out his hand

'Boots, come here.'

She put her fingers in his palm and let him pull her to his side. He didn't seem to care he was surrounded by industry people. Or that he was expressing his feelings for her in public. All that seemed to matter to him was that she was by his side. She gazed up into his deep brown eyes and the expression in them. She let out a little sigh. This just felt so right.

If all she got was his hand in hers, she could die a happy woman.

Chapter 27

Chase pulled Ava aside. He had wanted to get her alone for a little while. Once he had her secreted behind a stone pillar in a little alcove, he tipped her face up and claimed her with a kiss. Her response was immediate and passionate.

It was time to get her out of here. 'How about we take off?'

Her eyes were heavy-lidded and her lips partially open, as if waiting for him to kiss her again. He was tempted.

She nodded and whispered, 'Where to? Your house? My hotel room? The creek?' A slow smile curved her lips and he knew what she was thinking.

'Not now, Boots. I want to blow this pop stand and go somewhere fun. Remember Harper's? Then later ...' he said, nuzzling her ear.

'And my friends?' she asked him. She placed her hand on his chest and the warmth of her fingers seared through his shirt.

'Up to them. They can stay here if they like and we can arrange to get them back to their hotel. Or they can come along to Harper's.'

'Why don't you ask them?' Her hand slid up his chest to rest in the curve of his neck and shoulder. Her fingers tapped him slightly as if she was testing the merchandise. She could test the merchandise anytime she wanted as far as he was concerned.

'Let's go find them.' Taking Ava's hand, he led her back into the thick of the party and spotted the women hanging out around the bar. They were a vibrant lot and practically lit up the room. He knew they came with Ava, kit and caboodle, and he also knew it would be fun to have them in his life.

Walking up to them, they made room for Ava but looked at him expectantly. 'This party was a necessary stop but we can head on to our original destination if you want. If not, you can stay here. I'll make arrangements to get you back to your hotel, whether now or later. It's up to you if you want to come with Boots and me.'

'Boots?' Fredi said with surprise. 'This must be getting serious if nicknames are involved.'

Chase couldn't believe he felt a rush of heat up to his face. 'Ah, it's just a term of endearment. Nothing to get all excited about.' He didn't want them jumping to conclusions when he and Ava hadn't even talked about the future. Geez, they'd only just met, but one thing was for sure. He liked being with her, having her around, and the thought of her not being in his life almost made him suffocate.

'You guys have to decide quickly. Because we're outta here real soon.' He looked at his watch. 'Five minutes.' He put his arm around Ava's shoulder and pulled her tight. 'This one's definitely coming with me.'

Celia smiled and he saw the sparkle in her eyes. 'I, for one, wouldn't mind heading off to this other fun party,' she said.

'I'm in.' Bonni got off the stool and picked up her bag.

'Twist my arm – who wants to have fun anyway?' Fredi

stood and shook out her long curly hair. Chase chuckled. 'Besides, this party has a distinct lack of bad boys.'

'Ah, I'm sorry, Fredi. Only Lance's boring old agent came.'

'Are you going to sing with Lance?' Celia asked as they walked out of the building.

'Time will tell.'

The moon was still high overhead when they arrived at the Harper farm. Significant lighting was set up over an area of the field and Chase knew exactly what would be going on there. And that gave him the idea for the second competition.

Wheeling the truck into an empty spot, they all piled out and he led them toward the barn, also lit up like a Roman candle and with some great music coming from inside. Now this was way more up his alley than being at that industry shindig.

'Wow, this looks like fun.' Celia was bouncing. He watched her take everything in. She definitely was a firecracker. 'What are the lights for?'

'Tag football. These guys are serious about it and whenever there's any sort of gathering, day or night, there's a game.' He dipped his head to Ava and murmured, 'And that, Boots, is challenge number two.'

'What? Tag football?' She looked up at him and he chuckled at the shocked expression on her face.

'Any country girl worth her salt could hold her own in a game.' He pressed a kiss to her hair and inhaled her intoxicating scent.

'Well, I guess this is going to be the second new dress that gets ruined on a date with you,' Ava said ruefully.

'You look pretty damn fine in that dress, so we can't have that. I have some gym clothes in the truck. They'll be too big for you, but they're better than the dress.'

'If I'm going to be tackled, at least your clothes will bear the brunt of the grass stains. Although I'm not opposed to a little lying around with a particular someone.' She gave him a smoky look that held no room for misinterpretation.

'The grass just might come, Boots, but this is tag football, not tackle football. You'll be fine.' He ran his hand along her shoulders and under the thick fall of her hair.

She twisted her mouth with a dubious look. 'We'll see.'

Chase figured he'd be winning this contest, but he'd make damn sure she didn't get hurt.

'What kind of party do we have going on here?' Fredi said as she made herself at home inside the barn, claiming a chair next to the wide-open door by dropping her purse on it. The other women followed suit. 'This spot will let the breeze blow in. Now that's a bar!' She pointed to the typical Harper spread and took Celia's hand, hauling her off to inspect the situation.

Planks were set up on bales of straw that you could almost hear groan under the weight of all the bottles, tubs of ice, glasses, mix, fruit and beer, plus a fan that blew across the table to keep the flies off and the air moving. Another table was loaded down with all kinds of snacks and finger food, with another oscillating fan standing guard. This is what he loved about the country. The transformation of a barn to a party location.

'Wow, this is something,' Bonni said. 'Do they still keep livestock in here?'

'The Harpers started putting their hay up in another building. Livestock is also housed elsewhere. They wanted to expand their business so they revamped this to host events.'

'I think it's wonderful,' Ava said.

He watched Celia skip around then stop in front of a big tin tub full of ice and beer, glistening with condensation. She took a quick selfie then yanked out four bottles and held them up. 'Y'all want some?'

'Grab five,' Bonni called to her and held up a hand with her fingers splayed. 'Don't forget Chase.'

'Oh, no, thanks, Celia. I'm dry tonight. DD. Water would be fine.' He thumbed his chest.

Celia spun around and added a bottle of water to her haul before bringing everything back to their little group. Chase twisted off the caps for women and tossed them in the old battered milk can posing as a garbage can.

'If I didn't know that you were a California girl, Celia, I'd say you fit right well with the country life.' He took a swig from his bottle.

Celia gave him a big grin, taking his words as the compliment they were intended to be. He draped his arm over Ava's shoulder and liked that she leaned into him.

'Is this a normal thing, to have a party like this, well after dark?' Ava asked.

'You never know what might pop up around here. But because CMA Fest is going on right now, everybody's trying to hitch their wagon to the fun.'

It wasn't long before Bonni, Celia, and Fredi all went off to the dance floor while Ava stayed with Chase.

'Oh man, don't tell me there's going to be more line dances,' she moaned, and he chuckled.

'Don't worry, you don't have to do any line dances, but if you do, I don't mind showing you the steps,' he reassured her.

'I'll bear that in mind, twinkle toes.' She gave him a saucy smile.

A slow tune started up and Chase took her beer, putting it on the window ledge along with his water, and led her to the dance floor.

'I think a little slow dancing is what we need right now. It's been a bit of a wild day.' He lifted her hand and spun her gently. She twirled like an expert and took a few fancy steps that made him raise his eyebrows before stepping into his arms.

'I like your way of thinking, superstar.'

Her fit next to him was perfection. A sharp pain in his chest reminded him that she'd be leaving. Unless he did something about it.

Being in Chase's arms again was heaven on earth. Ava saw the looks they were getting from everybody, probably because he was a very eligible bachelor. *Off the market now. Sorry, ladies, he's mine.* Possessiveness flashed through her mind and she smiled, resting her cheek next to his shoulder and gazing out at the other dancers.

How did all his friends and the people here perceive them? As an item? A couple? Was she an interloper? She had no idea, but for these precious few days she'd be anything he wanted her to be. A sigh of contentment slipped from her and she turned her head, liking how his cowboy hat shadowed them. She no longer wanted to see the curious looks of those around them and tucked her nose into his neck. Ava inhaled his familiar and delicious scent.

Never had she felt safer, never had she felt more treasured and never have had she felt – dare she say it – *love*. She had to think of something or some way to broach the subject with him. And just see . . . see what he thought and where his heart was taking him. If it was taking him anywhere.

His knee pressed between hers, which made all thought drown under her rising desire. His hand was low on her hip and kept her tight next to his groin. She was pretty sure it was to partially to conceal his building erection, which amplified her own arousal, in addition to keeping her close. With one of her arms slung around his neck, she took his other hand. His large fingers curled around hers. He held their hands next to his chest and, while that was not the proper stance for this dance, it filled her heart with joy.

Dancing with Chase was the perfect thing to do. He was a great partner and they swayed against each other, sensuous, connected, breathing in time, their bodies pressed together so intimately. They were lost in the moment until the music stopped and a voice came over the loudspeaker. Everyone stopped and faced the stage.

'It's that time, ladies and gents. It's the party version of *Friday Night Lights*.

Ava looked up at Chase. 'You know, if I win this, I win the bet.'

He grinned down at her. 'Boots, you're talking to a former quarterback. You ain't got a chance in hell.'

Chapter 28

'Two baskets up here with the two colors in play. Come pick your pleasure.' The announcer pointed to the baskets in front of him.

'Clearly, we'll be on opposite teams,' Chase told her.

'Clearly. After we pick colors, you'll get me the change of clothes?'

'Absolutely,' Chase replied. 'I don't want any accusations later on that I had an unfair advantage.'

He crowded into her so he could steal a quick kiss. When he raised his head she pointed her finger at him. 'No more of that, mister. You're the enemy now!' Chase smiled down at her and she gently elbowed him away as she went to join her friends by the other basket.

'So competition number two is football, huh? The man has obviously deduced that you have no experience with organized sports,' Fredi said.

'I know,' Ava moaned. 'Why couldn't it have been beer pong or something? Anyway, you need to help me.'

They nodded.

'Don't worry,' Fredi said. 'We got your back.'

'So what is the third competition in this Nashville bet?' Bonni inquired.

Ava shrugged and the line shuffled forward. 'I have no idea. He makes it up as he goes along.'

They reached into the basket and grabbed their flags.

'This is too funny. Anyway, at least we're on the same team. Just don't trip,' Fredi told her.

'Did you just jinx me? Aww, Fredi, why'd you have to go and say that.' Ava let out a huff, 'I'll do my best. But I don't watch football, I know nothing about it.'

'It's not like this is going to be rules enforced by linesman and everything. Basically, you just want to get the football from your end into their end without losing your flag,' Bonni informed her.

'I'm going to fail this one. I know it. Especially since you jinxed me, Fredi.'

'Not if we can help it.' The girls stood around Ava and walked out of the barn to the playing field. On his way to get Ava the change of clothes, Chase had stopped by a bunch of other players on his team and Fredi did the two-finger I'm-looking-at-you from her eyes to his.

He threw back his head and roared with laughter, then said something to his friends. They all turned to look at the women. Nodding their heads, they crossed their arms.

'Ah, geez, this is not looking good,' Ava said.

Game on.

Chapter 29

They lost. Very badly. Chase had arranged for a limo to take her friends back to the hotel while he'd drawn her a bath at his place. Tag football, her patootie. She'd fallen more times than she'd run.

'I think this guy could be a keeper.' Celia nudged Ava when they settled in the back of the limo on Friday morning on their way for another day of tourist fun. Chase wasn't joining them this time as he had to go back into the studio, but he followed Celia on Instagram to be a virtual participant in their activities.

'I must say, he does know how to impress. The other thing I'll say is he seems to do it out of the goodness of his heart. No expectations. No fanfare, just considerate. He's just an all-round nice guy,' Fredi said, and they all turned to look at her.

'Fredi, am I hearing you right? You're actually complimenting him, and it isn't the first time on this trip. Could it be your icy heart is starting to melt?' Bonni teased, but with a hint of seriousness in her tone.

Fredi shook her head and her curls swung. 'Oh no, don't

get me wrong. My feelings about happily ever afters haven't changed. But Chase isn't the usual dumbass I see every day.'

Ava was both surprised and charmed that Fredi seemed to have Chase's back. That made her heart happy. If her friends liked him, well, then . . .

'You're right,' Ava agreed.

Her friends stared at her, glanced at each other then back at Ava.

'What?' she asked, not sure what the strange expressions on their faces meant.

'So, what does that mean for you, then? It's obvious he has a thing for you and I know you know that.' Fredi took a sip from the flat white she'd got from the hotel before they left and kept a keen eye on Ava.

Ava shrugged. She knew there was something between her and Chase, and they did need to discuss it . . . soon. She sensed that Chase felt it, too. However, she was not eager to bring up the topic with Chase; they were having too good of a time for seriousness,

Her friends were all watching her expectantly, like she had something important to say. But she didn't, not yet anyway. She did know it had to be done eventually, and that time was fast creeping up, since they really only had another full day and night after today. Her heart started to race with the impending timeline. This trip seemed to be flying by and the idea of only seeing him probably one or two more times filled her with a heavy sadness.

'Ava, what's wrong?' Bonni rested her hand on Ava's shoulder.

She shook her head and sat back, trying to calm her nerves. This was so unlike her. Emotional, yes; overthinking, yes; but being nervous wasn't really part of her repertoire.

'I–I'm fine.' She did her best not draw in ragged breaths and took slow and steady draws of air. Was she giving herself a panic attack with the stress of the looming deadline? Ava wasn't used to this kind of unsettling emotion. She was a rock, solid and tough in the business world. Why was she feeling uneasy now, to the point she almost felt like she could puke?

'You don't look fine. Put your head between your knees,' Celia instructed.

'Okay, okay. It's all good.' Ava sighed and relaxed back. 'It's never going to work between us anyway, so I—'

'What do you mean "never going to work"?' Celia asked.

'Us. Chase, me. If you don't mind, I don't really wanna talk about it now. Let's just have fun today.'

'Yes, let's have fun today. I'm especially looking forward to lunch on the riverboat.' Bonni was always good at deflecting a conversation away from something uncomfortable. Ava cast her a thankful smile. Bonni squeezed her hand in response.

'Yeah, it should be fun. We're also absolutely going to the Country Music Hall of Fame, the Bluebird Cafe, and oh geez, I had another spot on my list, but I can't remember,' Celia said.

'Once we see the main things, I'm pretty sure Dave might know of some other fun places.' Ava leaned forward and called up to the driver. 'Dave, think about some other places you can show us.'

'You got it,' the man said. They'd had the same driver each time Chase arranged for a car and Ava was incapable of not being friendly enough to learn the guy's name.

The first stop was the Country Music Hall of Fame. They hoped to beat the crowds and then head out to the river boat for lunch. The women piled out of the limo and stood in front of the doorway to country-music history.

'I can't believe I'm here.' Celia gazed at the front doors in awe.

'You know what? Me either,' Fredi said, and she stepped forward to be the first one through the door. Bonni hung back with Ava.

'Are you okay, honey?' she asked.

'Sure, why?' Her friends knew her well.

'I know you, Ava. I know how you open your heart and, remember, you told me about that guy in Texas. I know what's going on in your head.'

Ava sighed. She couldn't hide anything from Bonni. 'I don't know what to think.'

'How about you don't think right now? How about you just put it all away for a little while and have some fun? Give your brain a break and just let everything play out naturally. When it's time to act, you'll know,' Bonni said earnestly, and tapped her chest over her heart. 'Trust me, you'll know.'

She gave her a hug then they linked arms and followed Fredi and Celia inside.

'Oh look, there's a Little Big Town exhibit!' Ava said excitedly.

'I almost feel like I'm in hallowed halls,' Bonni said.

They walked through the rotunda, taking the time to look at all the exhibits in the displays. They purchased tickets for the museum proper.

'I wonder if they have new-performer information here,' Ava pondered.

'Do you mean, as in, there could be something here talking about a man named Chase Hudson? One of the CMA new artists of the year?' Celia asked her.

'Something like that.' Ava looked around.

'Why do you like Little Big Town so much?' Fredi asked Ava.

'For one thing, I love Kimberly Schlapman's hair. If I had curly hair, I'd totally get my hairdresser to cut it like that. But I think their song "Girl Crush"' is heart-wrenching, and "Better Man" – geez, all their songs are soooo good. They resonate with me. "Girl Crush" is just so sad.' Ava turned away, feeling the emotion rush into her, and tried not to let it take over, thinking about that song, but man, it was a hard thing to do. 'Could you imagine? Knowing your man was loving someone else and you couldn't cope with it, wanting to be all the things that the new woman was? It chokes me up every time.'

'Yeah, I suppose.' Fredi wandered around and stopped before a fashion display. 'I think I'm going to need more time than what we allotted. Just look at these clothes.' She reached out and touched the glass.

Bonni and Celia chattered away as they continued on their tour.

'Look at all these vintage instruments.' Celia was leaning down to read the inscriptions and taking photos.

'You can almost feel the history, can't you?' Bonni said. She put her hand beside Celia's. 'I often wonder, if I touch something, will it suck me back to the time or give me visions.'

Fredi hooted. 'Seriously? This isn't *Outlander*. Come on, guys.'

They were silent for a few minutes, each lost in their own thoughts. But all Ava could think of was her and Chase. About their future, what was to come tomorrow, and beyond that. Standing amidst all this history made her certain that there was no time like the present. It was time to talk.

They wandered through the exhibits for a while, each finding delight in something they saw, and finally Celia wrangled everyone. 'You know what? I think we'll have to come back here later, because we have to get going to catch that paddle boat for lunch.'

'Oh yes!' Ava didn't even bother to hide her excitement. 'It's lunchtime, and I'm hungry.'

'When are you not hungry?' Fredi asked her. 'We need to feed the beast, girls. And don't sneak anything off her plate or we could have a repeat of the meatball caper.'

'I'm not that bad,' Ava said, but that was a lie. She would also admit she was protective of her plate. 'That reminds me, what is the chicken-fry place in Nashville?'

'I don't know.' Celia shrugged her shoulders.

'Reese Witherspoon did a video a few months ago and she recommended it for hot chicken. I'll have to try and find that video when we get back to the hotel.' Ava led the charge out of the museum.

'No need,' Celia told her as she pulled out her phone. 'I'll find it and—'

Ava watched her and saw Fredi roll her eyes, then she commented, 'Celia, if yesterday at the distillery tour was any indication, you really need to curb your phone addiction.'

Celia didn't even lift her face from the screen but Ava saw the smirk on her face. 'Nope. And, come to think of it, I haven't done a group shot yet. Gather round, girls, it's selfie time.'

They pressed close together, with Bonni and Ava at the back and shorter Celia and Fredi in front. Celia held her phone out and they all leaned in.

'Everyone say cheeeeeese,' Celia instructed, and she captured it.

'This is definitely going on IG,' she said, sticking her nose back in her phone.

'Why I am not surprised?' Fredi muttered.

'And I'm tagging you all. I'll even tag Chase.' And before Ava could tell her not to Celia hit send and did jazz hands to prove it.

'Done and done.' Celia laughed, obviously quite pleased with herself.

'Now let's hightail it back out to the car. We have lunch waiting,' Ava said, and led the way. She hadn't heard from Chase yet this morning but she knew he was in the studio. She was going to have fun with her girls but she also had the sweet heat of desire, knowing she'd be seeing him later.

Chapter 30

After their lunch on the paddleboat, the girls took a drive by the Bluebird Café. They were hoping to get in, but it was closed for a special event. Some kind of birthday party was going on and no one uninvited was allowed in.

All four of them stood at the window, their hands shielding their eyes, and peered inside.

'I don't see anybody famous, do you?' Celia asked.

'It's hard to see anything,' Bonni answered her.

'This reminds me of that scene in the show *Nashville* when they had a big party for Deacon. You know, his birthday-party bash,' Celia told them.

'Imagine, wouldn't it be cool if we happen to stumble across some big-name birthday or anniversary, or even a filming of some show?' Ava said excitedly as she moved down to look in another spot at the window.

It didn't appear promising.

'Okay, guys, come on. This is really weird, staring inside like this. Let's get going. I don't want to be bailing us all out of jail or something for loitering or being a peeping Tom,' Fredi said, grabbing Ava's arm. 'Let's go.'

'Well, what are we going to do now?' Ava asked. She turned to look at Celia. 'Got a Plan B?'

'No, my next thing isn't until tomorrow. I kind of thought this day would draw out a little longer, what with visiting the Bluebird and all.'

Once they were back in the limo, they asked Dave if he'd come up with any ideas.

'There is one way to see Music Row, if you're up for some exercise. I can call ahead and see if there's room, plus, it's BYOB.'

Bonni said, 'I'm always up for exercise, you guys know that.' She raised her hand, fisted it and flexed her bicep.

Typically, Fredi groaned. Ava didn't say much, waiting to see what the rest decided. Her thoughts were mainly about seeing Chase later.

'Okay, what do you have?' Celia leaned back in the seat and pulled out her phone from her pocket.

'There's a pedal bar.'

'What's that?' Fredi asked, skepticism edging her voice.

'It's a pedal-bike bar that goes through the downtown streets. Basically, you drink and ride and, since you guys aren't driving, you can stop and bar hop as well if you want.'

'That sounds pretty cool,' Bonni said.

'Oh, look! It'll be a blast.' Celia held up her phone and they all leaned in to look at the image on the screen.

'I've heard, if you have too much to drink, they stick you on the back of the bike and put a helmet on you in case you fall out,' Dave told them.

'Oh, my God, that would be hilarious,' Celia said, and gave her friends an inquisitive look. 'We should go.'

'We are not repeating your drama from Fat Tuesdays in Vegas,' Fredi said sternly to Bonni, wagging her finger.

Bonni just laughed and shrugged her shoulders.

'We should make a bet on who'll end up with the helmet.' Celia was all over it.

'We're not in Vegas, we're in Nashville, and there's more talk of making bets here than there was there,' Ava said. 'I like the idea, but we don't need another bet to worry about, especially when it comes to getting drunk and wearing freaking helmets on the back of pedal bikes.' Ava shook her head. 'Nope. I won't get drunk where there's pedaling involved but I'm in for a fun time.'

'Are you in, then?' Celia asked Fredi and Bonni.

'I am,' Bonni answered.

'I guess majority rules,' Fredi grumbled.

'To the pedal bar, Dave,' Ava said.

Ava stared at the contraption; she wasn't quite sure what to think.

'That looks like it's a whole lotta work for a few drinks.' She put her hands on her hips and looked at her friends to see what they thought about it.

'Looks like loads of fun to me,' Bonni said, standing behind one of the seats, ready to jump on.

'I'm with you, Ava: not sure the drinks are worth all the effort.' Fredi had crossed her arms and tossed her head, giving everybody a narrow-eyed look. Her blue eyes suddenly looked stormy.

'Oh, come on, it'll be fun. Hop on.' Celia was already climbing up into the seat she had chosen, which was right near the front.

Bonni was next, then Fredi and Ava looked at each other, let out a joint sigh and took the next two seats.

Dave handed over a cooler of the beer they'd purchased along the way. The bartender took it and stashed it.

'I may as well start this drama off with a drink.' Celia slapped her hand on the bar surface. 'Pronto Tonto, please.'

The female bartender opened a beer and handed a bottle to Celia. 'Make sure you keep my friend liquored up as well.'

The woman looked like she loved her job. She was conversing with the other guests, laughing at her male counterpart, who was telling jokes. Ava was feeling a whole lot better, but then she always did with her friends. She knew they would have the time of their lives on this monster booze bike.

'This must be a super-fun job?' Ava leaned forward to get in the shade a little bit. It was going to be hot on this thing.

Fredi twirled her beer bottle between her fingers. Bonni and Celia were already guzzling down beer.

'It is. I like meeting people and having fun,' the woman told her. 'By the way, my name is Carolina, so don't be shy on calling me when you want something.'

'Perfect, thanks.'

Ava pulled her sunglasses out of her over-the-shoulder bag. She put them on and pulled her hair up into a topknot. It was going to be warm, pedaling around.

'Everybody settled? Everybody got a drink? Because we're about to get cracking,' Stephen, the driver upfront, shouted. 'Let's crank the tunes.'

'Come on, people! Let's let them know we're ready to pedal for the drinks!' Carolina called out, and blew a horn.

'And here we go.' Music came on the speakers, everybody started their pedaling and off they went. There were a couple other bikes coming up behind them.

Ava turned to look at Fredi, who was sipping at her beer. 'You're not pedaling, Fredi.'

'My little legs won't make the least bit of difference.' She cast Ava a challenging stare then blew her a kiss.

'You can at least make it look like you are, like, put your feet on the pedals. Everyone else is doing their part.' Ava pointed to the group of people across from them.

'Yes, that's a good idea.' Fredi looked down and got her feet settled on the pedals, doing a great job at faking her participation.

This wasn't just a drinking bike ride, it was also a great way to see downtown. You could pub crawl, too, if you wanted, but Ava hoped her friends would be happy with riding the bike around and not getting off.

'So what do you think of this, guys?' Celia, up front, leaned forward to look back at them.

Fredi raised her second bottle. 'Oh, this is just dandy. I've always wanted to ride a bike bar.' Then she downed a good portion of the bottle.

They laughed at Fredi and her antics. Even though she complained, she had herself a good time.

Celia had a huge grin on her face and Ava knew full well she was thrilled they were enjoying this bicycle trip. Even Fredi was still smiling and having fun. Which was what their girls' weekends were all about.

'At the rate you're going, though, Fredi, you're going to be the one sitting on the back with a helmet on.' Ava chuckled and sipped on her beer. No way was she going to get hammered. She had a date later.

Chapter 31

Chase placed his guitar on the stand and went into the control booth. Dozer was lounging on the couch with a shit-ass grin on his face.

'What are you smiling about?' Chase asked him, grabbing a soda out of the fridge, and a couple of sandwiches that were in there. He was hungry and inspected them to make sure they were still edible. He was so hungry his stomach thought his throat had been cut.

'I guess you created an impression last night.' Dozer spread his arms out along the back of the sofa and tapped his fingers. 'Yep, when you do the talk, you sure do know how to do it right.'

'So, I take it I'm performing with Lance?' A thrill of excitement made Chase feel pretty damn happy. Ava would be excited and he knew Fredi would demand a meeting.

'You betcha. They want you to do two songs and are asking that one of them be your latest hit. And you can choose the other one.'

Chase thought about it for minute. And he was fine singing

'You Drive Me Crazy'. Figuring out another one was a dilemma. 'I'll think on the second one.'

'What about the one you were doing just now?' Dozer lifted his finger and pointed at the booth.

'No, not that one.' Chase wasn't ready for the Ava song to be made public yet. She had to hear it first.

'What's wrong with it?' Dozer was insistent, and Chase knew, unless he shut him down right now, he'd be as relentless as a dog with a bone.

'No. I'm not singing it.' He stared Dozer down.

Dozer stood up and faced Chase, tilting his head back to make eye contact. Chase crossed his arms. Dozer narrowed his eyes and puffed up like a peacock trying to look big, ready to argue.

'No,' was all Chase said. 'But, *if* I feel it's ready, then I'll do it. There's a lot of factors involved in this song and it's only been kept within this circle here.' Chase hitched his thumb behind him at the live room, where his band was probably watching the exchange with interest.

'You know I don't like it when you go against what I think is the right thing to do,' Dozer told him.

'I know, and you're usually right. But this time I'm making the call.' Chase was determined. The anger and protectiveness rushing through him made him realize how special the song was.

To show the conversation was over, Chase took a bite of sandwich and dropped into the big old leather chair that had probably been in the room since the early days and seen all the artists that have come and gone over the years.

'One thing I do want is backstage passes.' Chase finished off the bottle of water then start working on the second sandwich.

'Backstage passes, for CMA Fest? Are you out of your

mind?' Dozer rested on the stool in front of the engineering console.

Chase shook his head. 'Nope. I know you can do it. That's why you're my agent.' Chase gave him a look from under the brim of his cowboy hat and his voice carried a message that was clear as a bell.

'How many?' Dozer sighed.

Chase smiled behind the sandwich he'd just bit into. He didn't like being tough with Dozer, but sometimes he had to be. He held up four fingers.

'Four! That's asking a lot.' Dozer ran his hand through his hair.

Chase swallowed his bite before answering, 'I understand. One, for sure, and the others if you can do it.'

He laughed when he saw Dozer relax.

'One, I can guarantee.' He stood and grabbed a flash drive sitting on the mixing board. He held it up and waved it. 'These are good. You're really going to be at the top, Chase. And I'm here to work hard for you, you know that, right?'

'Of course I do.' Chase washed down another bite of his ham and cheese sandwich with a big gulp of soda.

'Right, I'm off. I'll be in touch later with details.' Dozer left and Chase finished off his food, eager to get back to his new song. But he had a thought and whipped out his phone.

He texted Dozer. *If that song is on the drive you took, you're not to share it. Fair warning.*

As he opened up his contacts, seeing Ava's name gave him a burst of happiness. He was eager to see her later. He typed her a message.

Chase: *How's your day going, Boots?*

He didn't really expect to hear back from her, knowing they were being tourists today. He'd wanted to take them to more places yesterday but they'd run out of time. Chase was looking forward to later and wanted to cram in as much time with Ava as he could before she left. Unless he could talk her into staying a little bit longer.

The weight of the limited time they had together hung heavy in his chest. She'd just dropped into his life, turned it completely upside-down, and then it would be time for her to leave. The sandwich he'd just eaten felt like a rock in his gut now and he knew nothing would ever be the same again.

Tonight was the night they needed to talk.

His phone chimed.

Ava: *Just finishing up this pedal-bike bar tour. I think I could use a massage and a hot tub.*

Chase: *I have an idea for our last test for you.*

Ava: *Oh Lord, do I want to know?*

Chase: *Want to know or keep it a surprise? Can you get away after your bike tour?*

Ava: *We're supposed to go to the Nissan Center tonight . . . later?*

Chase: *Can I encourage you to send your friends off without you?*

He watched his phone and waited for a reply. Maybe he was putting her in an unfair position. He was about to type back to her not to stress it when his phone pinged.

Ava: *I think so.*

Chapter 32

Once he'd picked her up after their pedal bar tour and they were on the road she decided it was time to tell him something. 'Chase . . .' She paused, trying to find the words.

'What's up?'

'I kind of have a confession to make.' She wondered how he'd take the news.

'Oh no, I'm not sure this is going to be good.' Chase glanced at her and his mouth tipped up on one side in a very sexy smile that could quite easily distract her from *the talk*. She was determined to soldier on through.

'Oh, no, it's nothing really bad.' Ava twisted in her seat to look at him. It was important to see the expression on his face.

'OK, out with it, then.'

She chewed her bottom lip, wanting to be honest with him but, while it was the right thing to do, she was suddenly hesitant. It wasn't fair to keep hiding it.

She drew in a steadying breath. 'Okay, well, you know how you think I'm a city girl?'

'Yep.'

'I'm not, actually.' She paused, holding her breath she watched him closely and waited for his response. Ava expected him to be upset with her for keeping this from him.

He burst out laughing, which was not what she expected at all. 'You just want to get yourself out of this bet.'

'I do not! I can hold my own.' She crossed her arms and stared him down, quietly relieved he wasn't mad but also determined to prove him wrong.

He continued to chuckle and softened his voice, 'I'm sure you can. But I'm pretty sure I'm gonna win this one, too.'

'You're awful cocky and, you know what? I don't think you will.' She gave him the sternest glare she could muster. 'Bring it on, superstar.'

'Oh, I plan to. Trust me.' He tossed her a confident look which made her even more dogged she would win this last bet.

Ava sat behind the steering wheel of the all-terrain vehicle Chase had said was hers and looked ahead at the muddy, wet, dirty, track running along a low area that was clearly a mire. This was not what she had expected. At. All. Mudding, of all things. She'd never heard of it before and, sitting in an all-terrain vehicle – something she'd never driven before – wearing a helmet, goggles and gloves, Ava knew deep in her bones this was definitely not up her alley.

Nope.

But she had to win. If she didn't, then it was over and Chase was the winner. She gritted her teeth and gripped her gloved hands on the steering wheel a little tighter.

'This is your last test,' Chase had told her when they arrived. She had no choice but to do this. They had each won and this was the tiebreaker. She had to win this. She just had to, so she could prove him otherwise.

She glanced over at Chase.

'Whoa there, Boots, you're scaring me with that fierce look on your face.' He laughed and adjusted his goggles. He also wore a helmet, just like she was, and a great big smile shone through his beard.

She shook her head and focused on the track ahead of her. The countdown started, a horn blew and then she was off. Not flying as easy as she thought it would be. It was damn hard keeping control. The vehicle skidded all over and if she put the brakes on, it slid; if she gave it gas, it would fishtail. She was having a hard time controlling it and grew frustrated trying to keep up with Chase. He was a demon and doing his best to run her off the track. He zoomed in front of her, cut her off and sent a spray of mud raining down in her path all over her.

'Chase!' She screamed at him then realized she should've kept her mouth shut. The mouthful of muck was not appetizing. She spat it out with very unladylike gusto and pressed her lips together.

Ava accelerated and pulled on the steering, trying to get herself back in contention. He was ahead of her and she had a sinking feeling she was going to lose this bet, too, unless she stepped up her game.

For someone who wasn't a sports fan, she was beginning to feel at a disadvantage. Sure, she'd won the fishing. Failed abysmally at the football. And now this. Maybe she should've just settled for a game of poker.

Her emotions rode high and she was shouting at this machine to pay attention to her commands and quit getting stuck. It thwarted her and continually got bogged down in the gooey muck. She gave it gas and the tires spun in the mud, sending an impressive rooster tail out behind her.

Ava looked over her shoulder and gave a maniacal laugh. She didn't have to be girly right now, she could be tough and no nonsense. The true country girl she had been born and raised. Somehow, she had to get this cart moving. Rock it. That's what she'd do, rock it back and forth. So, she did reverse and forward, giving it gas and then the brakes, repeatedly, until finally it popped free.

She leaned over the steering wheel, gritted her teeth and followed Chase. Now she was going too fast and couldn't keep it in a straight line, nearly veering back into the bog, trying to catch up. Her saving grace was that he stopped to look over his shoulder to see where she was. It gave her a few precious moments. His eyes widened in surprise and he frantically tried to get his cart going again. She let out another crazy laugh and a loud whoop.

'Go faster! Go faster!' she shouted at the cart, then she was on Chase's bumper, then up at his side, and finally ahead of his front bumper and out in the lead.

'I got you, Chase Hudson! I'm going to win this!' And she zoomed past him. She was nosing ahead when he roared up beside her.

They looked at each other and he yelled, 'You don't stand a chance against this cham-peen driver. Me!'

'Wanna bet?' She leaned over the steering wheel again and took off. But he was right there. She couldn't shake him, and she thought about cutting him off, like he'd done to her. But she didn't have the guts. Then she hit some kind of bump and her vehicle launched itself off the ground.

She was airborne and let out a wailing screech. Ava didn't

want to look down and closed her eyes. Her scream ripped through the air and, when the vehicle came down with a crunch, her head snapped forward. The vehicle did a couple of precarious bounces on two wheels before jolting down to all fours. Chase zipped across the finish line just as she was gaining control.

'This isn't fair! You've done it before. I never have.' Ava crossed the finish line and slid to a stop. She pulled her helmet and goggles off and rubbed the back of her neck. 'I think I've got whiplash.'

Chase was waiting for her. He helped her out, rubbed the back of her neck and wiped her face and hands with a hot cloth. It felt like absolute heaven, and then he gave her a big kiss.

'You did good, Boots.' She wrapped her arms around him. 'But I won,' he murmured against her lips.

She looked up at him and gave him a playful swat on the arm, shaking her head. 'You may have won our bet but this loser demands a shower and a whole lot of TLC for this aching body.'

'I really do have to wonder what it is with you and showers.' He pulled her into a hug and rubbed her back and neck with his strong fingers.

'Mmm, then I suggest we find out what I find so appealing,' she purred into his neck then pressed her lips next to where his vein throbbed. The mud was beginning to harden on them both and she longed for a hot shower with her sexy superstar.

'Are your friends okay with you coming back to my house?' He took her hand and they walked back toward his truck.

She answered, 'Yes, they decided to go out and get something to eat before going to the concert tonight, and I told them I was going to be with you.' She placed a towel over the seat of his truck so she wouldn't get it dirty and climbed in. 'So, you've won. Just how are you going to exact your pound of flesh?'

Ava fully expected him to want some kind of sexual thing. Which, of course, she wasn't opposed to.

He looked at her, and something in his expression made her pause.

'I really want to keep seeing you after this weekend.' His words filled the cab of his truck and Ava fell silent, digesting what he'd just said.

'What do you mean?' She couldn't stop the wavering in her voice and cleared her throat.

'Well, keep seeing each other and see where it goes.' His words were clear and honest.

Ava looked out the window to try and figure out the right thing to say. 'I don't know. Long-distance relationships don't work.'

'That's not true. Your friends have made it work.' Ava was surprised he knew about Bonni and Celia.

'How do you know?'

'They told me yesterday when I showed them around the house.' He looked both ways before turning the truck back on the highway

'Things don't always happen perfectly for everybody. Just because they made it work out doesn't mean I can.' Ava watched the fields and trees whip by.

'We can make anything work if we want it bad enough.' His voice softened.

'That's them. Everybody's different.' She wasn't ready to tell him she'd been through this before. Ava stopped herself from looking at Chase. She was getting upset. She didn't want this to ruin their day; she wanted to enjoy it. She knew they had to talk about it, but not right now. 'Listen, maybe I should go back to the hotel. I don't have a change of clothes and I'm a mess.'

'If that's what you want.'

She heard the disappointment in his tone and wanted to scream, *No, it's not what I want.* But Ava felt at an utter loss right now. 'I think it's for the best.'

'Okay, I can tell this upsets you. But I want you to promise we'll talk about this later.' He certainly was an understanding man, and it made her even more upset.

Ava looked at him and gave a quick nod. 'Okay, that's fine.'

'Good. I'll pick you up around seven thirty.'

Ava felt like her heart was breaking, thinking about the impending conversation and its likely eventual outcome.

Ava was glad the girls had already left for their dinner and the hotel room was empty. She was in no mood to talk and her friends would want to know why she was here and not with Chase. The looming conversation with him later was upsetting enough.

She went into the bathroom, dropped the muddy clothes into the shower and stepped in. She turned the water to almost scalding hot. Steam filled the room and she rested her hands on the tiled wall, letting the water rain over her.

After she had scrubbed every inch of her body and her hair, she felt much better and wrung out her clothes, hanging them over the shower doors. She kept running the conversation through her head. With every new thing she learned about Chase, it made her want him more and more. Getting ready, she gave herself some time to sort out her thoughts before their talk.

She did it slowly, making sure her hair and makeup were casually perfect. Ava still had half an hour before he was coming to pick her up and she felt like a beer. She found a note scribbled on a piece of paper left on the bar.

Went out for some food then over to the NC. Have a great

night if you decide to indulge in Loverboy. If not, you know where we are. Xoxox B, C, F

She could relax and think for a while. Ava grabbed a beer from the fridge behind the bar and walked out on the balcony. She watched all the people below. There were families, kids running around, couples and lovers – it was everything she wanted and everything she feared she'd never have. Except . . . maybe . . . with Chase.

Ava sighed and leaned back in the chair, nursing her beer. She began to daydream and saw her and Chase as a couple, as lovers, as parents . . . with a family. But, how could they see a way around their distance and his fame?

Her cell phone chimed and she grabbed it.

Chase: *Hey, my beautiful Boots. Got the mud all off ya? I really would have liked to wash you down myself.* Ava's heart swelled with emotion for him. *I'm running a little bit late, but I'll be there shortly. Will text when I'm pulling in.*

Ava: *k, cu soon.*

Chapter 33

An hour later Ava was sitting under the stars on Chase's to-die-for patio. He hadn't broached the touchy subject of what would happen after this weekend and she assumed he was waiting for her to bring it up. It was cooler than last night and she cuddled on a comfy lounge chair. This was the first time she'd been out here, and she instantly fell in love with it. The pool was gorgeous, made with colorful tiles and a slate walkway around it. Tucked at the far end was a hot tub under a beautiful arbor draped with flowering vines.

It was wonderfully romantic and had the cozy feel of a magical grotto. Ava was bewitched and decided this was her favorite place, aside from the bedroom, of course. Just like the landscaping at the front of the house, back here the ambient lighting in the lush gardens ringing the pool gave a fairy-tale sparkle to the magnificent flowerbeds and waterfalls. She'd never seen anything like it.

'This is so beautiful, Chase. Did you design all this as well?' she asked, relaxing on the deep cushions.

'I'm glad you like it.' Chase settled in a chair beside her, his long legs stretched out in front of him.

'Mmm, yes, I do. It's so peaceful and . . . just lovely.' She was a little tense and tried to calm herself. But it was time and she decided she may as well just dive in.

'What is this?' she pointed between her and him.

'What do you mean, "what is this?"' he asked her, his beer bottle paused at his mouth.

She would never tire of looking at him; she was absolutely blown away by how handsome and breathtaking he was. How he made her feel alive. How he was a one-of-a-kind guy – she knew they had broken the mold after they made him.

'Us. We're two different people from two different worlds. We haven't even really talked about us and life, and what's next. Where we'll go from here.' She watched to see if he would display any kind of expression.

He was silent, and it frightened her. He'd alluded to it earlier, but what if there was more to what he wanted to discuss than she'd originally thought? What if he hadn't thought past the *now*? What if he was content with how things were and there was nowhere to go from here? Oh, she was just so damn confused.

He reached forward and put his bottle on the table between them then took her hand. 'Ava, I've been thinking the same. I've had the best time with you and I'll be upfront and honest.' He pulled his chair around and faced her. Her heart skipped a beat, waiting for the words she didn't want to hear again. 'I've been wanting to talk about this and I was kind of hoping it would be here, after we'd had a shower . . . together.' He gave her a teasing wink.

She felt a blush rush up her cheeks. 'I needed time to think. I know more about you than you do me. Like, what I do for a living, where I live, my interests. Why have you never asked? Didn't you really *want* to know?'

'Good Lord, no! I mean, yes, I wanted to know, not no I didn't. But, you're absolutely right. I haven't asked you and I was wrong not to. It just seemed we were having such a great time and those sorts of details were just lost in the background. So I'm asking now. Tell me more about you, Boots.'

One moment she had wanted him ask her and now, a second later, she was tongue-tied. She didn't know what to say. It surprised her.

'I live in the middle of prairie belt, I'm under a contractual obligation to the company I work for. Been with them for a few years, working my way up. I'm a numbers girl—'

He raised his eyebrows. 'Numbers?'

'Yup, numbers are my jam.' She gave him a quizzical look. 'What, you don't think I could be good with numbers?'

'I never said that. I just didn't expect it. Ah, you're a brainiac then?' The teasing look he cast her way calmed her down, easing the tension of the moment.

She laughed. 'That's exactly what my friends call me.' She remembered their jokey bantering back in Vegas when Bonni had won the jackpot and they insisted she go to make sure the money went through fine for Bonni.

'So, more about you, then. You admitted you're a country girl. What made you go to the city?'

She searched his eyes in the low lighting and saw his genuine interest in knowing her answer.

She shrugged. 'I needed to find myself. Small town, nothing going on, and I longed for the bright city lights. I danced when I was young and all through my teenage years, working toward my dream of Juilliard. But I had an injury and that was that.'

Ava shrugged. 'So I went to college and began a career I thought I wanted.'

'"Thought"?'

She nodded. 'Yeah, I wanted to climb the corporate ladder and break the glass ceiling but the higher I got, the more difficult it became.'

'Why?'

She let out a long, frustrated sigh and looked him dead in the eye. 'Because the more I achieved, the less I realized I wanted it. Backwards, huh?'

'Not really. Sometimes we don't know what we want until we don't have it anymore.'

She met his gaze. Those words spoke volumes to her. It made her look back on how hard she'd fought and clawed her way to get where she was now, and these last few days had made her long for a simpler, less complicated way of life. A life with someone like Chase.

'But I never stopped. I was driven.' She swung her legs over the edge of the lounge chair and slipped her knees between his thighs.

'Your parents?'

She shook her head. 'They decided to travel and see the world before they became "old and decrepit" – their words, not mine. Sold their home and headed off into the wild blue yonder, as they said. It was hard to say goodbye to them at the airport, and I feel terribly alone sometimes.'

'Good for them! You don't have to feel alone, though. You have your friends.' He reached out and cupped her cheek.

She waited for him to say she had him, but he didn't.

'Sooo – us? You were asking what we are?' His voice was low and intimate . . . it sent shivers along her spine.

'Yes. Us. What are we? Just a weekend fling, or something more?' She quietly held her breath.

'I know I want more. I mentioned this earlier and you didn't seem to want to talk about it, so—'

'I'm sorry, it's just that . . . I've been through this before.' Her voice was soft and he leaned in to her.

He looked at her from under his eyebrows and she couldn't pull her gaze away from him. Ava waited for his next words.

'How have you been through this before?' he asked, and he didn't give any of his thoughts away; the expression on his face didn't change at all.

'Years ago.' She wasn't entirely sure how much to share. 'I was away, at a conference, and met someone. We hit it off, but he lived in London and I was here.' She let out a deep sigh and told him the story, ending with, 'I vowed never to put myself through it again . . . and here I am.'

Chase reached over and took her hand, curling his fingers around hers. 'But that's a different situation and not me. You're painting me with the same brush and that's not fair.'

Ava let out a shaky breath and looked at him. 'How can it work? It's hard to see how it can.'

'Why not? Many people make a long-distance relationship work.'

Ava shook her head vigorously.

'Your friends—'

'Just because it worked for them doesn't mean it will work for me – us. Not to mention, I'd have to break my contract, which would carry significant financial penalties, I signed a non-disclosure agreement, *and* the loss of privacy. I've seen what you go through when we're out. I'm not sure I could deal with all the trappings of fame.'

Chase let out a deep sigh and sat back in his chair, letting her fingers fall from his. Ava's heart shattered a little bit more. She had known this was how it was going to be and was about to suggest she go back to her hotel.

'Okay, then, we have this weekend, right? Let's put all that away. No more talk about the future, let's just enjoy our time now. Confine what we have to this weekend.' She heard the disappointment in his tone, but Ava was relieved.

'I would like that.' She tried not to feel guilty.

They looked at each other for a long moment, the silence of the night surrounding them.

'Then let's make the most of it.' He stood and held his hand out to her. 'I'm starved. Shall we cook?'

Ava laughed, and relief flooded through her. 'Yes, I'm hungry, too.'

He pulled her up and wrapped her in a hug. It felt so damn good to be in his arms and the feelings he roused in her pushed her worry aside. They had more time together, and she would enjoy it. Enjoy him and take the memory of them home with her.

She reached for her glass of beer and let him lead her over to an outdoor kitchen she was ashamed to admit she hadn't noticed before.

'My goodness, what a set-up. I think Chef Ramsay would be envious of this.'

Chase's deep laughter warmed her from the inside out and she began to feel a little better. 'I'm pretty sure his kitchens are way more impressive than this one. What do you say I fire us up a couple of steaks?'

'You cook on an open fire and on a grill! You are full of surprises.' Ava let her gaze linger on him. She leaned on the counter and watched him move around the kitchen and prep the grill.

'Of course I cook anywhere. I've been on my own for quite

some time. If I didn't cook, I'd be long dead.' He pulled out a tray that had obviously been put in the refrigerator earlier. 'Like rib steaks?'

Her mood was lifting and Ava began to feel the way she had before their conversation had gotten all serious.

'I'm good with whatever you're cooking. Don't go to any trouble, though.'

'No trouble at all. I planned on grilling for you.' Chase placed the tray on the counter and gave her a wink. Ava sighed, so glad that they were getting past the heaviness. She didn't want their time to be full of tension she wanted the carefree fun they'd had.

'Do you always have food out here? Is that normal?' Ava took a deep drink of her beer and put the glass down on the mosaic countertop. She slid on to a stool.

'I asked my housekeeper to bring the food out, since I thought we might eat outside. I much prefer being outside than inside anyway.' He seasoned the steaks.

It was weird hearing him say he had a housekeeper or staff, even though she knew he did, but it seemed so unreal, since she hadn't seen anyone when she'd been here.

She raised the glass and said, 'This is good beer.'

'It is. It's a local brewery run by a friend of mine.' He wiped his hand on the tea towel tossed over his shoulder. 'He's starting to make a name for himself. I do what I can to help him out.'

'Shop local. I support it.' She liked his loyalty. 'My friends and I have discovered that Nashville has quite an active craft-brewery scene.' She took a couple big gulps of the beer then selected a few potato chips out of the bowl he'd pushed toward her. 'Mmm, chips and beer.' She popped a chip into her mouth and her tongue nearly caught fire. 'Oh my God!' Ava grabbed her beer and guzzled, trying to quell the heat on her tongue. 'What is that spice?'

Chase laughed. 'Don't like spice?'

'I do, but that's crazy.' She waved her hand in front of her mouth then drank some more. Slowly, the heat began to fade, leaving a rather nice taste in her mouth. 'Man-o-man.'

'Here, have some more beer.' He filled her glass. 'There are a lot of micro-breweries in Nashville and area. Caesar salad okay with you?' He opened the fridge and held up big head of romaine.

'Yes, Caesar would great. I must say, you're impressing the hell out of me right now.' He was obviously very handy in the kitchen. What wasn't sexy about a man who could cook? 'Is there anything I can do?'

'If you'd like, how about you melt down some butter and smash a few garlic cloves to simmer?'

Ava got up and carried her beer around to the other side of the counter. Since he was busy with the salad, she looked around for what she needed. Soon the aroma of sizzling butter and garlic rose on the air and Ava sliced a loaf of Italian bread.

'Can't beat home-made garlic bread,' he commented when Ava turned and shook the pan to keep the garlic from sticking. 'You seem to know your way around a kitchen as well.' Chase placed the steaks on the platter and showed them to her.

'Oh, look, you've put them in the shape of a heart!' He caught her gaze and she drew in a soft breath. Had he done it just for her? She liked to think he had. Boy, he was really working the charm.

Chase put the platter down and snaked his arm out around her waist and drew her in. She didn't even have time to think before his mouth covered hers. She melted in his arms. Oh, she was in so much trouble. She knew her heart was going to be broken. But right now, with his mouth slanting on hers, his hands holding her tight and her fingers pushing into his hair, she had no will to refuse him.

Her body reacted to him, as it did whenever they were close. Her breasts pressed his chest and her nipples hardened into aching points. All she could think of was how he'd suckled on them before and how badly she wanted him to do it now. Heat and desire boiled low in her belly and that sweet ache between her thighs – for him – grew to a fever pitch.

He was romancing the hell out of her, wanting to make her forget their conversation . . . and it was working. Ava closed her eyes and lost herself in him. Behind her eyelids she saw all the things she dreamed about: the diamond engagement ring, lace, satin and pearls, babies, and the shadowy face of the man always lurking on the edge of her visions, never allowing himself to be seen, suddenly materialized. And it was Chase.

Stop it, Ava!

He lifted from her and turned back to the counter. Ava didn't like the empty feeling that lingered. He was quickly becoming so much a part of her it was almost frightening. His deep voice snapped her from her wedding-bells daydream.

'I think steaks should be marketed this way around Valentine's Day.' Chase stared into her eyes

'W–what? Steaks . . . oh.' She was befuddled, then remembered the heart shape he'd made with the steaks and what had started her romantic daydream in which he played the starring role.

He covered the meat with wrap and place them beside the grill, which was warming up. 'I like to use charcoal – better flavor – and it won't be too much longer until the coals are ready.'

'I can wait. There's a bowl of chips here, and they are my weakness.' To prove her point, she reached for one, dragged it through the dip and popped it in her mouth. She was doing her best to regroup after that kiss.

'Now there's a girl after my own heart. No shame in eating

chips and dip and drinking beer.' He took a big chip and scooped out an impressive amount of dip.

She laughed and let the happy feeling wash over her, doing her best to let go of the tension from earlier. He was incredibly easy to be around and she was relieved they were falling back into their easy-going ways. She checked the simmering garlic and turned the heat down under the pan as he checked the grill. That done, he pulled another growler out of the fridge and topped up their glasses.

'Why don't we go and sit by the fire for a bit?' he suggested.

'Fire?' Ava turned around and saw a fire pit she'd noticed earlier, now glowing with flames licking up through the rocks.

The fire pit seemed carved out of stone. It was close to the edge, overlooking a small hill that fell away to a cedar rail fence separating the forest on the other side from creeping across the wooden boundary. The pool was on the other side of them and shone a lovely aqua from the submerged lighting.

'I'm just stunned how beautiful all this is. My eyes see it but my words can't describe it. It's simply magical.' She followed him to the grouping of chairs around the stone fire pit. 'When did you get the fire going?'

'It's gas.' He almost looked guilty when he said that. 'On-and-off switch back in the bar, and a remote here on the table. I much prefer a wood fire, but this is just easier here.' He put their glasses down on the iron table between two chairs.

Ava crawled on to the lounger. Night birds sang in the trees behind the fence. It was very secluded and the deeper the night grew, more twinkling lights materialized in the shrubbery and flowers. Fireflies began their mystical dance between the leaves and a horse neighed in the distance. She heard the thumping of hooves. It was wonderful.

Ava bloomed with happiness when he draped a throw

blanket over her legs. She snuggled down into the coziness. 'Thank you.' She was touched and brushed her fingers over the soft weave of the blanket, at the same time snared by the heated look in his eyes.

'In case you get chilly,' he said, leaning down to tuck the blanket around her hips. He didn't stand up, staying partially bowed over her. He was so close. Yet so far away.

Impulsively, she reached up with her hands and took the sides of his face in her palms, stroking her thumb over his beard. She pulled him down. He didn't resist and their eyes remained locked on each other the closer they got. Chase rested a knee on the edge of the chair and steadied himself with one hand on the chair back.

Ava held her breath as he lowered his face to hers, inhaling his scent and the wildness of the land around them.

'I wasn't expecting this,' he said in a low and crazy sexy voice that twisted her belly into a tight knot of arousal.

'Neither was I.' Ava tugged on him, drawing him closer. The pool lights reflected into his eyes and she melted even more.

Slowly, excruciatingly slowly, Chase decreased the distance between them until she felt the heat of his lips. It took only one little tug for their lips to meet.

The simple power his voice had over her was nothing compared to how much he rocked her world with a kiss.

Chapter 34

Chase tasted her lips and thought he'd never tasted anything sweeter. He moved on to the lounger a little more and gathered her in his arms. She didn't resist and fitted so perfectly next to him. Her hand slid around his neck and she came to life under him. He'd grown used to her response and, if it hadn't happened now, as a consequence of their talk earlier, then he would have been devastated.

Somehow, he had to make her see they were meant for each other. And now, knowing they had only a couple precious days left, Chase knew he'd fallen for her. Deep in his soul, he knew she was the one, and he had to find a way to let her know. But he also had to move delicately. Gradually. Prove to her he wouldn't run or leave her or not place her first.

Since the moment he'd seen her the other night, her hips swinging on the dance floor in front of him and her lovely legs, ending in those sparkly boots, he'd been completely under her spell. She'd made everything else fade away so his attention was totally focused on her. Ava pressed into him, her breasts against his chest, and his cock sprung to life. Chase groaned into their kiss and she breathed deeply. He inhaled her breath. She moaned softly, and he returned it with another deep, almost guttural growl of his own.

He was completely startled when, in the middle of their kiss, she stiffened and suddenly pushed him away. *What the hell?* Had she had a change of heart? Was she done with him now? He blinked and bolted to his feet, wavering slightly. His jeans far too uncomfortable against his hard-on. Dismayed by her change in behavior, he watched her struggle to her feet then reached out to steady her when she wobbled. She was clearly as aroused and unsteady as he felt, so what had happened? What had he done wrong? Chase was perplexed.

'Do you smell that?' She lifted her nose and sniffed.

'Holy shit,' he shouted. He smelled the burning.

'The garlic butter!' Ava cried, and dashed around him, sprinting to the kitchen. She grabbed a lid that was handy, slammed it on top of the flaming butter then yanked the pan off the burner, threw it in the sink and turned the water on.

Ava turned around and looked at him, her eyes were wild and her mouth open in shock. He stood with his arms out, feeling useless and utterly ridiculous that he hadn't noticed the smell before she did.

'That was close,' he said, and raked his hand through his hair.

She puffed out a breath and the shocked expression changed to relief, then she started to laugh. She held her belly as she laughed harder.

'Oh my God. I can even manage to set fire to an outdoor kitchen. Maybe I should leave all the cooking to you.' She laughed harder. 'That was stupid.'

Tears rolled down her face and he wasn't sure if crying was

mixed in with her laughing. But she was killing herself and, now that the drama had passed, he also began to see the humor in it. Her intermittent hiccups and gales of laughter infected him and he started to chuckle along with her.

Chase reached for her hand and drew her into his arms. He was glad to see she had relaxed and when she wrapped her arms around his waist his heart sung. They stood in their embrace, all the while her body vibrating against his with her laughter.

He kissed the top of her head. 'I never thought the night would turn out quite like this.'

'Me either.' She drew in a big breath, tipping her head back to look up at him, then glanced at the sink. 'Oh, wow, that was kind of intense. Do you believe in destiny?'

He was silent for a moment and considered it. 'I know you're a romantic, Boots. But destiny?' He shrugged. 'If you look hard enough, I suppose you could put it all down to destiny. Right now, I think my destiny is your lips.' And he didn't wait for her to answer, dropping a kiss on her mouth.

'You have no idea how romantic I am and I totally believe in destiny. Soul mates. Happily ever afters. Love,' she murmured against his mouth. This is what he wanted to hear from her. Not that she thought they could never find a way to be together.

Chase deepened the kiss; he was more determined than ever to win her over. Make her see they had a future. But for right now, he had a beautiful, funny, passionate, sensitive woman in his arms. And he couldn't ask for anything more.

Ava's eyelids drooped into a seductive gaze that made his lungs freeze. Leaning over her, he pushed her back down into the pillows on his bed. It hadn't taken them long to retreat to his room after dinner. Both of them had been teasing and flirting all through dinner. He'd been hard pressed not to resume the conversation about their future, but he was definitely formulating a plan.

Somehow, he had to make her see they owed it to themselves to see what they had together. How their bodies spoke so perfectly to each other would be the best conversation they could have right now.

Chase took her hands, gathering them in one of his, and held them above her head. Her eyes, deep gold like honey, watched him. He was nearly done for when she moistened her lips with her pink tongue. His other hand slid under the white lacy top she wore, the softness of her skin leaving him with a desperate craving. He pushed the top high up over her belly and rested his hands just below her breasts, feeling her rapid heartbeat. She inhaled sharply and arched her back.

Chase was thrilled, her reaction exactly what he'd anticipated. He leaned down and pressed his lips to her belly, liking how her flesh quivered under his touch. He pressed his nose to her and drew in the scent of her flesh, more intoxicating than any Tennessee whiskey he'd ever tasted. Chase ran his fingers over her skin and followed with his tongue. His fingers stopped at the top of her shorts, where he unsnapped the button and lowered the zipper.

He felt the soft material of her panties – a vision of her hot-pink panties from their first night was still seared into his brain. He slipped his fingers under the edge, and lower, until his fingers pressed into her warm flesh. At the same time, he swirled his tongue in her belly button.

She sighed and it was music to his ears. Chase explored deeper, stroking her sensitive folds until she gasped. He let go of her hands and they immediately held his head, gently pushing him lower. He kissed his way down and, lifting her hips, he slid her shorts and canary-yellow panties down her long, tanned legs. Chase hooked an elbow under her knee and lifted, opening her as he shifted between her legs.

His mouth followed his hand and she became alive under him. He explored her with his tongue and his fingers, seeking, pressing, licking and sucking until he found a combination that was magic to her. She moaned and lifted her hips, her fingers pressing urgently into his head to keep him tight to her.

He needed no encouragement and when her body stiffened and her knees clamped on him, Chase gripped her ass, holding his mouth to slick heat. He drew her orgasm until she cried out and went lifeless on the bed. He looked up at her and never had he seen anything more beautiful. Her arms flung wide, her white top jumbled around her breasts, clad in a canary-yellow bra, her auburn hair wild on the pillow and her shapely knees next to his ears.

Chase was happy he could bring her pleasure. It was something he never wanted to stop doing. He moved up the bed and lifted her shoulders to pull her top over her head. She raised her arms and he removed it completely. She opened her eyes, her lips partially open and shiny, as if begging him to kiss her again.

He stood, ready to get rid of his own clothes, but seeing her like that stole his breath away and he was frozen to the spot. The yellow bra was delicate and pretty yet unbelievably erotic with its little black bows. He would never tire of looking at her tanned, lean body.

Chase tossed off his shirt and reached for his belt. 'I could write a song about you.' He didn't tell her he already had.

She swung her legs over the side of the bed and reached for his hands.

'Is that so? Well, then, I'm going to give you something to

really write about.' Her voice was sexy and husky and she looked up at him with those eyes. He felt all his will vanish as she licked her lips and pushed his hands away.

'Are you now?' he said in a tight voice and thrust his fingers into her hair when she had his jeans undone and pushed down.

'Yes, I am,' she said softly, and lowered her face to him, running her hands around his hips to grab his ass, her hair falling in a curtain around her shoulders and his forearms. The dim lighting shone off the long, wavy strands and he locked his knees when the sweet heat of her tongue touched his cock.

But this wasn't how he wanted it to go. He wanted to make love to her. Cherish her. Bury himself in her. He gently pushed her away.

'Ava, no,' were the hardest two words he'd ever spoken.

She looked up at him, alarm and hurt reflected in her eyes. And he hated that he'd put it there.

Ava held his thick, hard length. She could barely contain the trembling of her body, she was so incredibly turned on. Plus, this was after he'd already given her an earth-shattering orgasm. She wanted to drag him down on to the bed next to her and taste him, just like he'd done to her. Seeing him without his shirt – the perfection of his shoulders, the muscled chest dusted with hair and his intricate tattoos, and oh, his extraordinarily toned torso and belly – she ached to see more of him again.

Getting his jeans off him had been her goal. But now she looked up at him, suddenly embarrassed by him stopping her. She was at a loss what to do. What man stopped you from giving him oral sex?

'I want to make love to you first,' he growled.

Apparently, this man did.

Relief flooded through her: she wasn't being rejected. Instead, he was only thinking of her and a shared intimacy. She squeezed her hand around him and stroked. She loved how his head dropped back and his great body trembled under her touch. He grew impressively harder. She stared up at him, not finding any words to express how wonderful he looked to her. It made her wish she was a writer so she could compose the perfect sonnet to describe him.

'Ava, keep that up and—'

'Are we just going to talk all night, superstar?'

He looked down at her. 'No, ma'am.'

She melted under the fiery heat of his gaze. Letting go of him, she grabbed his hand and fell back on the bed.

They tumbled on the sheets and he rolled on to his back, taking her with him, and she straddled his hips. He had her bra undone and off in a flash and reached into the bedside-table drawer. He pulled the package out and Ava fell off him, snuggling into his side, and watched as he sheathed the condom over him. One day, perhaps there'd be no need for one. The thought startled Ava so much it made her wonder why she'd been adamant about a long-distance relationship not working. But before she could think any more he moved over her, reached between them and she lifted her knees.

He drove into her, pushing her up in the bed with the force of his thrust. 'Oh, Chase.' She clutched him and met him thrust for powerful thrust. This was wild, passionate and raw. Ava locked her ankles around him and he gathered her in his arms. They molded together, moving in time, their sounds filling the room until he brought her to the edge and she exploded all over again. Squeezing her eyes shut, she didn't even try to stop the scream of pleasure that ripped from her and mingled with his roar of release in the quite solitude of his bedroom.

Chase buckled over her, his breath harsh; their bodies were coated in a sheen from their exertion. Ava didn't want him to move, the weight of him on her reassuring, domineering, possessive and . . . loving. She wanted him to stay there forever.

Chapter 35

Loving Ava all night long was what he was born to do. But not for just one night . . . every night. Right now, Chase needed to put Ava out of his mind. It was the hardest thing to do after their fantastic night last night. But waking up early on a Saturday morning for rehearsals and sound check for tonight's performance hadn't been easy. He needed to be focused. Singing with Lance and getting that down pat was a major career high. His initial set was for fifteen minutes early on in the program, but he also had the two songs later with Lance. The more he thought about it, the more he grew excited, thinking about singing Ava's song. He'd decided he wanted to. He had to sing it. Even if it wasn't perfected yet, he would sing it from his heart.

Backstage was a flurry, as it always was during the CMAs; this was what he loved about country-music life: the intensity, the hustle, the bustle, the music, the sounds, the people.

His Martin slung over his shoulder and holding a cappuccino, Chase leaned against a pillar and watched Kelly Clarkson do her thing. It was when he was in the company of talent like her that he was filled with awe and wondered just how he'd ever managed to get to this point.

She finished her set and as she walked off the stage Kelly stopped in front of him and he straightened, putting his cup down on a chair.

'Chase Hudson! I love "You Drive Me Crazy". It's such a great song. Maybe one day we can do a duet.'

'Ms Clarkson, I appreciate your words and I'd be more than honored to do a duet with you.' Chase was a little star-struck and did his best not to look like a buffoon.

She reached out her hand and he shook it. 'I look forward to it. I'll have my people call your people.' She gave him a big smile, and then she was off in the flurry of her entourage.

Chase had not expected that to happen; it actually made him feel giddy.

'It looks like you're about to swoon, big guy.' A familiar woman's voice behind him made him crack into a big grin. He spun around and saw Fiona Johns.

'Well, if it isn't the top entertainer of the year, or is it the last two or three years?' He was thrilled to see her. Fiona launched into his arms and he gave her a huge hug, swinging her around.

'Chase, it's so good to see you. What have you been up to? I love your new song, by the way! Has any woman snagged you yet? Are you going out on tour, because I want you to come with me if you're not? I hear you're singing with Lance tonight. Why aren't you singing with me?' She was a firecracker and shot a million questions at him, which was totally like her.

He laughed, tossing his head back. 'Whoa there, lady, you're making my head spin. One question at a time.'

'Listen, my rehearsal's soon. Once I'm done, how about we catch up?' She held his forearm and nodded. 'Yes?'

'Sounds perfect to me. Let's fit something in.' She stood on her toes and planted a big kiss on his cheek, then she was gone, her long, dark hair streaming out behind her.

He shook his head; she was something else. They had met way back – like, fifteen years ago – when both of them had started writing and singing, doing gigs at the local music holes and then finally the Bluebird. There was never anything romantic, just a strong friendship bond. He was looking forward to talking to her. Maybe a female perspective could help him figure out how to maneuver through the situation with Ava. It was times like these that he wished he had a sister.

'Chase Hudson, you're up. Sound check.'

Chase drew in a deep breath, suddenly feeling a little bit nervous. It wasn't like him to have nerves, but there was a hell of a lot going on emotionally for him. His biggest worry was Ava. All he had with her was the remainder of today and tomorrow before she left.

He was determined to do his damnedest to make sure it wasn't for good.

Fiona was waiting for him after his sound check and hooked her arm through his. 'Come on. We've just a few short minutes to catch up.'

They went and grabbed a coffee and found a quiet corner with a couple of chairs.

'So what's new?' Fiona leaned forward on her knees, a coffee cup dangling between her fingers.

'Geez, what's new? It's been a bit of a crazy ride the last little while. But I'm loving it. You, though, you have really done great. I'm happy for you.' Chase really was: it was good to see someone who worked so hard do well.

'It definitely has been a challenge. But I was up for it, grappled my way through, and you know how it goes,' she said in a secret tone of voice, her eyes wide. 'I love it, though, and my label is super-good to me.'

'Any man in your life?'

She waved her hand and made a *phssst* sound. 'When do I have time for a man? I have been on tour steadily for the past year and I'm booked out for the next eight months. And, by the way, I want you to join me at some point,' she said, and pointed her finger at him.

'I would like that. Give me some dates and I'll take a look at my schedule.'

'Now you,' she said. 'Tell me what's going on with you. I've seen those Instagram photos with you and this red-headed siren. Who is she?'

Chase put the cup down and sat back in the seat, crossing his arms. That came out of the blue, but if he could talk to anybody about Ava it would be Fiona. 'I just met her the other night. And we've pretty much spent every moment together since.'

Her eyebrows shot up. 'Really? So the elusive Chase has been caught? She must be something pretty special to have snagged you.'

Chase was quiet. Hearing Fiona say the words he'd been thinking only drove deeper that he needed to do something to make Ava see it.

'Yeah, something like that. She is pretty special. Only she's hesitant on any kind of future.'

'Why?' Fiona looked concerned.

'Because we'd have to have a long-distance relationship. Ava is the epitome of a dreamer and a romantic, but she's also insanely practical. Plus, she's not all that keen on being in the public eye. I'm trying to respect her space but also romance the hell out of her so that she doesn't want to end our relationship after this weekend.'

'What's your plan, then?'

'I need to make one last-ditch attempt. I think I'm going to do it tonight.' He drew in a deep breath and frowned. 'Yep, it has to be tonight.'

'What are you thinking? Are you going to do something public or something private?' Chase saw the look of concern on Fiona's face.

'Public. I've got a new song—'

'That you wrote for her?' Fiona leaned forward with interest.

Chase furrowed his brows 'Yeah, how did you know?'

She lifted a shoulder and said mysteriously, 'It's a small town. Anyway, forget it, just tell me more.'

Chase frowned. He'd have to find out who'd been talking. 'We just put the track down yesterday, and it's pretty damn good.'

'Uhm, are you sure putting her on the spot like that is the right thing to do? If she's skittish now, that might make her bolt.'

'I don't think so,' he said in a low and thoughtful voice, and shook his head. 'Even if our story isn't meant to have a happy ending, I know Ava, she'll appreciate me doing this. Like I said, she's a romantic and, if this isn't romantic, me bearing my heart and soul to her on stage in front of thousands of people and on television, I don't know what it is. I have to know I'm doing everything I can do in order to win her over.'

He saw tears fill Fiona's eyes. 'Oh, Chase, honey, I hope you know what you're doing. You could be in for a world of hurt.' She leaned forward and put her hand on his knee and squeezed.

'I know it. And I think it's the right thing to do. But how about we take a selfie? I know she'd get a kick out of that.'

'Anything for you.' Fiona hopped out of her seat and came over to stand beside Chase.

They both snapped a couple of selfies and Chase attached one to a text.

Chase: *Look who I found backstage after my sound check. Did I ever tell you we were good friends?*

He didn't expect to hear back from Ava quickly so when his phone chimed almost immediately he chuckled and held it up to show Fiona.

Ava: *OMG! You know that amazing superstar Fiona? OK, I demand that you get her autograph for me. Oh wait a minute, the girls saw the picture and they want autographs too.*

Chase laughed and showed Fiona the comment. She also chuckled and took Chase's phone from him.

Fiona: *Hi Ava, Chase told me all about you. I'd be happy to give you an in person autograph tonight. I'm pretty sure you're going to be here for his performance, right?*

Ava: *Holy crap, I'm actually texting w/ Fiona Johns? I can't believe it. Yes, I – WE – will be there. We have a suite, so you're more than welcome to pop up and see us.*

Fiona: *LOL, I'll see what I can do. Here's Chase back. Great to meet you by text. By the way, you have an awesome dude here.*

Ava: *I know.*

Ava was stunned, and her friends were gathered around, equally star struck she was texting with Fiona Johns.

'Oh my God!' Celia was nearly screeching. 'You were just texting with one of the biggest country superstars. And look at you, you're calm. I think I'd be a hot mess.'

'What am I going to do? I just have to talk back to her like a normal person. But wow, that was pretty mind-blowing.'

'No kidding.' Bonni was peering at Ava's phone to look at the texts and photo again.

'What have we just done? We have fallen down Alice's

rabbit hole. All this fantastic stuff that's been happening to us ever since we got to Nashville and met Chase.' Excitement bubbled in Fredi's voice, which was very unusual for her.

Ava plopped down on a bench in the rotunda. The girls had insisted on coming back to the Country Music Hall of Fame because they'd been rushed the last time. And here she was in the middle of this fantastic place with so much going on. She had a wonderful man who wanted them to have forever together. Ava was overwhelmed. With everything being thrown at her so quickly, her usual practical self was having difficulty digesting it all.

'I wonder if she'll come to our suite later?' Celia asked and sat down beside Ava.

'That would be super-cool,' Fredi said. 'But she's such a superstar, I doubt it. Hey, guys, I want to go over and look at those displays. There's some really amazing fashion here and I didn't get to see it all last time.' She wandered off and Bonni's phone rang.

She held up the phone. 'It's Quinn.' She answered it and found a quiet spot to talk to her love.

Celia put her arm around Ava. 'How are you doing, sweetie?

Ava sighed and closed her eyes. She didn't really want to answer the question because she knew, no matter what she said, it would raise the issue she was facing.

'What's the matter, Aves?'

'Oh, nothing and everything,' she moaned.

'Well, that doesn't make any sense. Tell me what's going on. Come on, fess up.'

Ava let out a big puff of air and turned her head to look at her friend. 'You know we had those bets, right?' Celia nodded. 'I won the first bet, and he won the next two. So I asked him what he wanted.'

'What he wanted? Do you mean, like, because he won the bets?' Celia leaned forward and hung her hands between her knees.

'Yeah, and he shocked me. I thought it would be something fun with a sexual nature to it, but it wasn't.'

Ava was quiet, thinking about it. Somehow, right now it didn't seem as terrifying as it had when they talked about it last night.

'Are you going to tell me or leave me in the dark guessing?' Celia nudged her arm.

'He wants to see me after this weekend.' There, she had said it.

'And that is bad how?' Celia inquired, and Ava heard a bit of humor in her voice.

'It's not funny.' Ava frowned and furrowed her eyebrows.

Celia held her hands up in supplication. 'I know it's not funny. I'm not trying to make it funny. But we talked about this before and I thought you were going to give it a go.'

'We may have discussed it, but I haven't made any decisions. All I know is a long-distance relationship rarely works.'

'I beg to differ with you on that one. I know two people who have successfully made a long-distance relationship work. And I think three times could be the charm.' Celia reached over and placed her hand on Ava's, squeezing it gently.

'Oh, I don't know. It just seems so complicated.' She was looking at all the negatives, none of the positives, which was so backwards for her. But, she was worried the negatives would overtake the positives before long.

'Listen, Aves, it's only complicated if you make it complicated. And it doesn't have to be complicated. If anybody had a complicated situation, it was me,' Celia said wisely. 'Look, I have two kids, dickhead for an ex-husband, and found a new man who is okay with my baggage. He helps carry it, for crying

out loud.' The love that flooded over Celia's face told Ava everything she needed to know. She was happy it had worked out so
wonderfully for her friend. She'd met a great man, taken a risk
and it had worked out for her.

'But I'm afraid,' Ava said in a low voice

'Oh, honey, what are you afraid of?' Celia scooted closer and
tightened her arm around her shoulder.

Ava looked at Celia, trying to decide if this was the moment
to own up to her fear.

'That I'll fall so hard and it won't work out and I'll be broken,'
she blurted.

Celia tightened her arm around Ava. 'Look, what if you
don't give it a try? You'll always wonder. And all you've talked
about all these years is finding your soul mate. The love of your
life. To fill your world with romance.'

'I know, right? I'm broken, aren't I?' Ava dropped her face
into her hands and didn't bother to hold back the tears.

'You're not broken. You're the most warm and compassion-
ate person I know. Why would you ever think you're broken?
You deserve this. You owe it to yourself to take that plunge and
see. If I can do it, you most certainly can, too.'

'Celia, I know everybody goes through their own dramas in
life. We all get hurt and we all either get over it or we don't. Yes,
the idea of romance and love is powerful for me and something
I so desperately want.'

Celia took Ava's hands in hers. 'I can't tell you what to do.
All I know is I was indecisive with Landon but you guys helped
me see it could work. I don't want you to miss out on this
opportunity with Chase. You deserve love.'

Ava sucked in a big breath and squeezed Celia's hands.

'At least I'll be able to say I knew him when,' she sniffed
through the tears.

'Look at you! Don't be such an idiot. We now have access to a private jet, Chase is loaded and there's absolutely no reason why you can't see each other every weekend if you want to. It can be done.' Celia was adamant.

'But I don't want to be a kept woman. I've fought hard for my independence,' Ava countered.

'Listen, you are young, have no kids and your business skills translate so well into telecommuting it wouldn't be hard for you to work remotely.' Ava opened her mouth to say something but Celia wouldn't let her talk. 'Geez, if the Beast hadn't trusted Belle, she would never have come back for him. And in *Notting Hill*! That's like you two, and they made it work. And what if Dorothy had given up – like you're talking about doing – and gave her ruby slippers to the Wicked Witch? She would never have found her way home.'

'*The Wizard of Oz* is not a love story,' Ava pointed out.

'But the metaphor still stands, dammit. Follow the yellow brick road, Dorothy, and find some courage, trust your heart and use your brains!'

Ava digested that, and a little bit of hope sparked inside her. Maybe it *could* work. But she still wasn't entirely sure.

Chapter 36

Ava ushered her friends into the suite. 'Hurry up! We're late as it is, and I don't want to miss any of the show. Chase is going to be on pretty soon.'

'If Celia hadn't been all caught up having phone sex with Landon, we wouldn't be in such a damn rush,' Fredi said, tossing her purse on the counter.

'Oh, but it was worth it. I'm all trembly now.' Celia had a faraway look in her eyes.

'Eesh, whatever. You could have waited until you got home tomorrow and then got all stupid with him. I can't bleach my ears, ya know.' Fredi gave a delicate shiver.

'Oh, come on, cranky pants. I miss my man's lovin'.' Celia eyed her when she took off her sweater.

'I got the only man I need, and he's replenishable.'

Bonni held up her hand. 'Don't wanna hear about B.O.B., please.'

They all chuckled. 'I certainly hope we don't have those

horrible people sharing the suite with us this time.' Celia went over and took a beer out of the fridge. 'Anyone else?'

They all said yes and she handed bottles around.

'Oh, I hope not. They were awful.' Bonni walked down to the railing and looked over.

'Everybody stay away from Ava's food. We learned our lesson the last time and we don't need a repeat,' Fredi reminded everyone.

'Okay, guys, enough. Chase is about to come on.' She rushed down to the railing and grabbed it with tight fingers. She couldn't believe how nervous she felt for him. He'd done this so many times, been on stage in front of thousands of people, but here she was, safely high up out of the limelight, and yet she was shaking for him. It was rather silly.

The current act played their finishing notes and left the stage. The crowd roared and the decibel level in the stadium nearly blew the roof off.

Ava's heart thumped painfully in her chest and she felt physically ill with nerves for Chase.

'Ava, calm down. You're hyperventilating,' Fredi told her, and rubbed her back.

'I can't believe how nervous I am. Why am I nervous? He's the one that should be nervous, not me. Oh my God.' Ava started to wring her hands and pace around.

Celia came up and took her arm. She leaned in and whispered, 'And you tell me you don't have powerful feelings for this man. Look how you're behaving when he's going to be on stage. You love him. Admit it. And don't be a stubborn fool and lose this chance with a great guy.' Ava stared at Celia and digested her words. She was right. She did love him. And she hadn't told him. Panic welled up inside her. All she'd done was try and push him away because of her own stupid fears. But those fears were still real. They were still legitimate. How could they possibly make things work?

The announcer came on and introduced Chase. He played a couple of his older tunes and the crowd was ecstatic. He was a natural. He worked the stage and the crowd like the pro he was. Ava could never, ever force him to give up something he was so good at, something he loved to do.

She watched, her chest swelling with pride for him. He was so damn amazing.

He finished his songs then took the microphone off the stand. He raised his hand in the air and the crowd went silent.

'Oh no, what's he going to do?' Ava asked, her nerves shooting through the roof.

'He's going to propose to you. Just like Luke did to Rayna on *Nashville!*' Celia squealed.

'He will not.' Fredi shook her head and frowned. 'No way would he do something like that.'

'Oh God,' Bonni said, and held her breath.

'Thank you, Nashville!' Chase shouted into the microphone. 'I'm thrilled to be here, and I have an exciting announcement to make.'

'Oh, here it comes,' Fredi said.

'I'll be coming back to sing for y'all with Lance Warrington.' The crowd erupted.

Ava felt relief and disappointment flood through her. What had she been expecting?

'Oh, shit. He didn't.' Celia sounded hugely disenchanted.

But Ava was conflicted. Part of her couldn't even imagine how she would feel if he had. What would she have done? Accepted, right?

'It certainly would've been TMZ-worthy,' Bonni commented.

Ava gripped the rail tighter and leaned on her arms; she was nearly panting again, but this time it was relief. Or was it? Had she wanted him to propose? Was she disappointed he hadn't? She shook her head and chastised herself. He'd never do anything like that on stage. It would be super-embarrassing for him and make him totally vulnerable.

Oh, but it would be romantic. She let out a soft sigh. Imagine if a man loved a woman so much he'd bare his soul in public to profess his love and propose!

'And now I'm giving a shout-out to some very special friends of mine that are watching from up there in one of the suites.' Chase lifted his arm and pointed in their direction. A sea of eyes turned toward them.

'He just outed us!' Celia was bouncing on her toes. She waved liked crazy and hooted her hellos to the crowd.

'Oh, man.' Fredi sank into the seat.

'They are the funnest bunch of gals. Give a big hello to Bonni, Fredi, Celia and my special friend, Ava!'

He touched his lips with his two fingers then blew the kiss up to them in the suite.

'Oh my God. Ava, he just blew you a kiss.' Celia was almost breathless with excitement.

Ava was paralyzed; the most she could do was lift her hand in a wave. She watched Chase turn and leave the stage, his arm in the air. Just before he went behind the curtain he paused for a moment and glanced up. He was too far away for her to see his eyes, but it was as if everything suddenly magnified and she knew he was looking at her. Her heart tumbled in her chest. He was really doing a number on her and she had no idea how she would have the strength to walk away from him.

'Is there an Ava in the house?' A woman's voice called from behind them and they all stood up and turned around.

'Can the night get any better?!' Celia could barely contain herself.

'I'm Ava.' She stepped in front of Celia then her mouth dropped open. 'I can't believe it! Fiona? You've come up to our suite! I'm floored!'

'Yep, I have. But I'm actually here to spirit you away. But first you have to put this on.' She handed Ava a T-shirt emblazoned with CHASE HUDSON IS ALWAYS RIGHT.

Ava burst out laughing and took it from her. 'I'd totally forgotten about this, but what do you mean "spirit me away"?' Ava couldn't comprehend everything that was going on. This was just becoming way too overwhelming. But she wouldn't trade it for a second.

'First, I'm doing some personal autographing at your request for your friends while you put that shirt on.' Fiona held up some photos and CDs and started signing them. Her friends gathered around her and they were all chattering up a storm. Ava dashed into the restroom and changed. When she came back out into the suite Fiona was finished and came forward to take Ava's hand. 'You and I have a little business to attend to.'

'We do?' Ava asked.

She followed Fiona out of the suite with a backward look to her friends. She shrugged her shoulders. 'I don't know. I'll text you.'

Her friends waved and all shouted for her to have a good time. They were looking shocked and very happy. Then they turned and rushed back down to the railing to see the rest of the show.

Bodyguards surrounded them as they made their way through the stadium, down some elevators into the backstage area.

'You're probably wondering what's going on,' Fiona said as she hurried along in the pocket of her bodyguards.

'Kind of, yes.' Ava trotted to keep up with the group as they rushed through the halls.

'I have to go on soon, but I wanted to bring you backstage.'

'But why?' Ava was still numb from the surprise of everything that had just happened.

'Because I wanted to tell you something. I want to talk to you about Chase. He told me about you. I've known Chase a lot of years, and it was never anything romantic, so don't worry about that, but I've not seen him taken with a woman like he is with you. Ever.'

She pulled her into her dressing room and shut the door. 'Here, have a glass of champagne.' Ava accepted the glass and drank it down like she'd been crawling through a desert and was absolutely parched.

'I can't tell you what to do. All I know is I can tell you what a great guy he is.' Fiona finished her glass of champagne and looked in the mirror, glancing at Ava in the reflection. 'I urge you to give it a chance.' She smoothed down her dark hair and took off her over shirt, revealing a fantastic sparkly mini-dress. She shoved her feet into screamingly high shoes that were equally as sparkly.

'Wow, you look amazing.' Ava finally found her voice. 'You surprised the heck out of me just now. Thank you for bringing me here and for treating my friends like you did. I'll never forget it. And thank you for what you said about Chase. If he's told you about me then I imagine he's told you my concerns. Trust me, this is not an easy decision to make.'

Fiona stepped forward and put her hands on her shoulders. 'I know it's not. Remember, the decision is as hard or as easy as you want to make it. Don't overthink it. Overthinking will ruin everything. I'm just giving my friend Chase a little help here. Remember what I said. Now, I have to go, but listen to your heart.' Fiona gave her a quick hug and was out the door, leaving Ava in a whirlwind of emotion, perfume and disquiet.

A bodyguard came in. 'Fiona asked me to escort you to the stage. You can watch the performances from back here now.'

Chapter 37

The excitement of being backstage was absolutely thrilling and Ava was having the time of her life. She hadn't seen Chase yet but figured he was off busy doing whatever singers do before they go on stage. A few minutes later she heard excited female voices and turned around to see her friends approaching with happy smiles.

'What are you guys doing here?' Ava opened her arms for a big hug. She soooo needed her friends now.

'Chase's agent, some dude named Dozer, came and got us. He said we had backstage passes. Here we are.' Celia fell into her arms and hugged her tight.

'Wow, this just couldn't get any better.' Ava was absolutely thrilled her friends were back here with her.

'I'm beyond words,' Fredi said, and pushed her way in front of them so she could see better.

'If I was stronger, I put you on my shoulders, Freds,' Bonni told her, humor in her voice. Fredi turned around and scowled.

They all focused on the stage when the next act was introduced. It was Lance with his special guest, Chase Hudson.

The four of them jumped up and down, clapping their hands and screaming like groupies. Ava was thrilled. She was backstage to watch her man sing. More and more as this day wore on, she was beginning to realize just how important he was to her. Her determination to have only this weekend with him was beginning to wane. She wanted more.

'There he is,' she said, and watched him walk out to the stage from the other side. He saw her and gave her a sexy, slow wink. She nearly fainted and her friends screamed like teenagers and waved back at him.

He looked wonderful. His hair was tousled about his shoulders and his hat, low on his forehead, reminded her of their first kiss under its brim. He had on a deep green shirt and his jeans were like a second skin. A whisper of desire that this was her man rippled through her. Ava was captivated.

Lance approached Chase and the two of them went up to the microphone.

Lance took the lead. 'Ladies and gentlemen, I am absolutely thrilled to have this amazing performer sing with me today. He's got a couple of songs for you I think you're gonna love, and I believe one of them is brand new. You heard it here first, folks.' Lance clapped Chase on the shoulder and stepped behind him as Chase began to play.

'I know this one, it's "You Drive Me Crazy". His number-one hit right now,' Celia said, and started to sing along with the rest of the crowd. Bonni and Fredi joined in and Ava was smiling like a fool before she also belted out the words.

'This is the best,' Celia said when the song ended. 'I thought we had it made when we were in the suite upstairs. But look at us now – backstage with all the great performers.'

'This certainly is a surprise,' Bonni replied.

'I'm just boggled,' Fredi said.

'Quiet, everybody, he's talking again,' Ava told them, and watched him up on the stage. She was so god damn proud she could bust.

'Lance was right, y'all, I have a new song for you tonight. It's so brand new I just wrote it the other day.' He had his hand around the microphone and leaned into it, looking up into the crowd, his other arm stretched out, pointing at everybody. 'I'm really glad all y'all are here to hear it, but most importantly there's one person I am especially glad to have hear it. Because I wrote it for her.'

Ava's heart catapulted into her chest and her friends let out gasps of delight. The crowd exploded.

'And that woman,' Chase continued, then turned to look at her in the wings and pointed in her direction, 'is standing right there, backstage, with her friends. This is for you, Boots.'

'I could die!' Celia screamed as if he'd just dedicated the song to her.

He began to sing, keeping his attention on Ava. She could barely hold back the tears. He sung about moonlit nights, fire-flies in the trees, the whisper of a creek and the soft sighs of a woman, about finding that woman he'd always known was there waiting for him, even before he met her.

Ava was moved to tears. She was almost sobbing and her friends gathered around to support her. And then Fiona was beside her, too.

Chase finished his set with Lance, waved goodbye to the crowd and came off stage. Ava broke free from her friends and threw herself at Chase. He caught her and swung her around. She sobbed into his neck and he held her as she cried. Never had she felt safer or more loved.

'Oh, Chase, I love you. I do. So much.' She gulped in air and wound her arms around his neck. 'But, but how—'

'And me, too, Boots. Shh, just let's get out of here,' he whispered into her ear, and she pressed her lips to his neck.

They walked past her friends; they waved and had happy smiles. Fiona gave a thumbs-up and then it was her turn on the stage. She bounced up there, wiping her eyes, then said into the microphone, 'Wasn't that just the most romantic thing you ever saw?' The crowd roared their agreement and she launched into her song 'Love is a Mystery'.

Within moments Chase and Ava were outside, leaving behind the chaos and the noise. Once in his car, they were cocooned in silence and simply stared at each other.

'Let's go back to my hotel, it's closer,' Ava said, and crawled into his lap, needing to be as close to him as possible.

'Your wish is my command.'

Chapter 38

It was all they could do to keep their hands off each other. Chase practically carried Ava through the lobby of the hotel. In the elevator, he pushed Ava into the corner and kissed her senseless. Dare he even hope she was going to stay with him? Hadn't he proved to her how important she was to him? But he wasn't even going to risk asking. At least not now. All he cared about was that she was here, with him, and in his arms.

The elevator door opened and he swept her up, carrying her into the hall.

'Which way?' He crashed his lips down on hers and she pointed. He drowned in her and went in the direction she indicated. At the door, she fumbled to get out the key card. Once inside, she pointed again and he headed to her bedroom. He kept kissing her as often as he could without walking them into a wall or piece of furniture.

Putting her down, they didn't waste any time and stripped the clothes from each other. Sending everything scattering around the room, they fell into each other's arms naked, their bodies sliding against each other, friction of skin to skin, chest to chest, thigh to thigh. It was excruciatingly wonderful. He could tell she was just as aroused as he, by the frantic way they kissed, touched and were unable to get enough of each other.

'Wait, hang on a moment,' Ava said breathlessly. She rummaged through the pile of clothes on the floor, looking for something.

'What are you doing?' He stroked the back of her head, loving the silky feel of her hair as the strands slid through his fingers. She stood up and her bra dangled from her fingers. This time, it was a beautiful black-cherry color and he hadn't even noticed it on her, they'd been so desperate to get naked.

'Give me a moment. Gotta put it on the door.' She opened the bedroom door, dropped the straps over the handle and shut the door again.

He laughed and said, 'Don't tell me you're signaling—'

She reached for him. 'Yep, our signal from college. Just in case they come home earlier than we anticipate.'

'Then we'd better get busy.'

'I agree.'

Chase strode over and grabbed her, lifting her up. Her back pressed against the wall, he handed her the package he'd taken from his pocket and she ripped it open. Ava rolled the condom over his hard cock and he moaned at the whisper of her touch. Both were panting with anticipation and he was barely able to stand the feel of her fingers on him.

She stroked, she squeezed, then guided him to her hot center. He didn't even wait, thrusting into her, and his knees nearly crumpled with the sensation that assaulted him. It took all his energy, his hands holding her ass, for him to stay upright. Her muscles tightened on him and he groaned, burying his face in her neck. Ava wrapped around his shoulders, her legs locked about his waist, and she molded to his chest.

This time, there was no gentle romancing, this was pure desire, a need coming from deep inside him only she could fulfill. Her moans and her little gasps of pleasure drove him on, she met his thrusts and the picture beside them on the wall banged in time with their cadence. Chase lost himself in her. And when his orgasm overtook him he felt her muscles clamp around his cock. She let out a long cry and shuddered in his arms as he ground into her.

After their orgasm subsided he cradled her in his arms. Holding her against him, he walked to the bed, ripped the covers back and laid her down. He crawled in beside her and pulled her to his side. Ava snuggled up to him, sliding her arm around his waist.

'I never want you to go,' he told her quietly, and the stress of the day, the performance, the emotional turmoil he'd been in, all due to Ava telling him she wasn't going to stay, took its toll.

'Mmhm.' Ava nodded her head and he knew she'd drifted off as he sunk down into the layers of sleep. He knew she'd be here in the morning.

Chapter 39

At a restaurant in the lobby of their hotel Ava and her friends were huddled around a table for breakfast. She was starving and wanted everything: bacon, eggs, hash browns, grits, toast. When her huge plate, fit for a lumberjack, was put before her, she could have dived in head first.

'Oh, Ava. One can never say your eyes are bigger than your stomach,' Celia said with a wink.

'You betcha,' Ava said, as she crinkled the bacon over her hash browns and dug in. 'I'm not ashamed.'

'Can you believe this is the last day of our vacation?' Bonni asked.

Fredi shook her head and carefully placed her poached egg on a piece of toast. 'No, actually, I can't. It seems like we've been here for ever and yet the time has flown by.'

Bonni swirled her coffee cup. 'I love our weekends away together. And I'm sad this one is ending now.'

Ava stopped eating long enough to say, 'Don't be sad, we'll

have more weekends. It's not even that long until Bonni's wedding!'

'True, and you all have to be there for that.' Bonni pointed at each one of them, giving them her cop stare. Fredi rolled her eyes and Ava couldn't exactly blame her.

'Like any of us would miss it,' Ava told Bonni. 'Something apocalypse-worthy would have to be happening to keep us from showing up.'

'Exactly,' Celia agreed. 'Oh, by the way, Ava, I know you already paid for your return ticket but we were talking and, if you can get a credit or your money back, we can give you a lift on the jet.'

'Thanks, but I won't need a lift. I'm not leaving.' She waited for the explosion of questions.

Her friends immediately fixed their eyes on her and she gave them a saucy look. 'What?'

She feigned innocence because she didn't want to tell them right away; she'd drag it out a little bit to build the drama. Ava speared more hash browns and bacon, swirled the forkful in the yolk of her fried egg and popped the gooey concoction into her mouth.

'Okay, we need more than that,' Fredi demanded.

'Damn straight. You don't say something like that without giving any further explanation,' Celia told her, and lifted her cup to take a drink of coffee.

Bonni sat back, nodding her head. 'What they said.'

'Well . . . I talked to Chase . . . then I talked to David . . . then I called Kate, my next-door neighbor . . . then I thought about it a little more . . .' Ava paused dramatically to take another large bite of her breakfast, chewing as slowly as possible. Celia looked ready to come over the table for her. 'I've decided to stay an extra couple of days with Chase. Leaving now just didn't seem right. It would be too rushed.'

'After his grand gesture last night, you would be a fool to leave,' Celia told her.

'Even I have to admit it was pretty special,' Fredi told her.

'Well, I'm glad you guys agree with my decision. I would hate to go against your wishes,' Ava teased gently, knowing her friends wouldn't give her a hard time about staying. In fact, they would probably give her a harder time if she'd decided to leave.

'So unless Chase and Ava decide to do something wildly impulsive, I guess the next time we'll be seeing each other is at Bonni's wedding.' Celia pushed her empty plate away.

'Yes, Quinn and I confirmed the location yesterday.' Ava could tell Bonni was excited and they all started chattering on top of each other, demanding to know where the wedding was going to be held.

Bonni held up her hands and they fell quiet. 'So, are you guys up for a trip to Monaco?'

Ava wanted to swoon. Oh, Monaco always sounded so glamorous, what with James Bond, gambling and Princess Grace! And now she was going to be a maid of honor at a wedding there! She made a mental note to see if Chase could be her plus one.

Bonni was nearly bouncing in her chair with excitement. 'Yes, I know, isn't it amazing! We're going to be going over there for a little while, before and after. Quinn swears up and down that he thinks it'll be a fantastic setting for a wedding but I suspect there's also a poker tournament there he wants to moonlight in.'

'I can't believe he's deciding your wedding locale based on a poker tournament,' Fredi said, shaking her head in disbelief.

'Hey, now, it was a joint decision. Besides, I knew who he was when I said yes and, remember, if it wasn't for a lucky win, Quinn and I would never have met,' Bonni replied.

'Wow, who would've ever thought the four of us little college girls would be going over to Monaco for one of our friends' weddings?' Celia was shaking her head in wonder.

'It'll be beee-autiful,' Ava sighed, just thinking about it. 'It's so lovely over there. It's been the setting of so many James Bond movies.'

'You guys up for hearing more news?' Fredi asked her friends, and they all turned to look at her.

'Of course, Fredi. You can always tell us anything,' Ava said to her.

Fredi drew in a deep breath and Ava started to get excited; she had a feeling she knew what Fredi was going to say.

Celia slightly rose from her seat. 'Are you finally—'

'You can't even let me make my own announcement but, yes, I've decided to open up my own studio.'

'It's about freaking time!' Celia told her, springing from her chair to hug Fredi.

Fredi tolerated it for a moment before saying, 'Get off me, you heathen.'

Celia was grinning as she retook her seat. 'Are you taking the space that Landon offered?'

'I rented a place for the studio off-property but I'm going to take him up on his offer to set up a showroom in some of his hotels. Is it still nepotism if it's via a friend and not family?' Fredi asked.

'We *are* family,' Bonni said quietly. 'And I can't wait to wear a Fredi original down the aisle at my wedding.'

'For sure, Bonni. I've already got ideas we can discuss. But I was actually inspired by someone else on this trip.' Fredi leaned down and pulled her sketchbook from her bag.

Fredi put the book on the table, placed her hand on it and caressed the cover lovingly. 'Ava, you have nearly driven me mad over the years with the back-and-forth about your perfect dress but, seeing you here in Nashville, it clicked for me.' She cast a glance at Ava and blew her a kiss. Turning the sketchbook around so her friends could see, she opened it. 'I give you the "Ava" dress. Take a look and tell me what you think.'

Silence fell around the table. Ava stared down at the dress and tears filled her eyes.

'Oh, Fredi, it's my dress. Fredi, it's my dress! I can't believe it,' she whispered, and reached out to touch the edge of the paper with her fingers. She glanced up at Fredi and was almost overcome. 'You've nailed it. All those ideas, all those designs, and you put everything together into this wonderful dress. It's perfection.'

'Look a little closer,' Fredi said softly.

Ava leaned in and let out an excited cry of delight. 'And the boots! The model's wearing my boots.' She couldn't believe what she was looking at. 'You did this while we were here?'

'You know I always have my sketchbook. It's your dress, Ava, for when you're ready. And I have a feeling it's not going to be too far off.' She glanced over Ava's shoulder and quickly shut the book.

Ava turned around to see Chase walking toward them. She burst from the seat and ran into his arms. The women watched the two and, when Ava looked back, they all had blissful smiles on their faces.

Chase took Ava's hand and they returned to the table.

'I just wanted to come and say goodbye. I know all you ladies are leaving, except this one.' He hitched his head in Ava's direction. She was helpless to stop the smile that went from ear to ear.

'Hopefully, we'll see you in Monaco as Ava's plus one?' Bonni inquired.

'Monaco?' He glanced at Ava then back to Bonni.

'We'll talk about it,' Ava said. 'There's a lot to talk about, and now we have the time to do it.'

Chase brushed his knuckles tenderly across her cheek before saying his goodbyes to the women. He touched the tip of his hat and stepped back to give Ava room for her own goodbyes.

'Stay in touch, girls. We have much to discuss,' Ava instructed, and they shared a big group hug. After extracting herself from them, Ava turned to Chase and held out her hand.

They walked through the lobby of the Opryland Hotel hand in hand. All Ava's angst about her decision had fled. She knew she was in the right place, with the right man, and was going to do her darndest to make it work.

'I have something to tell you,' Chase leaned down to her and continued. 'My label wants me to release the song I wrote for you, but I just want to make sure you're okay with that. Because once it's out there, it'll belong to everyone.'

'I don't mind. It's okay,' she replied to him. 'Because you belong only to me.'

'I've been waiting to hear you say that, Boots. I tell ya, I can't imagine being happier than I am right now,' Chase said.

Ava gave him a seductive pout. 'Wanna bet?'

Chapter 40

Ava leaned back against Chase's chest and thought she'd died and gone to heaven. The steaming hot-tub water swirled and a mist rose up around them. All the tension in her muscles slowly faded away and she was in complete bliss.

Once Bonni, Celia and Fredi had left, Chase and Ava had driven back to his house. It didn't matter how many times she had said goodbye to her friends, there was always the usual drama involving crying, tight hugs and promises of getting together soon.

It had taken the drive back to Chase's house from the Opryland Hotel for her to stop tearing up. He'd held her hand the whole way as she gazed out the window, the soft sound of country music filling the truck. Once they'd arrived he'd suggested that relaxing in the hot tub with a glass of wine was just what she needed.

The man knew her well, and he was absolutely right.

So here she was, naked and finally chilling with him. They were alone and she couldn't be happier. Before they'd shed their robes and eased themselves down into the heated water Chase had poured a delicious fragrance into the bubbles and Ava now inhaled the calming scent that floated on the air.

'Come here,' Chase said, and closed his fingers around her wrist, pulling her closer so she could settle between his powerful thighs.

'Mmm, I could get used to this.' She dropped her head back on his chest and gazed up at the starry sky filtering through the slatted roof of the arbor and the vines that wound along the wood. Beautiful flowers hung down, their exotic perfume mingling with the eucalyptus and citrus scent of the water.

'Good. I want you to, so that you'll never leave.' His voice was enticingly low and deep and Ava smiled. He gently massaged her scalp, pushing his fingers into the thick strands of her hair.

'You do know how to treat a girl.' She was hard pressed not to let her eyelids droop closed under his skilled hands. 'I can't believe it's only been a few days since we met. It feels like I've known you for ever.'

'I want to discover everything about you, and we've only just begun.' He pressed a kiss to her temple and Ava twisted in his arms to lie across his thighs. She wiggled a little so that his erection was nicely positioned between her legs. A distraction, indeed.

'I thought you wanted to talk,' he whispered against her lips. She nodded her head. 'I do.'

'We have all night to play, and hopefully many more as well.' He gazed down at her, his dark eyes full of passion and promise.

Ava rose a little higher and wrapped her arms around his neck. 'Yes, a whole lot longer than just tonight.'

He grinned, his teeth white against his beard and mustache.

The candles they'd lit and placed around the hot tub cast them in a romantic glow that filled Ava's heart. Fireflies winked on and off in the trees, creating an even more mystical mood.

'This place is just magical. I love it.' Ava drew in a very contented breath.

'Music to my ears, Boots,' Chase told her as he ran his hands up and down her back before cupping her bottom with a firm grip. 'I'll take that as an affirmation that you could live here.'

Ava nodded vigorously. Droplets of water sprinkled off the damp tendrils of hair that curled around her face. 'Oh yes, I definitely could. It's wonderful – you thought of everything when you designed it. Any woman would be thrilled to live here.'

'You're not just any woman, though, Ava. You're mine. So we need to figure out how to make us happen beyond tonight.'

'I know. And we will.' She was silent for a moment, just as determined as he was to figure out a solution to their tricky situation. 'I know we can.'

He tipped up her chin with his finger. 'It's not gonna be easy. I have a tour coming up and I know your contract isn't up for another year so you can't come with me. But have you thought about going freelance? You could base here out of Nashville and it would give you more flexibility to join me on the road when you wanted to.'

'I hadn't really thought of it from that perspective before.' It was encouraging, but then she deflated. 'Honestly, I could break my contract and just eat the financial penalties, but I don't want to do that to David or my clients. I want to be with you but I don't want to turn my back on my commitments,' she said forlornly, and raised her arms in the air then let them drop with a splash into the water. 'Stupid work ethic.'

He chuckled. 'That sense of loyalty is one of the many, many reasons I love you. And at the risk of sounding like a throw-back caveman from the fifties, you don't really have to worry about money. I've got plenty.'

Craning her head to look at him, she said primly, 'I'm aware of that, thank you very much. I myself have a very healthy brokerage account that would tide me over while I set up a free-lance consulting business. But I hate to leave money on the table. And David's been really good to me. I don't want to leave him in the lurch.'

Ava slid off his lap, her back and shoulders slightly chilled, since she wasn't completely submerged. She floated lower so the water rose up to her chin. Chase didn't seem bothered by the chilly air – the weather had taken a bit of a turn – and placed his arms along the back of the hot tub. It made his chest seem impossibly large and his tattoos glistened under a sheen of water. Her mouth went dry. She was a very lucky woman.

'Boots, I'd cancel the tour if I could, but that decision would affect more than just me: the fans, my crew, the promoters . . .' he told her, a very serious tone in his voice.

Ava shook her head and reached for his hand, taking it underneath the water. 'I appreciate the offer, but I can't ask you to do that. It's not right. We'll just have to work it out long dis-tance. I'm not crazy about that, but there's no other option.' Ava searched for something positive. She needed to spin it in a good light so she wouldn't get depressed. Pulling herself through the water to him, she said, 'You know what? We can do it. I know it. Just think of the anticipation. The sexual tension. Missing each other until our hearts grow so much fonder.'

The smile that broke out on Chase's face made her heart swell with love for him. 'I know we can. I was just waiting for you to say it.'

Ava giggled and looped her arms around his neck. 'I'm a

master scheduler, you know. I'll have us all figured out once I know your touring dates. I'll come and see you when you're home. And how about when you're on tour with a break – you'll come and see me? After all, you have a private jet, right?'

He threw back his head and let out a booming laugh. 'I never told you I had one. How did you know?'

She shrugged her shoulders. 'Don't all superstars have one to jet them around the world?' Ava moved closer to him, the tips of her breasts brushing nicely over his hard chest.

'To be honest, most celebrities don't own a jet these days. Not cost effective. They just reserve one when they need it. But I split the cost of buying one with the family business. I still use my tour bus a lot but during album-release week it's a lot more convenient to have a jet on standby for all the promotional appearances.'

'Ha, Bonni and Celia have to share one – won't they and Fredi be green with envy when I go flitting around the world with you! Speaking of which, there is one other thing we have to discuss. My role in your public life,' she said, pressing her mouth to his, liking the tickle of his mustache and beard against her.

He kissed her back, before saying, 'Your role is to be mine. And to give me lots of sex. And laughter. And make obscure movie references.'

'Chase, seriously. I know being with you means dealing with the fame thing and I'm willing to accept that, but what exactly does that mean? A bodyguard? Wearing make-up to get gas? No more food babies?' Chase's hand automatically dropped to her stomach when she said 'babies' and she could tell that was a discussion they would also need to have in the near future.

'We're going to be so normal and boring the paps will get disgusted with us and leave us alone eventually. It'll be a little rocky in the beginning. You won't need a bodyguard most of the time, maybe just at my shows or during release weeks. There will be a lot of promotional events you'll have to be my date for – award shows, release parties, radio events, things like that – but anyone who meets you is going to love you like I do,' Chase said, sliding his hands around her sides and pulling her tighter so that she felt every inch of him.

Ava cupped his cheek and he leaned in to her touch. 'And never, ever read the online comments, right?'

'Right,' he said. 'That's what publicists are for.'

Chase lifted his hips slightly and Ava was suddenly very conscious that they were both nude.

'I'm glad you told me that hot-tubbing naked is the only way to go.' She turned to lift the glass of wine off the ledge beside the tub and took a sip. 'Delicious.'

'Naked is the only way, and that's a fine French red, Châteauneuf du Pape.' His hands moved slightly on her belly and Ava gasped when one slid lower, the tips of his fingers teasing her sweetly. She was getting hot. And not just because of the water, but because of Chase.

She moaned, shifting slightly, and opened her thighs. 'Oh, I'm very glad you educated me on the correct way to hot-tub.' She put the glass down and leaned back on him; her breasts bobbed in the water and the peaks skimmed just below the surface of the bubbles. Chase's other hand slid up her ribcage and cradled one of them. She watched his thumb sweep across her stiffened nipple. 'So does this mean we're done talking?'

'It doesn't hurt to play with you a little, does it? I'm sweetening the pot so you know how much better it will be for you to stay with me.' His voice was husky and sent a delightful thrill skittering along her veins. 'After all, anytime you're naked with me is the best time.'

As if to prove his point, his hand finally dipped down between her thighs and found her clitoris while the other one gave tender attention to her aching nipple.

Even though the water was a hot, a hundred and four degrees, Ava shivered under his skilled touch.

'I like how you tremble with desire when I stroke you.' Chase's lips pressed against the back of her neck then seared a trail down to her shoulder. His cock was hard and insistent behind her, pushing so enticingly against her bottom. She wanted to turn around so she could fully enjoy him, but his hands were working magic on her and she held her breath, reluctant to move a muscle.

'So long as we acknowledge we're not done making decisions yet,' she mumbled, having a difficult time sorting out her thoughts under his wildly arousing fingers.

'Would you rather talk or—' He stilled his hands and lifted away from her slightly.

'No! No, don't stop. Please, we can talk . . . after.' And she groaned before falling silent, her eyelids fluttering closed.

His chuckle was deep and wrapped around her just as hotly as the steaming water. He had magic hands and knowing she would have him and his hands in her future thrilled Ava. She had found her man. Her soul mate. The love of her life.

His sweet stroking quickly brought her to the edge of delight and, when she came, his groan of arousal heightened her sensations. She quaked in his arms and he held her tight as the shudders of her orgasm lessened. Oh, yes, he had magic hands. Ava turned her head and pressed her cheek into his chest, savoring the brush of his hair next to her skin. Slowly, she relaxed back into him and let out a satisfied sigh.

'Oh my gosh! The only way the pot would be sweeter is if chocolate was involved.' Her body hummed, all her nerves finely tuned and aching for more. 'Mhmm,' she murmured.

'What'dya say we get out of the tub, take this inside, light a fire in the fireplace upstairs beside that big bed and continue our contractual negotiations?'

Ava lifted her head away from him and met his gaze. Humor, passion and, yes, love reflected back at her.

'Add in s'mores and I will follow you to the ends of the earth.'

He tipped an imaginary hat and said, 'For you, Boots, you bet.'

What Happens in Vegas

When the cop . . .
Meets the gambler . . .
The stakes have never been higher.

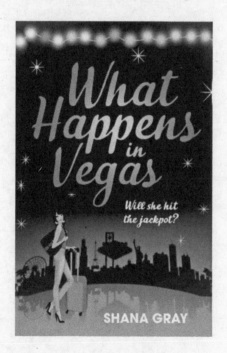

Available now from

HEADLINE
ETERNAL

Meet Me in San Francisco

The single mom . . .
And the playboy millionaire . . .
Are about to get wild.

Available now from

HEADLINE
ETERNAL

WORKING GIRL

A sexy seven-day job interview.
Seven irresistible interviewers.
Who will she choose at the end of the week?

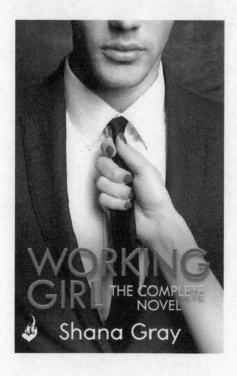

Available now from

HEADLINE
ETERNAL